THE
STARS DID
WANDER
DARKLING

COLIN MELOY

THE
STARS DID
WANDER
DARKLING

Illustrations by CARSON ELLIS

WALKER
BOOKS

For Mark

First published in Great Britain 2023 by Walker Books Ltd
87 Vauxhall Walk, London SE11 5HJ

2 4 6 8 10 9 7 5 3 1

Text © 2022 Unadoptable Books LLC
Illustrations © 2022 Carson Ellis

Poem credits: "The Seekers of Lice" by Arthur Rimbaud; "The Second Coming" by William Butler Yeats; "Lines: The cold earth slept below," by Percy Bysshe Shelley; "A Divine Image," by William Blake; "Darkness" by Lord Byron

The right of Colin Meloy to be identified as author of this work has been asserted in accordance with the Copyright, Designs and Patents Act 1988

This book has been typeset in Bembo

Printed and bound in Great Britain by CPI Group (UK) Ltd

British Library Cataloguing in Publication Data:
a catalogue record for this book is available from the British Library

ISBN 978-1-5295-1728-6

www.walker.co.uk

MIX
Paper | Supporting
responsible forestry
FSC® C171272

BEFORE

The rain-wet woods, a hover of mist just below the treetops, brief flurries of drizzle escaping through the boughs of the firs. The moss-thick floor, fountains of fern, primordial fern, bunching on the hillside, little explosions of green. Everywhere is green: dark green, lime green, sea green. The sound of the sea. No sign of the sea, but the sound of the sea. The wind, when it blows, is cool and wet and salty.

In a clearing, three men have appeared. No knowing how they got there – did they climb down from the trees or claw their way through the mossy forest floor? They have arrived, one after another, in the clearing. They are wearing suits and coats, brown as dirt, and brown hats. Their shirts are dingy, as if they spent the night somewhere dirty and dark. Their cuffs are yellowed from sweat.

A mist engulfs the clearing, obscuring everything beyond the first few stands of trees. One of the men kicks at the ground with a scuffed wing tip.

"What's this, Lugg?" says one.

"Don't know, Wart," says another.

"Seems spongy," responds the third.

"I believe it is earth," says the first. "I recall it; I have memory."

The third, Toff, kneels down and takes a fistful of moss in a grimy hand and holds it to his nose, sniffing. He recoils.

"Stinks," he says. He then proceeds to cram the stuff into his mouth. He chews. He chews like a cow on its cud. He stands and reports to his compatriots, barely intelligible through his mealy meal, "No good." Bits of moss fall from the corner of his mouth. His fellows look on disinterestedly.

They are all built mostly the same. They are of medium height, of medium stature, with little paunches of belly. Their facial hair distinguishes them: Toff with his bushy moustache, Lugg with his full beard, and Wart with neither beard nor moustache but with mutton chops that sprout from the sides of his cheeks like wiry dark cotton.

Toff has finished his meal of earth and moss and has swallowed. He has wiped his lips clean. The three men stand facing one another in the clearing, three points of a triangle.

"What's to be done, then?" asks Lugg.

"That's to be discovered," says Wart. "For now, we watch."

"And wait?" asks Lugg.

"And wait," says Wart.

Toff smiles at his compatriots. His teeth are black with dirt.

There is a rustle in the nearby vegetation. A small deer, having come upon the scene, has bolted. The three men track its movement as it races up the hillside.

"Is that one?" asks Toff.

"Nah," says Lugg. He has retrieved a small, well-worn book from his pocket. He begins leafing through it until he comes upon the sought-for page. "It's a deer, a mammal," says Lugg. "Related, though."

"Deer," says Wart.

"Deer," says Toff. "I recall now. Deer."

"Shall we kill it?" asks Wart.

Lugg refers to his book again and, having read it, shakes his head. "Lesser sentience," he says. He pulls out the small nub of a pencil and makes a note on the page. He places the book back in his interior pocket.

The other two men do likewise: pull book from pocket, note with stubby pencil. One returns his book to an interior jacket pocket, the other keeps it in his hand. This is Wart. He has remained on the page and begins to read: "'Coastal temperate rainforest, North America. More living and decaying biomass than anywhere on planet. Prime tree species include Douglas fir, Western hemlock, Sitka spruce, red cedar.'" Inhales deeply, grimaces. "Stinks."

The other two are listening, though.

Wart flips through more pages, reads, "'Programmable microwave oven. Percy Spencer, inventor. An oven that heats contents through electromagnetic radiation. Convenient features include selectable power level and presets for common preparations.'"

The other two nod, taking in the information.

Wart turns pages, reads more: "'Algebra. A variety of

mathematics that uses symbols to deduce sums. A core staple of modern primary education.'"

More nodding from his compatriots.

Thus emboldened, Wart flips more pages still and reads: "'Rimbaud, Arthur: When the child's forehead, full of red torments, implores the white swarm of indistinct dreams'" – here Wart digs his foot in the ground – "'There come near his bed two tall charming sisters with slim fingers that have silvery nails.'"

There is a quickness of breeze; it shakes the tree limbs and rustles the leaves. The mist begins to separate, to unweave. A veil is being lifted.

Wart continues, "'They seat the child in front of a wide open window,'" he reads, "'where the blue air bathes a mass of flowers and in his heavy hair where the dew falls move their delicate, fearful and enticing fingers.'"

The mist continues to dissipate; the light around them grows. Toff and Lugg exchange glances and then look out into the dark forest.

Wart is now reading from another page. "'Yeats, William Butler. Poet. Ireland, nineteenth and twentieth centuries. The darkness drops again…'"

The birds have stopped their song; the wind whistles through the boughs. It ruffles the pages of Wart's notebook. He grips the book tighter, his thick fingers holding back the paper, and reads again: "'But now I know that twenty centuries of stony sleep were vexed to nightmare by a rocking cradle…'"

Toff, looking out into the surrounding woods, sees something. A smile begins to break across his face, revealing his rutty, yellowed and dark teeth. Lugg sees it too, now, and smiles. Look: in the break between two trunks of trees is a lightening, the view of a horizon. Slowly, the surrounding forest reveals itself to the three men; it is as if a world outside themselves is emerging from thin air. Beyond the trees, the sky can be seen, a sky brightening as the mist retreats. This new light reveals, just below, a small town, its many buildings and houses arrayed before them as if in miniature. The ocean, the wide, grey ocean, heaves against a long strip of beach that extends beyond their vision.

Wart, his eyes now on the scene before them, finishes his recitation without looking at the page: "'And what rough beast, its hour come round at last, slouches towards Bethlehem to be born?'"

He smiles, closes book, places it in interior jacket pocket. The time has come.

SEAHAM, OREGON

1987

FRIDAY

There was a penny on the doormat.

It was there, Archie saw, just inside the second *O* of the family's name – COOMES – like the pupil of an eye. Archie had just come home from his last day of school before summer break and leaped the three front steps of his house in a bound. Something about the coin called his attention. It stopped him in his tracks.

He supposed someone had dropped it. *Find a penny, pick it up, all day long, have good luck*, he thought. He picked up the coin; it felt strangely cold to the touch. Like it hadn't wanted to be found. He recoiled a little from it. Just then, the front door swung open and nearly pitched him over sideways.

"Talking to the slugs, Arch?" asked his brother, Max.

Archie, embarrassed, quickly stood and threw the penny over the side of the porch. "No," he said, "I wasn't."

Max stared at him, a mocking grin on his face. The boy was equipped in his soccer kit: striped green shirt, *SEAHAM YMCA SOCCER* written across the breast. Striped shorts, striped socks pulled knee-high over shin guards. Max with his gelled hair and his one earring and his dogged acne that he lay siege to every night with a medicine cabinet's worth of creams and pads to little effect. He was sixteen, only three years older than Archie, but the divide between them could not have been more pronounced. Archie, to Max, was still a child. Max, to Max, was an adult.

"Out of my way, bug," said Max. The door slammed behind him, and he jumped the three steps of the porch to the pavement, the laces on his cleated shoes casually untied.

Archie watched him go. He slung his backpack over his shoulder and opened the front door. Just then, he looked down and froze.

The penny was there again. Back on the doormat. Exactly where it had been when he had picked it up.

"Close the door, dillnard!" came a voice from inside the house. It belonged to one of his twin sisters. He couldn't, in the moment, tell which one it was. All of his siblings seemed to have a competition going as to which of them could be crueller to their younger brother. He left the penny where it was and stepped into the house, letting the door slam behind him.

Olivia, fifteen, was sitting on the couch, playing Nintendo. One of the Mario brothers was leaping from a stack of blocks onto a flagpole. It was clear that Olivia had not yelled his name; she was too intent on the action on the screen. Annabelle, Olivia's twin, sat on the far side of the couch, twirling her brown wavy hair in her fingers.

"You're letting flies in, dork," she said.

12

"There's a penny on the doormat," said Archie, pointing behind him. "And when I…" His sisters fixed him with a disinterested look. "When I picked it up… Oh, never mind."

On the TV screen, three little fireworks exploded, in sequence, above a pixelated castle.

"It was your turn to take the rubbish out," said Annabelle.

"Sorry," said Archie. "Forgot. I'll do it now, OK?"

"Too late. Dad did it," said Olivia.

"Dad's home?"

Archie looked at the clock on the mantel; it was a quarter to four. Peter Coomes rarely came home from work before six. "Why did you even tell me that if Dad already did it?" he asked.

"'Cause you're in deep," said Olivia, returning her attention to the game.

"Double deep," said Annabelle.

Archie cast his eyes towards the kitchen. The door was closed, but he could hear his father's voice through it. Archie could tell he was talking on the phone; his sentences were punctuated with long pauses, during which he would grunt noises of understanding or assent. Archie walked to the door and pushed it slightly open, enough so he could see his father standing by the kitchen counter, his right hand cradling the yellow telephone receiver to his ear, the thumb and middle finger of his left hand kneading the edges of his forehead.

"I know that, Mrs Rockwell," he was saying. "Yes. I'm fully aware of that. Believe me, this is as hard for me as it is for you. I was relying on—" He was interrupted again; his left hand fell from his temples to worry the spiral cord that attached the receiver to the cradle. Archie could see his mother, her back to him, leaning against the fridge, watching her husband. He closed the door and returned to the living room.

"What's that all about?" asked Archie.

"Beats me," said Olivia.

"He was here when we got home," said Annabelle.

Archie sat down in the empty chair next to the couch and watched the action onscreen. He could still hear his father's muffled voice through the kitchen door.

"All I'm saying, Candace," Peter said. "All I'm saying. Let me finish. Let me finish. All I'm saying is that I can't be liable here. I spoke with the engineer. I mean, there were red flags everywhere, even before Wednesday. Yes, before Wednesday. We just can't..." This was followed by a lengthy pause, after which he continued, "Uh-huh. I get that. But see, the thing is, my engineer said that we just can't continue work. Not with the sort of seismic issues we're seeing on the site."

Archie exchanged a fleeting look with Olivia before her attention was drawn back to the screen.

"We don't know how far they go," his father was saying. "These ... fissures. And until we do, I just can't allow this work to continue. I'm sorry, Candace." This was followed by a series of "uh-huhs" and "I knows" plus several apologies before Archie heard the receiver being placed back on the cradle. His mother and father spoke in hushed tones for a moment before the door to the living room swung open. His mother, Liz, looked into the room and gave Archie a

14

forced smile. "Hiya, Arch," she said. "How was the last day of school?"

"Fine," said Archie. "What's up with Dad?"

Liz looked surprised, as if impressed by Archie's powers of deduction, then turned serious. "Well, I suppose you should know."

"Know what, Mom?" asked Olivia.

"Your dad's going to be home for a while," she said. "They've stopped work on the site."

Annabelle looked away from the television; a swell of sad bleeps accompanied Mario's fall into a gap between two beige pillars.

"It's not a big deal, guys," Liz said. "It's temporary. Till they can figure out what's going on."

But it did seem like a big deal to Archie. He knew the last year had been a difficult one for his parents. The nonprofit his mom had worked for, CoastAid, had dissolved her position in November, and she had been unemployed ever since. Seaham, like most coastal towns, had lived under a pall of depression for as long as Archie could remember. And so it had been some relief when Coomes Construction's bid on the new hotel project that was being planned on the headlands just north of town had been accepted.

"What does that mean?" asked Annabelle.

"Well, we don't really know what it means yet," answered Liz. "I suppose we'll have to tighten our belts just a bit."

"What does *that* mean?" asked Olivia.

"It means just what it sounds like," said Liz. "Until we

get a better idea of what our finances are, we'll have to hold off on a few things."

The kids knew where this was headed; they'd been planning a trip to Los Angeles at the end of the summer — there had been talk of a beach bungalow rental and a two-day visit to Disneyland.

"We're still going, right?" asked Olivia, glaring at her mother.

"Well," said Liz, "I mean, we'll have to…"

"This sucks," shouted Annabelle, blowing at the cloud of feathered bangs above her brow, a wave-like tangle she sculpted every morning inside a cloud of hairspray. She pushed herself off the couch angrily and stalked past her mother.

"Annabelle," said Liz. "Language."

"What, *sucks*?" Annabelle had stopped at the first step of the stairs to the second floor. "Sucks. Sucks. Sucky sucky sucky sucks."

"Annabelle!" said Liz helplessly.

Annabelle marched up the stairs; Olivia followed close behind, shooting her mother a glare as she passed.

The theme from *Super Mario Bros* was playing on a loop from the TV speaker; Archie picked up the remote and switched it off.

Peter appeared in the kitchen doorway. "Hey, Arch," he said. "Happy last day of school, kiddo. Eighth-grade graduate and all. Big day!"

Archie ignored him. "Is it true?" he asked.

Peter crossed his arms and rested against the doorjamb.

"Yeah," he said. He gave his wife a brief look. "Yeah, it's true. You know Joe – he was over for dinner a few weeks ago. The engineer. Well, he and his team were doing some early excavation on the site, just below the cliff, and they opened up this whole network of underground cavities. Like caves, fissures in the rock." He rubbed his brow and said, "Anyway, it's like Swiss cheese down there, that whole cliff under the Langdon place. Can't build on it."

"Can't they just find another spot?" asked Archie. He didn't know much about the job, just that Candace Rockwell, a developer from Portland, was going to put a five-million-dollar hotel on a cliff above the ocean, near where Langdon House was. It had been front-page news in the *Daily Astorian*; all the grown-ups were talking about it.

Peter shook his head and frowned. "Don't think so," he said. "Seems like the boss has her heart set on the place. She's bound and determined to make it happen. But it ain't gonna be me that builds it, that's for sure. And I don't think she'll have much luck finding anyone else to do it, either." He wound his hands together, his thick, leathery hands that always seemed to be crisscrossed with black lines of dirt and grime. He wasn't that old – he'd just turned forty-three – but his career had aged him, stooping his shoulders and tanning his skin.

"This doesn't sound temporary," said Archie, now looking at his mother.

Peter glanced at his wife. "No," he said. "I'm not sure it is." He took a deep breath and said, "But something'll turn up. You don't need to worry."

"He's right," put in Liz. She smiled at her son.

"And it doesn't mean we can't still have our pizza-and-movie night," said Peter. "Nothing a little Antonio's and a good flick can't fix, am I right?"

Archie was unmoved. "Yeah, OK," he said. Throwing his backpack over his shoulder, he made his way upstairs.

In his bedroom, Archie heaved his backpack onto his desk chair and threw himself on his bed, belly-first. He could hear his sisters talking to each other through the wall, tiny gusts of ghost-like murmurs, and he hit the play button on his yellow Sony boom box to drown them out. A singer's voice growled from the speakers, midsong; something about being given gold and pearls stolen from the sea.

The sea wind picked up and rattled the window; the tree boughs shook, and Archie, his chin in his palms, looked out at the street below. The Coomeses' house lay several blocks off Seaham's main drag and even farther from the ocean, but the wind off the ocean, the salt air, and the distant spray were inescapable in this seaside town.

He thought of the camping trip – that was enough to lift his spirits. Chris Pedersen, Archie's best and oldest friend, had suggested it. Two nights in the woods with his three closest friends – Chris, Oliver Fife and Athena Quest. It would be a fitting kickoff to the summer holidays. They had the perfect spot, a level clearing a few miles up an old forest-service road, just behind old Lee Novak's property. They'd scoped it out over spring break, spending most of their days clearing out brush and digging a firepit. They'd even built a kind of lean-to against a stand of trees, but who knew if it was still upright after April's windy and wet weather. They would meet Monday morning and head out – that was the plan. Spend the first afternoon cleaning up the site, adding some improvements.

He turned over on his back and let the music fall over him; spiky guitar arpeggios spiralled from the yellow boom box and Archie felt inspired to crank the volume until the speakers began to crackle and a barrage of angry knocks sounded against the wall between his and his sisters' rooms.

"TURN THAT DOWN!" shouted one of the girls. It was no longer a ghost-like murmur – it was a banshee howl. And Archie happily ignored it.

But first they had to decide on the movie.

"Something scary," said Max, home from soccer practice, towelling himself off from the shower. He'd leaped from the bathroom when he understood they were discussing movie rental options.

Liz wouldn't have it. "Nothing scary," she countered. "Or too violent." She looked at Archie.

Archie blushed. "I'm thirteen, Mom," he said.

"Still," responded his mom, as if she didn't believe him, as if she didn't want to believe him. He would always be the baby of the family. "Maybe when you're older."

"What about," put in Peter, "a scary movie, but for kids?"

The Coomes children all looked at him askance, as if he'd spoken some heinous blasphemy.

"What?" he said, his hands up defensively. "Ever heard of *Bride of Frankenstein*? Terrified me when I was your age."

"Dad doesn't get a vote," said Olivia firmly.

Max crossed his arms, incensed. The boy was in his scary-movie prime, and yet on family movie night he rarely got his way. "Maybe you shouldn't be such a wuss, Arch," he said.

"I'm not scared," said Archie angrily. "I watched *Texas Chainsaw Massacre* at Chris's."

"You *what*?" His mom's eyes were wide.

"Ooh," said Max, unimpressed. "Big, tough Archie."

"Whatever," said Archie. "Greg Sanders told Oliver that he was at Lauren Hamilton's house over spring break and they were watching *Alien* and you had your eyes closed through the whole last part."

"You watched *what* at Chris's?" repeated Liz.

"Just ask Randy what to get," suggested Olivia, quickly changing the subject. Archie inwardly thanked her.

"Yeah," said Peter. "Ask Randy. Something funny, something the whole family can watch."

"Ugh," moaned Max. "We're going to end up with some black-and-white Russian movie about, like, clowns or something." Randy Dean was the owner of Movie Mayhem, the Oregon coast's best – and only – exclusively Betamax video-rental store. He was a wellspring of film knowledge, an encyclopedia of esoteric movie trivia.

"But do it quick," instructed Peter. "I'm going to call in the pizza."

And so Archie was out the front door, racing down the

steps to his bike. He pedalled into the street and made his way towards the main strip of the town.

The day was warm, and the breeze that fed from the sea was warm. He pedalled twice and then coasted down the hill from his house, feeling the wind pick up as his speed grew. He laid on the brakes at the stop sign at Overland, but barely slowed through the intersection. Stop signs in Seaham were more like suggestions than mandates. Before long, he'd arrived at Charles Avenue, named after the town's founder, Charles Langdon, using his first name, Archie figured, because they'd already named the street that ran down from the highway Langdon Road.

Langdon, a fur magnate from the late nineteenth century, had his thumbprint on just about everything in the town: there was Dolly Park, named after his youngest daughter, dead of consumption at age eleven. Abigail Street, named after his wife, ran perpendicular to Charles Avenue, which, in turn, ran down to the ocean, where Bosun Drive cut a straight line along the perimeter of the beach, named after Charles's beloved Saint Bernard. Of course, the flagship of this whole memorial monopoly was Langdon House, a stately Victorian behemoth, in near ruins on the headlands north of town and which had been, until Peter Coomes's phone call this afternoon, at imminent risk of demolition. The Langdon family, despite having their name on half of the street signs in town, had quietly faded into the background. The house was abandoned. Of course, in its abandonment, the house served only to stoke the imaginations of schoolchildren up and down the coast. Kids traded stories of the ghosts that haunted Langdon House, and the gruesome murders that undoubtedly had taken place within its walls. It was a tradition among Seaham Elementary students to dare younger kids to enter the gates of Langdon House after dark and throw a rock through a window. Sadly, by Archie's time, there wasn't an intact pane of glass to shatter on the whole place, and he and his friends had to make do with trying to break a shutter or knock a piece of siding loose.

Archie took a right on Charles, heading towards the beach. A few cars were still cruising the main strip, but the early throng of tourists had left Seaham in the late afternoon, heading back towards their rental houses and oceanfront motels. The only bar in Seaham, the Sea Hag, was starting to get busy, and its smell, a heady blend of beer and cigarette smoke, infected the whole surrounding block. He rode past the grocery store; he waved at Mrs Parsons, who was rolling a cart of discounted paperbacks into the front door of the Bookstall, Seaham's only bookstore.

The next block was a series of kite shops and candy shops, shops that hibernated in the winter months like bears, living for the five months that made up Seaham's tourist season. But now the kites were on display on the pavement, and the taffy was being stretched in the storefront windows, all that pink gooey material being pulled and plied by two twirling robotic arms like some superhero being put through the wringer by his archnemesis.

On the corner of Charles and Devon (the Langdons'

English ancestral homeland) was a former diner that Randy Dean had bought and remodelled as a video-rental store. This was the intersection Archie was navigating when he nearly ran straight into a woman standing in the centre of the street.

Archie jammed on the brakes. His bike pitched forward, and he felt himself begin to fly over the handlebars. He managed to throw his weight back just in time, and the bike's rear tyre came thudding down on the pavement, skidding sideways. He yelled and kicked out his leg to stop the bike from falling over, but it was too late: he hit the ground hard, on his side.

He looked up to see the woman standing over him. She was elderly, perhaps seventy, and her face was lined with wrinkles. Her skin was deeply tanned from sun exposure, and she wore a ragged dress that was stained brown with dirt. She stared blankly down at Archie, seemingly unmoved by the fact that she'd almost been hit.

Archie expected some kind of acknowledgement from the woman, even if it was a *watch where you're going, kid* – but none came. Archie lifted himself off the ground and said, "Sorry, I didn't see you there."

The woman continued to stare at Archie. Her jaw was slack; her eyes were wide, as if she'd just witnessed something terrible. A chill shot through Archie's body.

"You OK?" asked Archie finally.

"They shoulda left it hid," said the woman, her voice low and broken. Spit flew from her lips as she spoke. "They shoulda left it well hid."

"Excuse me?"

The woman began to shuffle towards him, her eyes boring into Archie's. "They found somethin' down there," she said. "Down below the cliff. Somethin' that would better been left hid. Hear me?"

"Uh, yeah," said Archie. He lifted his bike from the ground and inched away from the woman. "I don't know what you're talking about."

The woman's look changed; her eyes narrowed and her mouth curled down. Archie realized she had begun to cry. "They shoulda left it hid! They shoulda left it hid!" As she spoke, her voice was strained with panic, and Archie began to look around to see if anyone else was watching. He wondered if the woman needed help, if she was having some sort of mental breakdown. Archie didn't think he'd be able to handle such a thing. But then, abruptly, the emotion left the woman's face and she turned away from Archie, continuing down the street. Archie could hear her muttering as she shuffled along, saying, "They shoulda left it hid" over and over to herself.

Archie felt oddly shaken; he stood very still on the corner, watching the woman walk away.

Just then, he felt a nagging sting on his right leg. Hiking up his jeans, he saw he'd skinned the side of his shin pretty well. He winced and let the trouser leg fall. He walked his bike over to a street sign and locked it against the pole. He looked after the woman, to see if she was still on the street, but could not see her anywhere. Archie suppressed a shiver and walked into the video store.

"Hey – there's the guy we need to see," said Randy Dean as the bell above the door announced Archie's entrance. The man was standing behind a counter, busily feeding a stack of tapes into an auto-rewinding machine. Oliver Fife was sitting on the counter, chewing on a Red Vine he'd taken from the bucket that sat by the cash register. The Vines were five cents a pop, but Archie and Oliver, being such regulars, were allowed to freely pilfer from the stash – within reason.

"Hey, Arch," said Oliver. He spoke through a mouthful of red liquorice. "You gotta tell us."

"Tell you what?" asked Archie.

"Mr Fife here is very curious about what's happening up at the Langdon place," said Randy, studying the spools inside a videocassette to gauge its state of winding. There were *Bee Kind, Rewind* stickers (an image of a bee floated above the words) affixed on every tape that Movie Mayhem owned. Randy's main job, he complained, was rewinding tapes for customers who had ignored the sticker's instruction. Randy Dean wore his hair in long ringlets, and his blocky brown glasses were at least a decade out of fashion. He wore a pink Izod shirt and a pair of jeans hiked up high to the waist and clasped around his pear-shaped body with a brown weave belt.

"I heard they just suddenly stopped working up there," said Oliver. He went for another Red Vine from the bucket but was stopped by a "tut-tut" from Randy. He continued, "Figured you'd know what that's all about."

"How'd you guys find out?" asked Archie.

"Brody Tyke," said Randy. "He was just in here. He was on the crew, I guess."

"A cave, Archie," said Oliver, his eyes wide. "They opened up, like, a big cave in the cliff." Archie had known Oliver since the second grade, when the boy's family had moved into town from Arizona. They'd hit it off immediately, two kids under the spell of *Star Wars* and superhero comic books. Movie Mayhem had become a sort of home base for Oliver – his Fortress of Solitude, as he sometimes called it. There he was surrounded by the relics and icons of his favourite imaginary worlds: the shelves and shelves of tape boxes, the movie posters on the walls advertising sunglassed spies and leather-clad warriors. He was an odd one and seemed to be getting more odd as the years progressed. The idea of a cave being unearthed beneath the Langdon place was bound to get Oliver Fife going.

"What do you think they found down there? Must be something serious, if they're gonna stop building that hotel now," said Oliver.

"You probably know more than me," said Archie

26

defensively. "Dad said something about it not being safe to build on. That's all."

A couple, a man and a woman, came through the door. Randy gave them a mumbled welcome, and they wandered down to the far end of the store.

Oliver shook his head. "Uh-uh," he said. "That's too simple. And when something's too simple, it can't be true."

"Occam's sledgehammer," Randy said quietly.

"I think they found something down there," said Oliver. "And they're trying to keep it secret. I've got a *feeling*."

The strange woman's words echoed in Archie's mind. "I don't think so," he said.

"What do you think, Randy?" asked Oliver.

"*Bring Up the Dead*," said Randy cryptically. "1977. Leo DeSanto. One of his first films." He stepped from behind the counter and walked over to the wall of tapes that made up the horror section. It was Archie and Oliver's favourite corner in the whole store. The tape boxes here made a mosaic of trauma and terror against the wall of the store – screaming women, clutching at their chests in horror, stood beneath giant clawed fingers; blood-spattered typeface scrawled out such titles as *Demon Birthright* and *The Chainsaw Cheerleader* and *Dracula's Daughter*; gleaming airbrushed knives hung pendulum-like over unsuspecting teenagers; demons leered, and haunted houses loomed. Archie didn't need to have seen the movies to imagine what they promised – he could make up the stories in his head just by looking at the cover art, by scanning the breathless plot descriptions on the backs of the boxes.

Randy took one such box from the shelf. On the cover, an old brick schoolhouse stood on a dark lawn, jagged cracks erupting across the ground beneath it. The title, *Bring Up the Dead*, was written in dripping red type. The tagline below the image read, SCHOOL'S OUT – FOR ETERNITY. Randy gave the synopsis. "Turns out this school is built on top of an ancient Egyptian burial mound. Some kids find a passage into the tomb through the janitor's closet, and, as you can imagine, all hell breaks loose. Literally. Scared the crap out of me, truth be told. Not DeSanto's finest film, but is fairly pertinent, wouldn't you say?"

"You think there's an Egyptian tomb beneath the Langdon place?" asked Archie.

"Well, no," said Randy. "But it could be some other kind of tomb. Or something, perhaps, that was buried long ago. And the folks who did the burying didn't want it dug up."

Archie looked sharply at Randy. He began to say something, to describe his exchange with the woman outside the store, but stopped himself. It seemed too outlandish.

"Where's this movie set?" asked Oliver.

"Good question," Randy said. "Pennsylvania, I believe. Pittsburgh. It was cheap to shoot there in the seventies, I think."

"How is there an Egyptian tomb under a school in Pittsburgh?" asked Archie.

Randy smiled and said, "Movie magic, my friend."

Oliver and Archie looked at each other and laughed. "Yeah, right," said Archie.

"But what if," began Oliver, "what if there's, like, treasure down there? You know, maybe the Langdons, sometime a long time ago, like, hid some treasure down there. That'd seem realistic, right? I mean, what about the Langdon curse?"

"The Langdon curse?" asked Randy.

Oliver rolled his eyes. "C'mon, Randy. You know. The Langdons – they're all crazy, like, over time. Each generation. More crazy than the one before."

"Oh, *that* Langdon curse," said Randy. He smirked.

"Definitely some treasure, somewhere up there. Am I right?" Oliver looked at both Randy and Archie impatiently.

"Maybe so. Maybe so," said Randy as he returned to the counter. Archie and Oliver remained in front of the horror section, browsing its forbidden riches.

"I don't know, dude," said Archie, pulling a movie called *C.H.U.D.* from the wall and reading its back copy.

"Oh, come on, Archie," said Oliver. "We gotta check it out."

"Ollie, the whole place is fenced off," said Archie. He'd gone to visit his dad once or twice during the spring, and even then it was near impossible to get into the site.

"Betcha we could find a hole in the fence somewhere," said Oliver. "Especially if no one's there now. C'mon, I've got a *feeling*."

"That's what I'm worried about," said Archie. "You and your *feelings*. Remember the last time you had one of those?"

Oliver grew serious. "That was different," he said.

Archie didn't need to go into detail; ever since they'd been friends, Oliver had been known to lapse into what the grown-ups called "unexplained episodes". Last autumn, for instance, Ollie had become convinced – had been in the grips of a *feeling* – that the new maths teacher at their school was some kind of "eldritch being", as he'd called it. A resurrected dead soul. He'd become so convinced that he confronted the teacher after school one day; the teacher, of course, was taken aback. The man had only begun to defend himself when Oliver's face went pale and his eyes had rolled back in his head. Chris Pedersen, who'd been standing nearby, had managed to catch him before he hit the floor. Ollie had ended up in the nurse's office; his mother had to come get him. There'd been no explanation – not even from Oliver himself – except for the murmurings around the halls of Seaham Elementary that the boy had had an epileptic seizure of some kind.

"Right," said Archie quietly.

"Come *on*, Arch," said Oliver. He grabbed the tape box from Archie's hand and returned it to the shelf. "We don't have to go in; we just have to go look at it."

Archie looked sidelong at Oliver, knowing that the needling would never end unless he gave in. "Just to look?"

Oliver's face broke into a smile. "Just to look," he said.

"OK," Archie said. "But we do not go inside the fence. My dad would kill me if we got caught. I'd be grounded for, like, the whole summer. Goodbye, camping trip."

Oliver put his hand on his chest, straightening his face into a solemn frown. "No one's going to get in the way of the camping trip. We don't go past the fence. On my word."

"Swear by something," said Archie.

Oliver glanced around the room; his eyes caught on a tape.

He walked over to one of the neighbouring racks and pulled the movie from its shelf. Bringing it back to Archie, he handed it over; it was *Excalibur*, the 1981 John Boorman film that both Archie and Oliver loved. As Archie held the box, Oliver placed his hand on it and solemnly spoke in his best version of a British accent. "In the name of God, Saint Michael and Saint George…" said Oliver, beginning to quote, word for word, Uryens's knighting of Arthur after the battle at Cameliard.

Archie rolled his eyes. "Just swear," he said, interrupting him.

"I swear we won't go past the fence," said Oliver.

Satisfied, Archie returned the movie to its spot in the fantasy section; Oliver followed him, talking excitedly as he went. "Let's meet at the benches, tomorrow, ten a.m. I'll call Chris and Athena. They'd kill us if they found out we did it without them."

"Hey, do you have this on VHS?" The voice was from a man from across the room, one half of the tourist couple who had walked in earlier. He was holding up a videotape case.

Randy, at the counter, abruptly lifted his hand from the auto-rewinder, making it judder to a sudden stop. He looked at the man over the top of his glasses, studying him briefly before pointing to the sign above the counter that read *BETA ONLY*.

The man said, "Our rental house doesn't have a Betamax player."

Randy shrugged and returned to his rewinding. The couple, discouraged, replaced the box on the shelf and exited the store.

After they'd gone, Oliver asked, "What's the deal with that, anyway? Beta only. Everyone has VHS players these days. Everyone outside of Seaham anyway."

"It's the superior technology, Ollie," Randy responded loftily. "Better fidelity, crisper picture. Trust me. Beta'll win out in the end. VHS is a passing fad. Those big clunky tapes." He shook his head in disapproval.

"Shoot," said Oliver, glancing up at the clock behind the counter. "I gotta go." He looked at Archie. "Tomorrow. Ten a.m. By the benches."

Archie sighed. "Yep, see you then."

"See ya, Randy," said Ollie as he left the store.

"Always a pleasure, Mr Fife," Randy replied.

Just then, the phone rang at the counter and Randy answered it, saying, "Movie Mayhem, all Beta all the time. Randy Dean speaking. How can I help you?" Archie wandered to the section marked *COMEDY* and let his eyes drift over the titles, the designs, the photos on the fronts of the boxes. Randy continued his seemingly endless task of rewinding videotapes, the store's clunky phone now balanced between his shoulder and cheek.

"Uh-huh," said Randy. "Sure. I think we have that." He let the mouthpiece of the phone slip down his chin as he called out to Archie, "Hey, Archie – can you look there and see if we have *A Funny Thing Happened on the Way to the Forum*? It should be just above your left hand."

Archie looked. "Yeah, it's in," he said.

"Yeah, we've got it," said Randy into the phone. "Hmm?

Yeah, that's Archie Coomes. I can ask. One sec." Again, he let the mouthpiece drop and called to Archie, "Would you mind running a movie up to Birgitta Woodley's place on your way home?"

"Sure," said Archie. "I mean, I don't mind."

"Yep, we got you, Birgitta," Randy said into the phone. In the meantime, Archie had narrowed in on the movie *Fletch*, which he remembered had played at the theatre in Astoria two summers before. He removed the plastic tape case from behind the box and walked to the counter holding the two movies.

"Ah, yes," Randy said, having hung up the phone. "A good caper. Should satisfy the whole brood." He took the plastic cases from Archie and, double-checking the tapes were in the cases, ran a wand over the bar codes on the bottom of each case. Little beeps on the computer console on his desk registered their status, and he handed them over to Archie. "*Fletch* needs to be back Wednesday; tell Birgitta that's when *Forum* is due as well."

"Got it."

"Say hi to the fam for me," said Randy.

"Will do," said Archie. He turned to leave but had only got as far as the door when Randy called, "Oh, and Archie?"

"Yeah?"

"Careful up there, up at the cliffside," Randy said, his face suddenly serious.

Archie rolled his eyes. "We'll look out for mummies; don't worry." He raised his arms in a zombie-like fashion but almost lost the videotapes he'd tucked under his arm. Randy remained solemn as Archie pushed the door open and left the store.

Outside, people were coming off the beach, their arms laden with kites, blankets and umbrellas. Dogs danced alongside their owners while children were hustled into awaiting station wagons, oversunned and overtired. Archie shoved the two videotapes into the bag on his handlebars and unlocked his bike. He pedalled out into the street, navigating the trickle of traffic with the confidence of someone who'd spent his life winding through vehicles driven by lost tourists. He crossed Charles Avenue and turned up the alley behind the Sea Hag, piloting his bike through a waft of fryer exhaust. He took a quick left onto Abigail, and that was when he saw Brody Tyke.

Rather, he heard Brody Tyke before he saw him, as Brody was sitting in his pickup truck, shouting along to the heavy music that was blasting from his stereo and drumming madly on the top of his steering wheel.

"Hey! Archie!" Brody shouted over the snarl of distorted guitar coming from the truck cabin. "Archie Coomes!"

Archie pretended not to hear; he kept riding up the street. To his dismay, he heard the truck behind him rev and peel away from the kerb.

"Where you going in such a hurry?" asked Brody, pulling up alongside Archie.

"Just going home, Brody," responded Archie, his eyes glued to the road in front of him.

34

"I want to talk to you." He had to shout over the rumble of the truck engine and the squall of the heavy metal.

"I'd really love to, but I gotta get home," said Archie, and he laid into the pedals, pushing away from Brody's truck.

Brody gave the pickup a boost of gas, and a cloud of black smoke poured from the exhaust pipe. The truck shot ahead and veered in front of Archie, nearly knocking him off his bike.

"Jesus!" shouted Archie, screeching to a halt.

Brody stopped his truck in the middle of the street, blocking the way. He turned off the stereo and looked at Archie through the passenger-side window over the rims of his black sunglasses.

"Thing is, I had a job a couple days ago, and now I don't," he said. "Why'd your dad pull out of that hotel at the headlands? That's what I wanna know."

Brody was nineteen; he'd notoriously dropped out of Harrisburg High his junior year. He wore his stringy blond hair long and covered it with an ever-present baseball hat worn backwards. A black T-shirt emblazoned with the jagged logo of some metal band was his daily uniform.

"I don't know why," said Archie. "Why's everybody think I do?"

"It's your dad that took everyone off it. And I gotta know what for. I was counting on that job, man."

Yeah, he wasn't the only one, thought Archie. "Get off my back, Brody."

"What'd you say?"

"I said, get off my back." Archie began pedalling his bike around the front of Brody's truck.

"What is happening?" A woman's voice, steeped in a vaguely European accent, came from just up the street. Archie looked and saw Birgitta Woodley standing on her front porch, taking in the confrontation.

Brody seemed to ignore her. "Tell your dad he owes me back pay," he said through the rolled-down window. "He owes them whole crew that money. He better pay up." He gave Birgitta a dismissive look and then revved the truck engine and peeled away down the street.

Archie watched him go. Once the truck had disappeared around a corner, he walked his bike up onto the pavement. Arriving at the Woodleys' house, he retrieved the videotape from his bike bag and climbed up the steps to Birgitta's porch.

"Thank you," said Birgitta, taking the tape from Archie. She was Swedish by birth and wore her long grey hair tucked up in a stately bun. "So why do you let that boy bother you?"

"I don't mean to," he said. "I wish he wouldn't."

Birgitta made a kind of *tsk-tsk* noise with her mouth, and Archie couldn't tell if she was reprimanding him or Brody Tyke. Birgitta Woodley always seemed to carry herself with a kind of severity that Archie assumed to be uniquely European. "Well, anyway," she said, "thank you for bringing the film. Please tell your mother I said hello."

"I will," said Archie. "Bye, Birgitta."

The door closed behind her, and Archie was left on

the porch. He turned to go, to head back to his bike on the pavement, but something strange caught his eye. He looked down at his feet, at the dust-clotted woven mat that lay on the threshold of the Woodleys' house.

There was a penny on the doormat.

The movie selection had only been a partial success; Max had already seen it. Olivia and Annabelle had wanted something more like a high school comedy; but Liz and Peter, both in the dark about any movie that had been made after 1975, seemed excited – Liz thought Chevy Chase was cute and laughed at all the gags, even the ones that weren't that funny. Peter watched the movie in stony silence, his viewing interrupted regularly by the ring of the telephone in the kitchen. Initially, they paused the film each time he left the couch, but the calls became so unrelenting that finally Peter insisted they watch without him while he stood in the kitchen, answering the concerns of yet another engineer or designer, architect or day worker. The kitchen was right off the living room, so Archie couldn't help but keep an ear trained on the conversations.

Throughout the movie, Archie found his mind straying to the penny he'd seen on the Woodleys' doormat. He'd returned home, wanting to see if the penny was still there on his own doormat, but he was surprised – and somewhat relieved – to see that it was gone.

When the credits rolled, Peter came into the living room, having fielded yet another call. "What, it's over?" he asked, staring at the scrolling names on the screen. "What happened? You know, to the guy?"

"*Dad*," groaned Annabelle, "you missed, like, half the movie."

The phone rang again; Liz and Peter exchanged an exasperated glance, and Peter went to answer it. "Max, it's for you," he called, sounding relieved. Max leaped from the couch and jogged into the kitchen; Olivia and Annabelle disappeared up the stairs to their room. Liz had begun looking through a pile of mail on the side table, and Archie, guessing no one else was going to take on the task, knelt by the VCR and pressed the rewind button.

"Hey," said Liz as the machine whirred, "the Corkers are having a garage sale up in Cannon Beach tomorrow. Their oldest is going to college. Cindy said there'd be a bunch of tapes for sale if you want to go and check it out."

"Uh, no," said Archie. "I can't, really. I mean, I couldn't."

"You've got something going on?"

"Yeah," said Archie. "Nothing really. Just meeting with, y'know, Ollie and Chris and Athena."

"Sounds fun," said Liz. "Making plans for the camping trip?"

"Yeah," said Archie. "You know, figuring out who's bringing what. And all that."

"That reminds me," said Liz, "if you're taking the tent, you should really give it an airing out. It's been in the shed since August."

"Got it," said Archie. The VCR came to a sudden stop,

and Archie ejected the tape. He placed it in its case and set the case on top of the TV. "Night, Mom," he said.

"Night, honey," said Liz, lost in a magazine article.

There was still light in the sky, glowing over the rooftops and through the clouds, when Archie walked into his room. The band of rain he had seen earlier had never made land, but the lingering clouds were a canvas for a spectacular sunset, all pinks and purples. He waited there at his window, watching the light die until the streetlights flickered on and the street was dark, save for the lamps' little cones of orange light. He pressed play on his boom box and was about to climb into bed when something caught his eye on the street below.

Someone was on the pavement, staring up at the house.

Something about the figure gave Archie a fright; he quickly turned off his bedside lamp. The reflective flare of its bulb disappeared from the window, and he could see clearly down onto the dark street. There, standing below one of the leafy cherry trees that sprouted from Pam Applegate's front garden, was a strange man.

He was no one Archie recognized, so Archie at first took him to be a tourist. But there was something odd in the way he carried himself. What's more, he was not dressed in the way a tourist visiting the Oregon coast in June should be dressed. He wore a brown suit; a dark tie was knotted around his collar. There was an old-fashioned hat on his head, a floppy, worn-looking thing, and prodigious mutton chops sprouted from his cheeks. He was an adult, but he was not *old*; there was no grey in his hair. But the thing that Archie found most alarming was the fact that he seemed to be staring directly at the Coomeses' front door.

Archie felt his heart rate quicken; he willed the man to walk on, to leave his house alone, but the man continued to stand there, watching from beneath the slender branches of the cherry tree. He was standing straight and still – and Archie had begun to think he was frozen in place when the man reached into the lining of his jacket and removed what appeared to be a little book and a pencil. The man had just begun to make an annotation in this book when suddenly Archie's room was flooded with light.

The man's head jolted upward, and he looked directly at Archie.

"Hey, bug," said Max from behind him. He'd thrown open the door; light poured in from the hallway.

Archie quickly ducked below the windowsill and stared wildly at his brother. "Max!" he said in a hoarse whisper.

"Do you have my—" his brother began, before seeing Archie hunched down in the pitch dark. "What's your major damage?"

Archie waved at him, hissing, "Close the door!"

"Why?" asked Max, looking around the room. "Why's it so dark in here?" He flipped the switch near the door. The overhead light came on.

"Turn it off," Archie said angrily.

Max, perplexed, did as he was told. "What are you doing, Arch?" he asked.

"Close the door and I'll tell you," said Archie. Max shut

the door behind him and walked over to where Archie was crouched. "There's someone outside, watching the house."

Max's eyes went wide. He crouched by Archie, hidden beneath the sill.

"Who?" he asked.

"I don't know," said Archie. "Some guy in a suit. He was writing something in a book. Look."

Max slowly raised himself from the floor and peered out the window. "Oh my God," he said, his voice pitched in terror.

"What?" asked Archie.

"Oh my God," repeated Max, this time louder. "No!"

"What is it?" Archie couldn't stand the suspense; he pushed himself up and looked out the window at the street below.

There was no one there.

Max landed a punch on his brother's arm. He was laughing. "You're such a weirdo, Arch," he said. "I don't see anyone."

Archie searched the length of the pavement, trying to find the man – but he'd gone. "He was right there," said Archie, "I swear to God."

"It was probably Ron Applegate, dude," said Max.

"It wasn't Ron Applegate," replied Archie, dejected. "It was a guy with sideburns. In a hat."

"Oh my God, not a hat," said Max.

"Shut up, Max."

Max got up and turned on the light. He started searching the room, scrutinizing the padded rectangular case that

Archie kept his tapes in. "Did you take my Whitesnake tape?"

Archie was still looking out the window, scanning the street below. "No," he said. "Ask Olivia or Annabelle. I don't even like Whitesnake."

Max angled his head towards Archie's boom box. An ambient keyboard drone, the beginning of side A, was coming from the speakers. "Yeah, because you listen to this pansy stuff," he said, and left the room.

Archie waited until he heard Max's footsteps on the stairs, then he flipped off the light switch again. He looked out the window onto the street; the sky had gone totally black now, and the trees shuddered in the wind. He tried to dispel the feeling of dread in his chest – it wasn't unusual to see someone standing on the pavement on a June evening. The man might've been on a walk, lost in thought, maybe temporarily arrested by some idea until the light from Archie's window reminded him to move on. But there was no denying that the man had been staring at their house – and that the sudden eye contact between the man and Archie had been a real shock. Something about the man's look, even obscured in the night's darkness, had seemed almost inhuman.

Archie shook the thought away and turned on his lamp. He tried to focus on the music coming from his boom box; he picked up the book from his bedside table to read. It was a long time before Archie could fall asleep.

SATURDAY

Athena woke to a book being waved inches from her just-opening eyes.

Her full name was Athena Moonbeam Quest. It had been a charming name, even magical, when she was younger. It was like having a name straight out of a fairy tale. It was the pride of her first-grade class at Seaham Elementary – she'd won friends because of it, had been given first pick of toys at playdates because of it. She proudly announced herself wherever she went, using her full name, and was always buoyed by the smiles she got in response. But by the time fourth grade rolled around, the name had lost some of its glimmer. Suddenly, it was not so cool to have a name that might've better suited a cartoon unicorn. By sixth grade, she'd ditched the middle name altogether. Athena, as a first name, was innocuous enough. It didn't raise any eyebrows, at least. Not like Moonbeam. As for Quest – well, that was her family name. Not much she could do about that. Even if it was a name invented by her parents.

"It was different times, you see," her mother, Cynthia,

had said. "Coming out of the sixties. We were fighting the patriarchy, right? Why should I change my last name to your papa's? Who made that rule?"

"We agreed to not take either last name," her dad said. "So we came up with a new one. One that actually, y'know, had our spirit. As a family." And so Jordan Jones – a name that was extraordinary in its ordinariness – became Jordan Quest. His wife, née Woodson, became Cynthia Quest; their first child, Athena Quest. The Moonbeam part was some allusion to an all-night party they'd been at when Athena had been conceived; the story never failed to make Athena cringe.

"We were searching" was the explanation from them both. "We were on a quest – to find ourselves. To find our place in the world."

That quest brought them from San Francisco to Seaham just after Athena was born. There was a picture on top of the piano in the living room of Cynthia changing Athena's nappy on the fender of the old school bus that had carried them up the coast to Oregon, her blonde hair held back by a red bandanna. Jordan, bearded and shirtless, stood nearby, a tool belt strapped around his waist. In the background was the wooden frame of the home they were building, on a few acres just south of this small coastal town. Two – now three – questers, finding their home.

A second girl, Becky, was born six years after the photo had been taken. "After your great-grandmother, Rebecca," replied her mother when then-sixth-grade Athena asked why her sister got the normal name and she got the one from a

Greek goddess who was birthed from her father's forehead. "We always loved that name."

It was Becky, in fact, who was standing over Athena as she woke that morning, the first morning after the end of her eighth-grade year, waving a slim picture book in front of her sister's face.

"Can you read me this, Thena?" Becky asked.

"What time is it?"

"Dunno. Can you read it to me?"

"What about Mom and Papa? Can't you get them to?"

Becky shrugged. She waved the book again. Athena could make out the title: *The Little Brute Family*.

"Becky, it's the first day of summer break. Leave me alone." She turned over on her side and pulled a pillow over her head.

"Please, Thena? Pleeeeeease?"

Athena knew her sister well enough; the sun would burn out and the earth would wither before Becky Quest gave up her pleading. And so Athena rose, put on her clothes, and found herself in the living room of their family home, reading *The Little Brute Family* to her sister. A fitting start to her summer break, indeed.

She'd just got to the part where Baby Brute finds the "little wandering lost good feeling in a field of daisies", a glint of gold emanating from the top of the page like rays of light, when the phone rang. The side door to the kitchen opened and Cynthia Quest came in, her hair back in her requisite bandanna, a streak of dirt across her cheek. Athena absently watched her peel her gardening gloves from her hands and answer the phone.

"Thenie," she said, her ear to the receiver, "it's for you. It's Oliver."

Athena placed the book in Becky's lap and walked to the phone. "Hello?" she asked.

"Athena, it's me," said the voice on the other end.

"Oh, hey."

"Oliver," said the voice.

"I know," said Athena. The boy's voice was unmistakable – slightly nasal with the smallest warp on his *th* sounds that made them sound like *f*s. They'd been friends since third grade; she'd become used to hearing her name pronounced *Afena*.

"Did you get my message?"

Athena glanced down at the answering machine near the phone; a red light blinked on its beige plastic surface.

"Sorry," she said. "I guess I didn't. We got home last night kinda late and—"

"Doesn't matter. Meet at the benches. Ten o'clock."

"Ten?" She looked at the clock. It was just after nine. "Like, this morning?"

"Uh, yes," was the exasperated response. "It's important."

"What's up?"

"They found something. Up at the cliff. Y'know, at the headlands. Where they're building that hotel."

Athena knew all too well about the hotel they were building at the headlands. It had been all her parents could

46

talk about for the last several months. Some developer from Portland was planning a huge resort there – something that was going to transform Seaham and the coast. The Quests had taken it upon themselves, as self-appointed protectors of the local environment, to fight the plan tooth and nail. It put Athena in an awkward position; the contractor running the job was the father of one of her best friends.

"What?" she asked quietly, unconsciously turning away from her mother, who was pouring herself a glass of water from the kitchen tap. The last thing she wanted was another lecture about the destruction of the coast's natural beauty. "This isn't one of your, y'know, visions or whatever?"

There was a moment of silence on the other end before Oliver responded defensively. "No. It's not. It's like a cave or something. They've stopped work – that's what Archie says."

"Stopped?" She glanced at her mom.

"Yeah. Something about what they found. Anyway, we're going over there to check it out. You gotta come."

"Yeah, OK," said Athena. "Ten?"

"At the benches."

"Got it. See you there."

She hung up the phone; she zoned out, staring at the receiver for a moment. A cave. What kind of cave?

"What's that all about?" asked her mother.

"Something about the resort. The building thing. Up at the headlands. I guess they're not doing it now."

Cynthia's eyes widened. "No kidding," she said. "That's great news, Ath."

"They broke open some kinda cave." Athena shrugged. "Ollie wants to go check it out."

"With Archie too?"

"And Chris, yeah."

Cynthia took a drink of water. "Well, be careful. And let me know what you see." She looked out the window absently; Athena's dad, Jordan, was standing in the doorway of his cinder-block pottery studio, wiping clay dust from his apron. "That's great news," she repeated. "Your dad's going to be thrilled."

Athena looked at the clock; the benches were near Movie Mayhem, which was in Seaham proper. To get there in time, she'd have to leave now. She climbed onto the counter and grabbed a granola bar from the top shelf of a cupboard. She opened it and held it in her mouth as she retrieved her trainers from a hutch in the living room. Colourful light splashed down on the hardwood floors from the two stained-glass windows on either side of the front door. Becky was still on the sofa, flipping through her book.

"Where you going?" Becky asked.

"Going to go look at a cave," said Athena, between mouthfuls of granola bar.

"What's in the cave?"

"Dunno." Athena shrugged. "Guess we're gonna find out."

"Ooh," her sister said, brightening. "Maybe you'll find a little wandering lost good feeling."

48

Athena paused in her chewing and looked at Becky. "Yeah," she said. "Yeah, maybe."

And she was out the door on her way.

There it was, on the concrete floor of the shed. All rimed in a layer of dirt and grass stains; the word *HONDA* barely decipherable through the grime.

The lawn mower.

Chris Pedersen stared it down like it was an old nemesis; he felt a pit grow in his stomach. He was barely an hour into the first morning of his summer break, and how was he going to spend it? Diving into the chore that had haunted his summers since he'd been old enough to push this old two-stroke engine around. Mowing the lawn. The bane of every child's summer break. *Or,* Chris thought, *every child who had the sort of parents who felt like it was important to teach their kids the "value of hard work".* The thing was, not only was he expected to mow his family's own lawn on a roughly bi-weekly basis, he'd been contracted (through no consent of his own) to mow the Lindgrens' lawn and the Chus' lawn and the Frickes' lawn – like he was some kind of landscaping entrepreneur. Which was something he definitely didn't aspire to be.

But nevertheless, here he was. On a sunny Saturday morning, newly freed from his eighth-grade year of school. Ready to begin a summer of slashing through people's weedy yards. And the very first lawn to be mowed would be his own.

He yanked the mower out from a tangle of garden hoses and tomato cages. He dragged it into a dirty patch in the yard and checked the fuel level. He pressed the primer and set his foot on the side of the mower deck. *Here we go*, he thought. He grabbed the starter rope and pulled.

Nothing happened.

He let the cord snap back into the interior of the machine, pressed the primer another time for good measure, and pulled again.

Still nothing.

Thank the good lord, thought Chris Pedersen.

"Dad!" he yelled. "It's not working!"

"What?" The voice came from inside the house.

"The mower. It's not working."

Ted Pedersen appeared at the back door of their home. He was still dressed in his office clothes – tan suit and red tie, pressed slacks. "Well, did you prime it?" he asked.

Chris bent over and gave the primer button a few performative pushes and yanked the starter rope. Again, nothing happened.

"Did you check—"

"Fuel's totally full."

Ted put his hands on his hips and frowned; Chris did the same thing, mirroring his father.

"Well," said Ted, after a moment, "guess I'll have to tinker with it, see if I can't get it running."

"Darn," said Chris. "Guess I can't mow the lawn, then."

Ted grinned and shook his head. "I can tell you're disappointed."

"I was really looking forward to it."

Just then, the phone rang from inside the house. Ted withdrew to answer it. Chris remained, looking down at the silent mower. It was a temporary reprieve, Chris knew. But he would take it.

"Chris, it's for you," shouted his father from inside the house.

It was Oliver Fife, speaking breathlessly on the other end of the line. He'd left a message, the night before, and why hadn't Chris called him back? Something about a crack in a cliff, the Langdon property, the headlands, and Archie's dad. A *feeling*, he said. Oliver Fife had a *feeling*.

"Sorry, man," said Chris. "You're going to have to slow down. The *what* now?"

There was a long, dramatic pause on the other end of the line. Chris waited.

Chris had known Oliver since second grade, ever since Archie had brought the boy over to Chris's house for a playdate after school. He'd initially been a little stung by this introduction, worried that the unbreakable bond between him and his best friend would somehow become more … breakable – but he was quickly put at ease. Oliver was funny and weird; he said hilarious things sometimes and didn't seem to mind being the butt of a joke himself. Chris knew that Oliver would never supplant him in Archie's world, and he guessed Archie felt the same.

"They found something," Oliver said finally. "Up at the headlands. Below the Langdon House. A cave. Didn't you get my message? I wanna check it out."

"Did you talk to Archie?" Chris pinched the receiver between his ear and his shoulder as he began searching the cupboards for something to eat.

"And I can't really explain it. It's like I've got this feeling, you know? Like something's there. They stopped working on it, that's what Brody Tyke said. He's all mad, but that's—"

Chris interjected, "Dude, did you talk to Archie?"

"Yes, I talked to Archie. Saw him at Movie Mayhem last night. He said it was cool."

"Huh," said Chris through a mouthful of chips. "OK, I'm in."

"Awesome. Awesome, man. Meet at the benches. I'm heading over there now."

"Uh-huh," said Chris. He'd become distracted; through the kitchen window, he could see his dad leaning over the lawn mower, inspecting it. Ted Pedersen's jacket was off, and his shirt sleeves were rolled to his elbows. "Benches," said Chris absently.

"We'll bike up from there. This is going to be so *rad*."

"Yep," said Chris. "Rad."

He mumbled a goodbye into the receiver as he heard the end of the line go dead; the phone remained cradled at his shoulder. He watched as his father bent down and pulled on the starter cord of the mower – once, twice, three times.

A puff of black smoke; a reluctant engine chugged to life. Chris sighed heavily and hung up the phone.

Archie counted three familiar bikes laid at the corner of Bosun and Charles, where the pavement ended and the sand encroached on the streets in little drifts: Chris's striped white Bridgestone mountain bike, Oliver's hand-me-down red Schwinn, and Athena's sparkle-blue ten-speed – three incongruous models toppled over on top of one another. Their owners were camped on a bench some ways down a little path through the grassy dunes. Athena and Chris were sitting while Oliver was standing in front of them, animatedly recounting some story.

"Thought you might skip out on us," said Chris, seeing Archie come up.

"Never," said Archie.

"Good, 'cause I got out of mowing for this," said Chris. "That's like my one get-out-of-mowing pass for the month."

Archie and Chris exchanged slapped fives; Athena gave Archie a playful kick to the shins as Oliver leaned into him with his shoulder.

"So are we gonna do this?" asked Oliver.

Archie sighed and said, "I guess so."

Chris grinned. Oliver clapped his hands excitedly, rubbing them together like he was some movie villain. "Oh, this is gonna be good," he said.

Their bicycles unchained, they began pedalling up Bosun Street along the oceanfront, weaving around the beach-bound tourists.

"It's got to be connected to the Langdon place," said Chris.

"Wait, did you guys see *The Last Unicorn*?" asked Athena, sitting upright on her ten-speed, one hand steering on the top of the curled handlebars. She was wearing a canary-yellow Esprit shirt tucked into her 501s; her long brown hair flew behind her as she rode. "There are caves below the guy's castle, where the demon thing is."

"Ooh – yeah," said Chris. "There's got to be some kinda chained beast there."

Oliver added in his best movie-trailer voice: "The Langdons' demon, finally unearthed!" He looked at Archie and grinned, revealing the gap between his two front teeth.

Archie could only listen and agree. To him, the expedition seemed altogether more serious than they were treating it. He also had a grave suspicion that all the strange things he'd witnessed the day before – the ranting vagrant, the pennies on the doorsteps, the man outside his house – they all had some connection to this cave in the cliff.

But now Bosun Street began a small incline up the hillside, and the beachfront houses became less frequent, replaced by sloping, empty lots filled with tall fir trees. Soon, they'd left the main part of Seaham behind them altogether and were climbing, standing high on their pedals, where the road twisted into the forest. A wrought-iron fence began to parallel the left side of the road, enclosing a wide, grassy meadow. Scotch broom and blackberries had overtaken the clearing long ago, and it looked as if it would take the swordsmanship of a maiden-seeking fairy-tale hero to clear a path through the thick bramble. Not far off, in the centre of the field, Archie could see the spire of Langdon House.

"Always gives me the creeps," said Athena, coming up alongside Archie.

"Seriously," he replied.

Chris, riding ahead, stopped at the locked gate that guarded the drive to the front door of house; he waited there for everyone to catch up, his hands shoved into the pockets of his brightly patterned Jams. The cobbles of the drive beyond the fence were buckled and overgrown with weeds. Here, they could see the house in all its decrepitude: cracked white paint revealing weather-grey wood, broken windows and a warped roof.

"I was gonna miss this place," said Oliver, peering through the bars of the fence. The gate was bent and rusted with age, but had at one point, no doubt, been the very picture of well-to-do opulence. The initials *C.L.* were worked into the iron of the gate – presumably after the great patriarch of the family, Charles Langdon. Twin pillars anchored the two pieces of the gate; ornamental markings, covered in decades' worth of grime, could be seen etched into the concrete.

"Good riddance," said Archie. "Creep city." Archie's dad had often referred to the Langdon House as an eyesore and a lawsuit waiting to happen.

"Aw," said Athena, "I always kinda liked the flowers on these things." She was tracing one of the gatepost markings with her finger. "Sad to see 'em go."

"Wait," said Chris. "Is there someone inside?"

"Where?" asked Archie; he pressed his face against the gate, trying to see into one of the house's broken windows.

"You see someone?" asked Oliver, pushing alongside Archie and Athena.

"There – in the attic window," said Chris.

Archie felt Athena's hand seize his arm; he strained his eyes to look into the single oval window at the top of the house, searching for movement. He felt his pulse quicken.

Chris came behind them, and said, "Right… THERE!" Just as he exclaimed this last word, he grabbed Athena and Archie by the shoulders, hard. They both jumped; Athena let out a scream.

Chris erupted in laughter, clutching his side.

"Oh, grow up," said Athena, turning red.

"You about gave me a heart attack, doofus," said Archie.

The imagination did want to populate the old house, though – it wanted to put gaunt, staring butlers at the front door and pale children in pinafores in the second-floor windows, where the house sent out a decorated turret; it wanted to put a man staring out to the hills on the balcony above the wide front porch and a woman, a ghostly woman, pacing the widow's walk on the broken roof, staring forever out to sea. It was the kind of house that invited stories to be made around it.

"C'mon," said Chris, "let's head down to the beach."

The gravel road was rutted and worn from the heavy equipment that had been taxiing back and forth from Seaham down the cliffside below the house, and so the four friends dismounted their bikes and walked the steep grade to the beach. Chris and Athena pushed ahead; Oliver tailed along behind them. Archie took up the rear, as if forestalling his arrival there.

A chain-link fence now ran along the Langdon property; it took an improbable dive down the face of the cliff to the beach below. Here, the fence extended out to where the ocean met the sand, to keep all would-be invaders off the job site. To the north and south, twin promontories jutted out from the headlands, sealing off the beach. Even though it was technically public land, the only access was the road that ran by the Langdon place. Several large, imposing signs that read *DANGER! DO NOT ENTER* and *CONSTRUCTION AREA – KEEP OUT* were zip-tied to the chain-link; a padlocked gate barred any entrance. On the other side of the fencing, a few pieces of heavy construction machinery lay quiet on the sand, safe from the reach of the tides. One, a front-end loader, was parked near the cliff face, just in front of a massive gash that ran up the mudstone-and-basalt rock of the cliff. It seemed to sever the rocky face, like a bolt of lightning, from the base of the cliff to the top of the promontory, where little patches of grass could be seen clinging to the edge. The machine was surrounded by piles of newly made boulders.

The four kids ditched their bikes on the sand and approached the fence, fishing their fingers between the chain links.

"Can you see anything?" asked Oliver, peering through the fence.

"Nah, that machine's in the way," said Athena.

"That must be the cave," said Chris. "There, down below that crack. Can you see it?"

"Barely," said Oliver.

Archie's skin was crawling; he couldn't wait to get out of there. "Well," he said, after a moment passed and they'd all taken in the sight. "There it is. I guess we can—"

"Hey, guys – look," said Chris. He was pointing to where the fence ended. It seemed as if the barrier had been constructed during a high tide, when the chain-link would have extended into the ocean. Now, at low tide, there was a gap between the end of the fence and the water.

Archie glanced at Oliver. "We're not getting any closer," he said. "Oliver swore."

"I guess I did," said Oliver. He looked sheepishly at his friends.

"Dudes," said Chris, "we've come all this way. Can we just, y'know, get a *little* closer? I mean, we can't really see anything from here." He looked at the other three kids as he said this. "All in favour of getting a closer look?"

Three hands were raised in the air. Archie kept his close to his sides. He glanced around nervously. "Oliver, what about Saint Michael and Saint George and whoever?"

Oliver shrugged; he pushed his glasses up the bridge of his nose.

"No one's gonna see us," said Chris, walking to the edge of the fence. "We're just gonna take a quick peek."

But before Archie could be convinced and won to their side, both Chris and Oliver had slipped around the end of the fence and begun approaching the cliff. Soon, Chris's voice came from behind the machine, shouting, "You guys! You have to come look at this!"

It looked more like a crack than a cave, a jagged scar at the base of the cliff. At its widest, it was barely four feet across. But the darkness beyond suggested that it opened onto a deep seam in the earth. Archie and Athena came up from behind their two friends, who were standing just in front of the cave. They were all staring at it, mystified.

Athena was the first to speak. "This is what they stopped everything for?" she asked.

"Look," said Oliver, pointing up the cliffside. "The crack goes all the way up to the top."

"Dad said that the whole cliff was like Swiss cheese," said Archie. "Holes in the rock everywhere."

"So this must just be the opening," said Chris.

"Swiss cheese," said Oliver wistfully.

"Careful, Ollie," said Archie. "Don't get too close." A knot had developed in his stomach; he could feel it coiling, there below his ribcage.

"I want to see what's in it," Oliver said. He placed his hand on the edge of the fissure and craned his neck to look inside.

He adjusted his glasses on the bridge of his nose. "Whoa," he said. "It's really deep."

"Oliver," said Archie, suddenly overcome by his fear. "Back up."

"Yeah, Ollie," said Athena. "Maybe you shouldn't go too far."

"Just a sec," said Oliver. "I just want to see…" He stopped speaking. He let go of the edge of the crack and quickly began to back away from the wall.

"What's up, Oliver?" asked Chris.

The boy continued to steadily walk backwards, his eyes fixed on the hole. "Oh God," he murmured. And then he froze in place.

"Oliver?" asked Athena meekly.

But then something strange happened: the boy, continuing to stand upright, became locked into a kind of rigor mortis stance, his hands clenched at his sides and his lips tightly pursed. His eyelids fluttered wildly for a moment before, in a flash, his irises flew back in his head, revealing the whites of his eyes.

"Oliver!" shouted Athena. She ran to grab him. But the boy jerked back and fell to the ground. There was a dull thud as his head struck a piece of rock jutting from the sand; his glasses flew from his face. His eyes focused heavenward again, his pupils visible. He was staring blankly at the sky. He began to mutter odd, unintelligible bits of words. Spittle flew from his lips as he spoke.

"It's one of his … his *whatevers*!" shouted Chris, running to Oliver's side. "It's happening again."

"What do we do?" yelled Athena.

"I don't know!" said Chris. He was gripping Oliver's shoulders.

The first time Archie had witnessed one of his friend's *whatevers*, as Chris had called them, had been at a sleepover at Oliver's house, years before. They'd stayed up late that night, telling ghost stories. Chris had been there. Oliver was in the middle of his own story when he suddenly became quiet. In the glow of his torch, Archie could see his friend's muscles tense and his eyes flit back in his head. He'd been sitting upright in bed, but his head lolled to one side and his body went slack. Archie and Chris, terrified, had run to get Agnes, Oliver's mom. When they returned, the boy had regained consciousness; he acted as if nothing had happened. But the experience left a mark on Archie's memory.

"Oliver!" shouted Chris. "Wake up, dude." Athena was kneeling by Oliver's side. The boy was clearly unconscious; his body was still. She patted his cheeks; she cradled the back of his head and gave him a shake. Oliver continued to mutter, his eyes locked skyward.

"What is he saying?" asked Archie.

"I don't know," said Chris. "Dude, Ollie, come on."

"Oh God," said Athena. She'd removed her hands from the back of the boy's head; there was blood on her fingers.

"Hey! What are you doing over there?" shouted a voice. Archie turned and saw Emilio Hernandez, one of the partners in his father's business, standing on the other side of the fence. "Archie Coomes, is that you?"

"Emilio!" cried Archie. "Something's wrong with my friend. He's hurt!"

The man quickly pulled a key from his pocket and undid the padlock on the gate; he flung the chain-link open and ran over to where Oliver lay.

"What in God's name?" said Emilio, lifting the back of Oliver's head. He gave a frantic wave and said, "Everyone – get out of the way. Stand back."

The kids did as they were told; they watched as Emilio turned Oliver over on his side. Saliva dribbled from the corner of the boy's mouth. Emilio pulled a radio from his belt and thumbed the switch. "Hey, Joe," he said. "Emilio here."

There was a thrum of static and then a voice came over the radio: "What's up?"

"We got a kid down here, having some kind of seizure or something."

"What? Who—" came the reply.

Emilio didn't let him finish. "He hit his head. It's bad. We gotta get an ambulance down here right away."

"Roger that," said the voice. "Over."

The radio went silent. Kneeling at Oliver's side, Emilio looked up at Archie and shook his head, frowning. "Archie Coomes," he said. "Of all people. Archie Coomes."

Oliver had gained some semblance of consciousness by the time the paramedics arrived from Harrisburg General Hospital. He'd been making eye contact with his friends and was able to nod and shake his head to basic questions. They'd stopped the blood flow from the back of his skull with a rag Emilio had supplied. The boy looked as scared as Archie had ever seen him.

"Did something bring it on?" one of the paramedics asked the kids while Oliver was loaded onto a stretcher and belted in.

The kids looked at one another helplessly. Chris finally said, "He looked into the cave."

"He did what?"

"The cave. He looked into it. And then this happened."

"What cave?" asked the paramedic.

"Down by the cliff," said Archie.

Emilio, who was standing by Archie, interjected, "The gate was locked. It was clearly marked. I don't know how they got around the fence."

The paramedics loaded Oliver into the back of the ambulance and drove away up the road from the beach, lights flashing. Emilio and the three remaining kids were left standing on the sand.

"Emilio," began Archie, "I'm so—"

"Archie," interrupted Emilio, "what were you doing back there?"

"It wasn't his idea," said Chris. "He didn't have anything to do with it. Promise."

"I'm not talking to you, kid," said Emilio, shooting a glare at Chris. He looked back at Archie. "What were you doing?"

"We just wanted to check out the cave, that's all."

"The cave," repeated Emilio, exasperated. "You wanted to check out the cave. Let me tell you something about that cave:

you got no business getting close to that cave, you got it?"

"Got it," murmured Archie.

"You all got me?" asked Emilio, surveying the other two kids now.

They all mumbled their assent.

"You're lucky nothin' else happened to none of you. That woulda been my ass, got it?" said Emilio, fuming. He looked at Archie. "What am I gonna tell your dad, Archie, huh?"

"I don't know," said Archie. He hesitated, then said, "Do you … do you have to tell him?"

Everyone waited for Emilio's response; when none came, Athena put in, "The fence didn't go all the way to the water. Look – it's real easy to get around."

"That don't make a difference," said Emilio. "You see these signs? You guys can read, can't you?"

Everyone nodded, answering the man's question earnestly. Emilio frowned, and said, "Aw, hell." He looked back at Archie. "OK, here's the deal. I'm gonna put another section of fence there – so it does go to the water – and we're gonna just keep this to ourselves, OK? Your buddy had his little episode right here, on this side of the fence."

"Yes, sir," Chris said in chorus with Archie and Athena.

"Your dad would have my ass as much as yours," said Emilio to Archie, "and I'm not in the mood, not since we all been put off this job. You got me?"

"Got it," said Archie.

"And don't none of you come back here, OK? Not on this side, and damn sure not on that side of the fence. If I catch you – if anyone catches you – back here, I'm not gonna be inclined to cut another deal. Got it?"

"Got it," said Chris, before adding, "sir."

"Awright," said Emilio. "You all get out of here. I got work to do."

The three kids moved quickly to their bikes, eager to leave the scene before Emilio changed his mind or felt inspired to chew them out further. They were a sombre crew walking their bikes back along the road down into town.

"That was the worst one I've seen. For sure," said Athena.

"They seem to be getting worse," said Chris. "Hope it's not too serious, like, I dunno, brain cancer or something."

"I think he saw something in that cave," said Archie. "That's what made it happen."

"We don't know that," said Chris. "He's been doing this weird stuff for years."

Archie stopped, bringing everyone to a halt. He looked at each of his friends in turn, saying, "Don't tell me you didn't feel it. There's something weird about that hole. I don't know what, but it's not good."

No one spoke. Finally, it was Athena who broke the silence. "You know," she said, then paused again. Then, "We had a cat when I was little. I think I knew you guys then. Moksha. Remember him? Maybe not. He was super old – I think my parents had had him since they were in California. And one day he disappeared. Papa said cats do that when they die – they find some place to go. You know, to die. And one day, I…" She looked at the ground, frowning. "I was out in the

65

woods, behind our place, and I found his collar. Just outside of this big hole in the ground, some big pit that a fallen tree had left behind, I think. And I looked into that hole and I knew – I can't explain it – but I could, like, feel his death there." She looked up at Archie, her face red as if she'd been embarrassed to admit the feeling, and said, "That's what it felt like."

A moment passed. "That's really creepy," said Chris.

Athena had her eyes downcast. "You felt it, didn't you?"

"Let's go, you guys," Chris said. He started walking away down the hill towards town. "I was supposed to be home like an hour ago."

Archie and Athena exchanged worried glances before they, too, began walking their bikes after Chris.

That night, after dinner, when Archie was back in his room, a soft knock came at the door. It was his father.

"Hey, Arch," Peter said.

"Hey, Dad."

"I wanted to talk to you. Now a good time?" He walked into the room and closed the door behind him.

"Sure," said Archie, setting down his book.

"We heard from Agnes again," said Peter.

"How's Oliver?" asked Archie. He'd been consumed with worry all afternoon and evening; he'd found it hard to concentrate on his book – his thoughts kept going to Oliver, laid out on the sand, his eyes shot back in his head. The strange mumbling. The dark stain in the crotch of his jeans.

"He's fine," said Peter, sitting down at the end of Archie's bed. Archie had laid his book down by his side and Peter picked it up now; he studied the cover. "This any good?" he asked.

"It's all right," said Archie. "More of the same." It was a fantasy novel – the fifth in a series. He knew his dad didn't really care about the book or its contents; Peter Coomes didn't read much aside from the occasional thriller he picked up from the library.

Peter made to read the back of the book, but Archie knew he was just stalling for time. Finally, he spoke. "Seems like Oliver had a good fright," he said. "I don't know what sets him off when he gets these things, but Agnes seemed to think this one was a doozy." He paused and looked at his son, setting the book back on the bed. "You guys must've been real scared."

Hearing his dad say this released a torrent of emotion in Archie and he felt himself suddenly fighting the urge to cry. "Mm-hmm," was all he managed, for fear of sliding into sobs – something he just couldn't do. Not at thirteen. Not in front of his dad.

"Sounds like you guys did the right thing," said Peter. "Thank God Emilio was heading down there. But I betcha you would've been all right if he hadn't. Might've been scary, but you guys are good with each other. You look after each other."

Archie nodded, biting his lip, still fighting tears.

"Agnes said he's doing good, though," Peter continued. "He's awake and feeling all right. They did a CT scan; sounds like they didn't find anything. They're keeping an eye on him for a concussion, but that's about it. Looks like he cracked his noggin pretty good when he fell."

"He's probably not going on the camping trip, huh?"

Peter shook his head. "I don't think so," he said. "At least that's what his mom says. Guess they want to, you know, monitor him for a bit." He paused again and looked at Archie directly. "Listen," he said. "I know you said you were just going to check out the site, that you were just looking through the fence. But I want you to steer clear of that place – the beach and the cliff. I don't want you going back until we can do some work down there. You got me?"

Archie nodded. "What kinda work?"

His father became suddenly very serious. "I told Emilio to fill in that hole. To patch up that cliff as best as we can. He's gonna throw a ton of cement down into that place and dump a bunch of dirt to fill in that crack. Then we're out of there. Our job is done."

"OK," said Archie, surprised by his father's sudden determination. "Thanks."

"Uh-huh," said Peter. He reached up and tousled Archie's hair. "Love you, kiddo," he said. He stood up slowly from the bed; his knees gave a resounding crack. He walked to the door, opened it, and paused at the threshold just as Archie spoke.

"Dad?"

"Yeah?"

"What's in that hole?"

Peter ran a finger along the grain of the doorjamb, thinking. Finally, he said, "That hole's not gonna be there any more in a few days. So that's all there is to it," and walked out of the room, closing the door behind him.

SUNDAY

"The hospital's right on your way, sweetie," said Liz. She wasn't even looking at Max as she spoke to him; she was rifling through a pile of coupons in one of the kitchen drawers. "You can just drop them at the door."

"They're gonna make me late," said Max. "I was supposed to meet Chad at eleven."

"I'm sure Chad won't mind," said Liz. "They can come find you at the mall after."

Archie, standing in the doorway, chimed in. "Please, can you take us, Mom?" Max had only just received his licence, though he'd failed the driver's test twice before they finally passed him. Riding with him didn't really instil confidence.

Liz sighed. "I already said, Arch, I can't. I've got the shopping to do and — and there's a million things to do around here. It's right on his way. Plus, it'll give your brother some practice." She smiled at Max; Max frowned.

"OK, if you want us all to die," said Archie.

Max blushed and glared at his brother. "Shut up, bug," he said.

"You shut up."

Liz, rolling her eyes, said, "Boys. Boys. Please. Can you please be civil to each other once in your life?"

"Fine," said Max. "Whatever. But your weird friends better be ready, like, now." He grabbed the keys from the hook by the door. "And driver picks the music."

Fifteen minutes later, they were all packed into the Coomes family's 1984 Dodge Omni. Archie rode in the passenger seat while Athena and Chris were in the back. A Def Leppard tape played loudly on the stereo. Max drummed his fingers on the steering wheel as he drove. Archie looked out the window all the way, staring thoughtfully at the passing scenery, the wind-bent trees and the wide, raging ocean.

Over the whine of a guitar solo, Max spoke to Athena in the back seat. "I hear you're trying out for JV soccer next year."

Athena sat forward. "Yeah," she said.

"Good luck with that," said Max. "Squad's gonna be tough this year."

"Who told you, anyway?" asked Athena.

Max paused before saying, "Chris's sister."

"Ooh," crowed Archie, "Megan."

"Shut up," said Max. "She was in my chem lab." He went back to tapping on the steering wheel, but Archie could see that his face had reddened.

"What?" said Chris, evidently noticing the change his sister's name had on the boy. "You *like* her?"

Max sneered. "I don't *like* her. I mean, she's all right."

"Dude," said Chris. "I have to share a bathroom with that girl. She leaves her moustache hairs all over the sink."

Archie looked into the back seat just in time to see Athena give Chris a hard elbow to the rib. "Don't make fun of that," she said. "Girls have hair, too, y'know. Chauvinist."

"Yeah," said Max, glaring at Chris in the rearview. "Don't be one of those." He reached down and cranked the volume knob on the stereo; Def Leppard wiped out all possibility of further conversation.

Harrisburg had a population that was double that of Seaham's; the area's high school was here. It was also where the main hospital was – Archie and Chris had both been born at Harrisburg General. And now here they were, returning to see Oliver, bed-bound, in the short-term-stay wing.

"Two hours, bug," said Max, leaning over the centre console to speak through the rolled-down window. Athena, Archie and Chris were standing below the portico of the hospital's front doors. "At the Orange Julius."

"Got it," said Chris. "At Victoria's Secret. If you're in the changing room, we'll wait."

Max stared at Chris silently for a moment before saying, "If you're late, I'm skid-marking you and you can walk home up the 101. Got it?"

"Got it," said Archie.

"And watch your mouth, Pedersen," added Max, "or they're going to have a second dweeb in the intensive care wing."

Chris laughed; Athena made a face. "Just go," said Archie. "See you in a few hours."

Max turned the music back up, loud, and revved the engine. He put the car noisily into gear. It promptly stalled.

Archie and his friends burst into laughter.

Red-faced, Max cranked the ignition again and peeled away from the hospital entrance, a wake of squealing guitar following him.

"Super-cool guy," said Chris, watching him go.

"Brothers," said Archie. "What can you do?"

"Sisters are no better," said Chris.

"Come on, guys," said Athena. "Let's find Ollie."

He was sitting up when they walked in the room, his back supported by a pile of pillows. The television was on in the corner, and an old episode of *CHiPs* was playing, the sound off. The room smelled like bleach and applesauce. Oliver smiled when he saw them, though he looked pale and exhausted – there were dark purple bags under his eyes, and his lips quivered as he spoke. A ribbon of gauze encircled his skull, keeping a large compression pad in place on the back of his head.

"Hey, guys," he said. "Thanks for coming."

"Oliver," said Athena, rushing to the bed. "Oh my God, you scared us so bad."

"I'm OK, really," he said, though his voice was hollow, used up. "It's just this thing I have. It's not a big deal."

"Hi, you guys," said Andrew Fife, Oliver's father. He was sitting in a chair near the window. He and Agnes had divorced when Oliver was five. Andrew now lived in Harrisburg and shared custody of his two children with his ex-wife. He had Oliver's thick, brown hair and wore a bushy moustache. "Sorry you had to be the first responders on this one."

"Oh, it's no big deal," said Chris. "We're just glad he's OK."

"They did a CAT scan," said Oliver, glowing a little at the excitement of it. "Put me in this big machine. Like in *The Exorcist*!"

"Jeez," said Athena. "Is everything all right?"

"All good," said Andrew. "Thank God." He then stood and gave Oliver's shoulder a little push. "Just the normal brain damage, huh, Ollie?"

"Dad," he said, embarrassed. He rolled his eyes.

Athena grew serious as she asked, "Still don't know what it is, though?"

Andrew shook his head. "They've got some ideas, but … y'know…" He trailed off. "Always been a mystery, this one," he said brightly. His look remained on his son for a moment before he blinked and said, "Well, I'll get out of your hair, let you meet with your friends." He left the room and closed the door behind him, leaving the four kids alone.

"Oliver, the magical mystery boy," said Athena playfully.

"We brought you comic books," said Archie, retrieving from his backpack a small stack of *Conan the Barbarian* comics they'd picked up at a news-stand that morning. He set them down at the foot of the bed.

"Thanks, guys," said Oliver. He suddenly looked

73

stricken; he smoothed his hands along the bedsheets and stared up at his friends.

"What's up, Ollie?" asked Archie, sitting on the side of the bed.

"I can't get it out of my head," said Oliver. "I had dreams, all night. I couldn't shake it."

"What about?" asked Athena.

"The crack in the cliff," said Oliver.

Athena and Archie exchanged a look. "They're just dreams, Ollie," said Athena.

Chris moved in closer. "You never told us what you saw down there. What was it?" he asked.

"Give him a sec, Chris," said Athena. But Archie could see she was curious too.

Oliver closed his eyes tightly, as if willing the memory back to the surface. He pursed his lips and shook his head. "I can't remember," he said. "It's all blank. One moment I'm walking to the cave – Archie, I heard you calling me – and the next thing I know, I'm in the ambulance." He opened his eyes again; he was staring blankly at the television screen. "Can't remember a thing before that – there's just nothing there. But whatever I saw, it's like it's there, in my mind, somewhere." He paused, then said, "It's really scaring me, you guys."

"Hey," said Chris, "don't get all worked up. A lot of people have seizures. I think epilepsy is really common."

"It's not epilepsy," said Oliver. "I keep telling people that. No one believes me. The doctors – they don't even know. I mean, this isn't the first time. It's maybe the worst, but it's not the first time. I'll be OK."

"Well, hey – you're in a hospital," said Archie. "You'll get all the ice cream you can handle."

Oliver laughed politely, and they all laughed with him, but their laughter rang hollow, like they were actors in some play, trying to dredge up the emotion for another performance.

"But I get this feeling," said Oliver, pushing himself farther upright against his pillow supports. "I get this feeling like it wasn't a good thing, what they did."

"What do you mean? What who did?" asked Archie.

"Your dad, or your dad's crew, or whatever. They did a bad thing, Arch, finding that cave. I get this feeling…"

They shoulda left it hid.

Archie flinched. "What feeling?" he asked faintly.

"Like they should've left it buried."

The words took Archie's breath away. He quickly said, "Well, it's not going to be there much longer. My dad says they're going to fill it in. Emilio's doing it tomorrow. They're gonna patch up the whole cliffside, like nothing happened."

"For real?" asked Oliver, his eyes brightening for the first time that afternoon.

"That's what he says. Told me last night."

"Then that's the end of it," said Chris, letting out a huff of breath.

Oliver had rested back against his pillows and closed his

eyes. "Maybe I'll sleep better now," he said. He opened his eyes again and said, "You guys still going camping tomorrow?"

"That's the plan," said Archie.

"Good," said Oliver. "You should go. Don't let me hold you up."

"Why don't you hike in on Tuesday," suggested Athena, "when you're home and feeling better? We're going to be at the fort, just fixing things up."

"Yeah, maybe," said Oliver, drifting off. "Yeah. Maybe."

A dulcet stream of Muzak played; it echoed off the shiny tiled floor of the Harrisburg Hill Mall as Chris received three drinks from the girl behind the Orange Julius counter and handed them out to his friends.

"I'll get you back," said Archie, taking his cup.

"Don't worry about it," said Chris. "I'm flush. It's mowing season."

"Thanks, Chris," said Athena. She took a long pull from her straw; they found a seat at a nearby bench.

"Of course we're the ones waiting," said Archie after a time. "I'd be in such Dutch if I was a second late, but Max can take all the time he wants."

"Can't wait to get my licence," said Chris. "You know, Samantha MacDonagh got her permit when she was fifteen."

"Yeah, I guess it depends on when you enrol and all that," said Athena. She frowned. "My dad doesn't want me driving. Says I should stick with riding my bike. Better for the environment. Like, one less driver."

"Easy for him to say," said Archie.

They waited; they slurped at their drinks. The arcade could be heard, just down the hall, a symphony of digital bleeps and dings. They began discussing plans for the camping trip. They'd be leaving tomorrow, first thing, from Chris's house. Since Oliver wasn't coming, they had to decide who would bring the handsaw and the cookstove, two things Oliver had volunteered to bring.

"I hope he can make it," said Athena. "Once he feels better."

"It's just weird," said Archie. "What happened. I've never seen him act that way. I mean, he's been weird, but not *that* weird."

"You haven't noticed?" asked Chris.

"Noticed what?"

"They're getting worse. His visions. These – whatever they are – seizures. I mean, when we were little, these sorts of things would happen. But they weren't that big of a deal, right? It was just Oliver being Oliver." Chris threw his empty cup into a nearby rubbish bin. He stood up in front of Archie and Athena and continued, "But now – I mean, this. And then the thing last year with Mr Gibbons, remember, the maths teacher? Something's up."

"Like what?" asked Athena.

Chris shrugged. "I don't know. Guess that's up to the doctors. But something's not right. With, like, his brain."

Athena frowned. "Did you ever think that maybe it's a good thing? Like what he's said all along – these feelings he

77

has. That they make him special somehow? That they're…" She searched for the word.

"Magic?" Chris smirked.

"Yeah," said Athena defiantly. "Maybe they are."

Chris gave a dismissive laugh; Athena reddened. Archie was thankful to see his brother appear; he had a paper bag bearing the words PEGASUS MUSIC in neon. He glanced at Archie and his friends briefly before walking by, spinning the Omni's key chain in his fingers.

"Let's go," he said over his shoulder.

Athena and Chris exchanged a glare; Archie pushed himself up from the bench, and they all followed Max Coomes out the doors of the mall into the car park.

The road back to Seaham wound along the rugged, tree-strewn cliffs far above the ocean. They drove slowly, hampered by the weekend traffic of early summer vacationers and Portland day-trippers, forever rubbernecking the wild landscape and the vast, churning ocean. Max had bought a new tape at the mall and it played in the stereo. He was back to improvising a drumbeat to the music on the steering wheel. Occasionally, he turned to Archie and lip-synched the lyrics to the song; Archie tried to tune his brother out.

"See you guys tomorrow," Athena said when they arrived at her house, an odd-shaped building made of salvaged wood and stained-glass windows. A string of Tibetan prayer flags hung fluttering across the porch. Climbing from the car, she said, "Thanks for the ride, Max."

"No prob, Moonbeam," said Max. Athena made a face at him.

"Eleven at my place!" shouted Chris from the back seat. "And don't forget the camping knife!"

She turned and gave a thumbs-up from the porch, then disappeared into the house.

Pulling onto Charles Avenue, back in town, they were stopped by a long line of cars. Max rolled down his window and peered out, trying to get a better view of the obstacle. "What's up with this?" he murmured.

Archie, in the passenger seat, craned his neck forward. He could see flashing police lights a few intersections from where they were stopped. A group of pedestrians had congregated on the pavement, their eyes fixed on something playing out on the street before them.

As Max crept the car closer, they could see a police officer waving drivers onto a side street off Charles; beyond that, a yellow convertible was stopped in the middle of the road. Two police cars were parked there, their red-and-blue lights little pinpricks in the afternoon sun. As they drew closer, the car idled alongside a police officer. Max stuck his head out the window and asked, "What happened?"

"Some transient," said the cop, his hands on his belt. "Got hit. Keep moving, please."

"Yes, sir," said Max, a hint of attitude in his voice. But the car suddenly stalled. Max swore. He tried the ignition, but the car wouldn't start. That's when Archie threw open his door and leaped out.

"Hey!" shouted Max. "Where are you going?"

But Archie was already out on the pavement, pushing his way through the crush of onlookers.

"Arch!" shouted Chris. He'd left the car, too, and was chasing after his friend.

At the intersection, Archie could see the driver of the convertible leaning against the front panel of his car, a cigarette in his hand. He was talking to another police officer; his face was drawn and serious. The officer took notes in a small pad while the man spoke. Beyond that, just in front of the grille of the convertible, lay the body of a woman.

Archie edged closer, looking over the shoulders of the spectators, trying to get a better view – and then he saw.

It was the woman who'd spoken to him just days before. The homeless lady with the wild stare.

They found somethin' down there.

Archie pushed himself sideways between two kids who were gawping at the corner and stepped out into the street. There was no doubt – it was the same lady. She lay crooked on the street, her left leg cocked sideways in a grotesque position. A pool of blood was building beneath the back of her head; her eyes were wide and staring up into the sky. Her mouth, dotted with broken teeth, was slack and open.

They shoulda left it hid.

"Hey, you – kid!" shouted a police officer. "Back up. Police business. Get back to the sidewalk."

Archie felt Chris's hand at his shoulder, dragging him back.

"It's her," croaked Archie, staring at the body on the ground. "It's that lady."

"Archie, Jesus," said Chris, escorting him through the crowd, back onto the pavement. "What are you doing?"

"I know that woman, Chris."

"You what?"

"I saw her, two days ago. She spoke to me. She said something – she said something about that hole in the cliffside. I know it now. She said they should've left it hidden, that's what she said." Archie's heart was thundering in his chest. He could feel his blood pulsing through his ears.

"Archie, what the hell?" said a voice behind him. It was Max, standing at his shoulder. "You can't just…" Max's voice dropped away as he saw the gruesome sight laid out before them. "Jesus," the boy intoned quietly.

They all watched as an ambulance, its siren emitting sharp squawks, nosed its way through the idling traffic. The homeless woman, at this point, had been covered with a sheet. Archie and Chris watched as the medics carefully heaved her broken body onto a stretcher. Within moments, the crowd was parting again for the ambulance's hasty exit from the scene, and the police officers began ushering people on their way.

Max put his hand on Archie's shoulder. "Come on, man," he said in a tone of voice that Archie hadn't heard for a very long time. It almost sounded like concern. "Let's go."

A stunned silence had descended over the occupants of the car as Max drove the Omni through the neighbourhood streets towards Chris's house. When they arrived, Chris climbed out of the car and stood at the passenger-side window.

"See you tomorrow," he said.

"Yep," said Archie. "I'll be here."

Chris gave the top of the car a friendly pat and then jogged off towards his house.

Max looked at his brother. "You good?" he asked.

"Yeah," said Archie.

Max noisily put the car into gear and made a U-turn in the gravel of the Pedersens' driveway. He headed back down the hill towards town. "We don't need to tell Mom or Dad about that dead lady," said Max after a time. "Especially Mom. It's just going to freak her out."

"You think she was dead?" asked Archie.

Max sucked at his teeth. "Kinda looked like that. I mean, they put a sheet on her. They only do that to dead people on TV."

"I've never seen a dead person before," said Archie.

"Me neither."

Archie shook his head. "That lady was super out of it. Yesterday, when I saw her, she was just walking out in the middle of the road. I almost ran into her on my bike. It's like she was asking for it."

"Yup," said Max. "She was probably wasted."

"I keep thinking about what she said, about the cliff. About how they found something."

"Dude, I wouldn't pay much mind to that," said Max. "Probably the whiskey talking. Or whatever she was on."

"But still—"

Max interrupted him. "Didn't Dad say they were done with that place? They were gonna fill the hole with cement and leave it alone. So who cares what that lady said?"

Archie didn't respond. Max gave him a slug in the shoulder. "C'mon," said Max. "Don't be such a wuss."

And yet, the remainder of their drive was notably silent, with the windows rolled down and the volume of the stereo quiet, the music of the newly purchased tape a forgotten background to the sound of the road, the sound of the wheels.

MONDAY

"How'd you get a refrigerator in here?" asked Chris, peering at Archie's backpack. The two boys were standing in Chris's front yard; Archie's mom had just pulled away from the kerb, the Omni disappearing down the dirt drive. Chris mimed lifting the camo-green pack like it was a three-hundred-pound barbell.

"Ha, ha," said Archie flatly. It had become a kind of ritual between the two of them, ever since they'd begun camping without parents – this gauging who had packed the best and packed the lightest. He reached into the top pocket of the pack and retrieved a worn hardcover book. "This is like half the weight," he said.

"Can't leave without that," said Chris.

"No way," said Archie. The book had been, in fact, the first thing he'd set aside to pack. It was a hefty hardcover collection of ghost stories that belonged to his dad, a Modern Library edition from 1940. Archie had brought it on every camping trip they'd taken, and they were slowly making their way through the stories. "As if this weekend wasn't scary enough," he said.

"How about the stove?" asked Chris.

"The what now?" asked Archie.

"You didn't," said Chris.

Archie slapped his hands to his cheeks in mock-mortification, and Chris glared. Archie smiled. "Yes, I brought the stove," he said. "I'm not *that* clued out."

Just then a car arrived, a beige Volkswagen Rabbit, and Athena appeared from the passenger side with an excited leap. "Hey, guys," she said.

"The goddess of wisdom," said Chris triumphantly. He made a play bow.

Athena smiled and opened the hatchback of the car, retrieving her pack. Jordan Quest climbed out of the driver's seat and waved at the boys. He wore a threadbare *Orion* magazine T-shirt; his face was obscured by a thick beard and a pair of wire-rimmed glasses. He followed Athena from the car, chatting with her while she nodded impatiently.

"Hey there, boys," said Jordan, surveying the kids' backpacks. "Looks like everyone's ready to go."

"You can go now, Papa," said Athena.

"OK, OK, I'll get out of here," said Jordan. "See you Wednesday, Ath. Have fun. And Archie – tell your dad he made the right choice, shutting down that job. Tell him, will you?"

"I will," said Archie.

"Keep the headlands wild!" he shouted as he climbed back into the car and drove away.

"Oh my God, you guys," said Athena. "My dad. What a nerd."

"No nukes, man," said Chris. He held up his fingers in a peace sign.

Athena smirked at Chris and set down her backpack next to Archie's.

Megan, Chris's older sister, was sitting on the front porch, eating a bowl of cereal, even though it was well past breakfast time. She spoke to them through a full mouth. "Don't get eaten by bears," she said.

"There are no bears up there," said Chris.

"You never know," responded his sister.

"I do know," said Chris.

"You're a smart-ass," said Megan. "I hope you do get eaten."

And with that benediction laid on their journey, the three hikers headed out into the woods.

They each knew the way: a neighbourhood trail behind Chris's house led to a culvert beneath the highway; from there it was a short walk to a gravel road that led up the hill and away from town.

They stopped at the first stand of trees, just where the forest began encroaching on the wheel tracks of the road, where the gravel was patched with weeds and the wheel ruts were deep. Athena pulled a ziplock bag of muffins from her pack and held it open to her friends.

"My mom made 'em," she said. "Honey whole wheat."

Chris took one and inspected it as if it were some alien specimen. "Looks healthy," he said.

"Chocolate chips?" asked Archie.

"Carob," said Athena.

"Of course," said Archie. He took a bite. The muffin had the consistency of compacted sawdust, but it was a little sweet, and the taste was welcome after their march up the hillside. He spoke through mouthfuls. "I guess Oliver's going home today," he said.

"Oh yeah?" asked Athena. "Where'd you hear that?"

"Agnes called my mom this morning."

"Well, that's good news anyway."

Chris chewed thoughtfully, looking out over the stands of new-growth fir, the tangles of blackberries. "Dad says this all is going to be developed soon. Won't be long."

"Doesn't the forest service own it now?" asked Archie.

"Yeah," said Chris. "But you know how it is. This is all going to be houses someday."

They sat quiet for a moment as they imagined the rows of houses, clapboard white and beige, where there was now a spindly barrier of trees.

"That sucks," said Athena. She stood up and wiped the crumbs from her jeans. "Shall we?"

"We shall," said Chris.

Their destination was a meadow some three miles back from the highway, one that Chris and Archie had discovered two summers prior. The land bordered a parcel of private property owned by a man named Lee Novak. Lee still lived in a house on his land – they'd seen the smoke from his wood stove rising above the tree line on past trips – but the outbuildings of what once had been a massive timber holding were all but abandoned.

The forest-service road they followed took them just above one such building — a long rectangular warehouse. It sat in a narrow draw below the road. The roof, or what remained of it, was carpeted in moss, and bushes sprouted from the blown-out window frames. It was just one of the many mile markers along the trek to their campsite, and they would have likely passed it without comment except for the fact that something was different about the building today. Today there was a truck parked in front of it.

"Check it out," said Chris, pointing to the vehicle.

Archie immediately recognized it as Brody Tyke's pickup. Plumes of exhaust were puffing from the tailpipe, and its driver was sitting behind the wheel — Archie could just make out Brody's shadow through the windscreen.

"Shhh," warned Athena, and she waved them to the side of the road, into the bushes, to be better hidden.

Just then Brody emerged from the truck, all stringy hair and tattooed arms. He stood in front of the idling vehicle and placed a cigarette between his lips. After lighting it, he waved out the match and threw it to the ground; he took a long drag and adjusted his baseball cap, looking around.

"Brody," said Archie in a whisper. "What's he doing here?"

"Beats me," said Chris.

There was some distant family connection between Brody and Lee Novak — Archie thought that maybe Brody's mom was Lee's cousin — because Brody had been heard bragging about his claim on the Novaks' remaining land, how he was going to develop it someday, sell off all the timber and become a millionaire. No one believed him. And yet here he was, parking his truck on Lee's land, taking in the scenery like he owned the place.

Brody's head cocked sideways, and he looked up the hillside towards where the three friends were crouching.

"Shoot," said Chris. "Stay down, you guys. The last thing I want to do is deal with Brody Tyke."

They all ducked behind the cover of the roadside weeds and waited; when they looked up again, Brody was nowhere to be seen, though the truck remained parked in front of the warehouse.

"Let's keep going," said Archie. "I don't want him to see us up here."

They all agreed and, standing up, made their way up the road and out of sight of the truck.

It was just after three o'clock when they arrived at the meadow.

Over spring break, they'd built a lean-to at the edge of a stone-ringed firepit, and they were relieved to see that it was still standing, though the fir boughs they'd laid over the roof for thatching had mostly caved in. They dropped their backpacks at the mouth of the structure with a collective yawn of relief. Chris began checking out the structural integrity of the lean-to, pulling away the dried branches and tossing them into the empty firepit.

"Needs a little work," said Chris proudly, "but looks like it's still holding up nice."

They passed around a wineskin of water and shared an already-dwindling bag of snacks, its M&M's having been picked out over the course of their hike. Chris produced a Frisbee from his pack, and they arranged themselves across the meadow, tossing the disc to one another. Once they'd tired of that, they got to work setting up their camp: Chris scoured the surrounding forest for firewood while Athena and Archie bumbled their way through the construction of the tent Archie had brought.

Hours passed in this way. Soon, the sun began to sink on the horizon. The shadows of the trees grew longer, crawling across the empty grass like barbed fingers towards the kids' campsite; the shadows found the three campers in various stations around the firepit while Chris busied himself with getting the tinder lit and Archie stirred a boiling pot of ramen noodles on the little stove. Athena sat half reclining in a camp chair, idly drawing a pencil sketch in her notebook.

"How's that ramen coming along?" asked Athena, her pencil now wedged behind her ear.

"Everyone knows the best Top Ramen takes time, madam," said Archie.

"You're a real connoisseur," replied Athena.

"Only the finest for my paying customers."

The sunset was unspectacular; there were no clouds in the sky to reflect the rose hue of the sinking sun. The bright blue slowly shifted from one shade to another until, with a blink of pinkish yellow on the fringe of the evening sky, the light went out and the sky was filled with stars, a wild spray of static against the blackness. The three kids ate their noodles and watched the day disappear, talking quietly.

Once the stars had really arrived, Athena jumped up from her camp chair and gave a kind of celebratory dance around the firepit, in dedication to the twinkling stars.

When the dishes had been put away and the marsh-mallows they'd packed had been roasted, Archie grabbed the ghost-story book and sat at the edge of the fire, wiping the ash from the cover like a priest preparing for a holy rite. "You guys ready?" he asked.

Everyone nodded. "Pick a scary one this time," said Athena. She and Chris were huddled together on the other side of the fire from Archie.

Archie chose a story called "The Willows" by Algernon Blackwood. It was one of the longer stories, but the title seemed ominous enough.

"'After leaving Vienna,'" Archie began, "'and long before you come to Budapest, the Danube enters a region of singular loneliness and desolation...'" It was the story of two men on a canoe trip through the wilds of turn-of-the-century Hungary, and the two kids who made up Archie's audience listened raptly through the whole telling, though it was well past ten o'clock by the time he finished. Just as he read the last page, Chris pointed to the horizon, saying, "Oh man, look!"

A full moon had risen above the trees, bathing the meadow in an unearthly glow, and the three friends leaped to their feet, struck by the sudden change in their surroundings.

"Oh my God," said Athena. "Now that's a moon."

Chris, with a shout of joy, ran into the centre of the meadow. He threw his head back and gave a wild howl, like a man whose bloody transformation into his wolf form was nearly complete. Archie laughed loudly. "Save him from himself!" he shouted.

"He'll tear the village apart!" yelled Athena, running after Chris. They were all diving into the performance with gusto.

The moonlight was so bright, it was like someone had switched on a massive, glowing lamp in the sky, and the meadow and the surrounding trees were clear as day, cast in an eerie grey light. The air was uncommonly warm; it felt good on Archie's bare arms.

Chris caught Archie first and pretended to sink his teeth into his neck. Abiding by the unspoken rules of the game, Archie fell to the ground, screaming. When he'd stood back up, he, too, had been transformed. He joined Chris in his wild rampage and they were both leaping through the meadow. Athena laughed and slipped the lycanthropes' grasps time after time, but soon Athena surrendered to the moment. She fell in with the two leaping boys, and they were now three werewolves with no further victims to claim, exulting in their wildness and the full, radiant moon.

Their howls became songs and their leaps became dances, and they were no longer werewolves but ecstatic revellers. They sang "Puttin' on the Ritz" and "Walk Like an Egyptian" in a kind of absurd kick line till they collapsed on the carpet of grass, laughing so hard they were crying.

The stars were out now, despite the white moon, and they pinpricked the dark canvas of sky like fireflies. Athena had begun pointing them out, the ones she knew, when Chris suddenly spoke.

"I'm moving," he said.

"What?" asked Archie, suppressing a laugh. His heart still thrummed in his chest from their running.

"I'm moving," he repeated. "We're moving. My family."

Archie looked over at his friend. "You're joking."

Chris didn't say anything. Archie could feel a swell of anger rising in his stomach. He said, "Dude, cut it out."

"Where to?" asked Athena. She somehow intuited the seriousness of the moment sooner than Archie. In the blond glow of the moon, Archie could see her eyes boring into Chris.

"Ohio, I guess," said Chris. "Columbus. Mom got a job."

"How long have you known this?" asked Archie.

"Since last week."

"Last week?" Archie was incredulous. He pulled himself up from the grass and sat cross-legged, looking at his friend. "Why didn't you say anything?"

"I am now."

"But – the whole last week – the end of school, going to the cliff, Oliver, all that stuff. And you were just sitting on it?"

"Why Ohio?" asked Athena.

Still lying with his back on the grass, Chris gave a shrug. "University there, I guess."

"Dude—" Archie began again, but Chris interrupted him.

"Dude, what?" Chris had propped himself up on his elbow; he was now meeting Archie's glare. "You think I want to move to Ohio? You think I want to leave?"

Archie stared at his friend, dumbfounded.

Chris continued, "It's not till the end of August. Mom's leaving in a couple weeks, and Dad and Megan and me, we're going to meet her at the end of the summer."

"I just think it's selfish, that's all," said Archie. "You not saying anything. I mean, you just left us hanging."

"I'm sorry," said Chris.

"Yeah, that doesn't cut it," said Archie. He stood up and walked away from Chris and Athena, out into the middle of the meadow.

The stars were brightest here, now that the moon had begun descending behind the spires of trees. Archie could feel the night air, cool as he stared up at the blackness of the sky. Despite the stars, Archie only saw the darkness between them. He could hear Chris and Athena talking, quietly, where they'd all been sitting. The sounds filled him with nausea; how could she be so casual about this? Chris, his oldest and best friend, was leaving Seaham. Archie felt angry; he felt betrayed. He also felt embarrassed that the news had affected him so much.

He didn't know how long he'd stayed there, staring at the sky. He heard Chris and Athena return to the campfire; he glanced over his shoulder once and saw the glow of the flames. He started to feel the coolness of the night under his clothing. His initial burst of anger had passed; only the embarrassment remained. He walked back to the campsite. Chris and Athena were there, sitting around the fire. They watched him as he silently took his seat.

Finally, it was Athena who spoke. "You OK?" she asked.

Archie murmured a yes, his eyes intent on the flames.

"We were just talking," said Chris. "We thought maybe we could build like a bike track, just up there, where the hills start. Kind of fun to bring up our bikes sometime."

Archie nodded.

Chris said, "Hey – we've got the whole summer."

"Summer's a long time," said Athena.

Archie finally looked up from the fire; he looked at Chris. Their eyes met. "Yeah," he said. "We've got the summer."

"So let's make the most of it," said Athena.

It was after midnight when they crawled into their sleeping bags in the Coomes family's tent, Archie sardined between Athena and Chris. The conversation had eventually drifted away from Chris's leaving. By the time they'd turned in, it was almost as if the subject had never been raised. Now, in the tent, Archie could hear Athena breathing rhythmically, her hair tied into a braid and piled against her pillow. Archie whispered into the silence: "Chris?"

"Huh?"

"You awake?"

"Yeah."

"You'll be back, right? I mean, you'll come and visit."

"Oh, for sure," said Chris. "How could I not?"

There was quiet then between the friends. Chris said, "And you can come visit me, too, you know."

"Yeah," said Archie. "For sure."

And then they both lapsed into silence, each of them staring up at the dark ceiling of the tent until they'd fallen asleep, lulled by the quiet wind and the grass hushing against the canvas of the tent wall.

And then:

Tchok.

Archie first registered the noise in the depths of his sleep, his mind incorporating it into the events of his dream. It wasn't until he'd heard it a third or fourth time that he began to emerge from sleep, realizing that the noise was real.

Tchok.

"Archie," came Athena's voice. She was gripping his shoulder and shaking it. "Archie, wake up."

The sound came again: *Tchok.*

He opened his eyes. "What's that?"

"We don't know," hissed Athena.

Archie looked around the tent. Athena was at his side, a look of wide-eyed terror on her face. Chris was on his knees, his brow knotted with determination while he listened at the wall of the tent. "What's going on, guys?" asked Archie loudly.

Chris waved at him: *Be quiet!*

Tchok.

Athena flinched at the sound. Chris said: "Sounds like someone chopping wood."

"What time is it?" asked Archie.

Chris looked at his watch. "Just after four," he said.

"Who would be chopping wood *now*?" asked Athena.

It came again, twice now, quickly: *Tchok. Tchok.*

"Is it getting closer?" asked Archie.

There came another noise; Archie started at it: a woman's voice letting out a kind of shrill moan. It sounded like a lamentation. The sound reverberated against the hills surrounding the meadow in a lonely echo.

They all seized up as if a live wire had connected them, binding their bodies into a tense, quaking chain. Archie felt like each of his muscles was contracting at once, as if trying to squeeze him into a tiny ball.

"What was that?" said Athena slowly, enunciating each word.

"I'm going to see what's happening," said Chris.

"No!" shouted Archie. He gripped Chris's arm. "Don't go," he said. "Dude, do not go out there."

But the boy's fingers were already at the door zipper. The sound of the axe fell again just as the tent flap flew open – *tchok* – and Archie dropped his hand from Chris's arm. Chris looked back at his friends once and then exited the tent into the darkness.

"I'm going too," said Athena.

"Ath," said Archie, "don't. We don't know what's out there."

But then she was gone. Archie was suddenly alone, his body tense against the fabric of his sleeping bag, his ears attuned to every sound that was coming from beyond the walls of the tent.

He took a deep breath; he crept forward and stuck his head out the door.

The moon was gone; the meadow was completely dark. A cool wind tousled the grass outside the tent, and the air felt almost wet on Archie's skin. He could see the light from Chris's torch dancing in the distance, and then it blinked out and was gone.

Tchok. It came again. Each time it sounded, it rang Archie's body like a bell.

He began to wrestle with himself internally – should he follow his friends? Or stay in the safety of the tent? Maybe it was wiser to stay; Athena and Chris could probably figure out what was going on without him.

The sound became more frequent now, as if there were several axes laying into a tree, pounding in rhythm – *Tchok. Tchok. Tchok. Tchok.*

A spasm of horror tore through his body, and he whipped his head back into the tent, grabbing defensively at his sleeping bag. He heard footsteps outside the tent. Archie recoiled from the door, pushing himself against the back wall. The door was violently zipped open, and in tumbled Athena and Chris.

"Jesus," said Archie. "You guys scared the—"

"Shhh," said Athena. "Be quiet. Don't talk."

"Turn off that light," demanded Chris. He had a stricken look on his face; Archie stared at him. He extinguished his torch, and they were all in the darkness of the tent together.

"What did you see?" asked Archie.

"There's someone out there, in the woods," said Chris.

"I don't think they saw us. But they're close. I don't think they know we're here."

"What are they doing?" asked Archie.

"I don't know," said Athena. "Chopping something. I don't know."

"We couldn't see," said Chris.

The sound continued unabated in the woods outside the tent.

"Won't be long till daylight," said Athena.

"Maybe if we don't mess with them, they won't mess with us," suggested Archie.

They found each other by reaching out their hands and feeling one another's sleeping bags. They pulled themselves together this way, close, and lay back on the floor of the tent, staring into the darkness and listening to the chopping, away out in the black forest.

TUESDAY

It was a bright day when they awoke. At some point in that early morning, they all, improbably, had fallen asleep. The sun was streaming in through the mesh windows of the tent, and the air felt hot and close. Archie was dripping with sweat in his sleeping bag, and his first thought, before he'd fully recollected the events of the night before, was to get himself out of the bag and into the fresh air. He ripped open the tent door and looked out on the scene before him: the smouldering campfire, their emptied backpacks, the black plastic bag of rubbish. Everything was there as they'd left it, as if nothing had happened.

The chopping noise had stopped. The meadow was blessedly silent, save for the occasional birdsong and the soughing of the fir trees. He heard the crinkle of sleeping bags behind him and saw his friends shake themselves from sleep to join him at the tent flap.

"All clear?" asked Chris.

"Think so," said Archie.

They emerged from the tent like survivors of some

100

natural disaster, climbing from their underground shelter and blinking at the sun. There was no sign of any intruder on their campsite; the meadow and the surrounding forest seemed to keep its secret, behaving very much like the quiet and serene landscape it had been the day before. They wordlessly set about making their breakfast – boiling water on the campstove for instant oatmeal.

Finally, it was Chris who spoke. "You guys," he said. "We can't let this ruin our trip. It's not a big deal."

It was true: here, in the light of day, every frightful explanation for the sounds they'd heard seemed ridiculous – the product of imaginations stewed in ghost stories and isolation. Why wouldn't someone be chopping wood in the middle of the night? This was Oregon, the wild western frontier, a country populated by men and women who did as they pleased, when they pleased. There had been wood that needed chopping, and someone had decided that the middle of the night was the time to do it. Simple as that.

They made no mention of the woman's cry – that strange, howling moan. That, they all had decided on their own, was simply the sound of the wind.

It was almost eleven o'clock by the time they'd finished breakfast and washed the dishes. Slowly, the mood of the day before had returned, the terror of the night having been ushered away. They talked excitedly about the improvements they would make to the campsite.

"I'm thinking a crow's nest there," said Chris, pointing to a cluster of three hemlock trees near the edge of the meadow.

"Ladder up the side of the tree trunk, we're good to go."

"We need to replace the lean-to roof first," said Athena. "And I was thinking it'd be cool to have a little room off to the side here. For storage or something."

They'd carried a few assorted tools in their packs: two hammers and a box of nails, a saw, and a measuring tape. Athena scoured the low-hanging branches of the nearby fir trees for suitable roof thatching while Archie helped Chris saw the sturdiest limbs from whatever deadfall they could find.

It went on this way until well into the afternoon, when the lean-to had been completely renovated with a fresh roof and a little alcove off to the side, and the first beams had been nailed to the stand of trees for the crow's nest. They ate a late lunch in the lean-to, enjoying the shade it provided from the afternoon sun, and Chris suggested they explore the nearby hills.

"Maybe there are caves up there or something," he said.

"No caves," said Athena. "Done with caves."

"Fine," said Chris, laughing. "Let's just see what's up there."

There was a saddle between the two highest hills to one side of the meadow; they decided that would be their destination. Athena volunteered to stay at camp, to keep working on the addition to the fort. "I'll keep an eye out for axe-wielding maniacs," she said.

"You sure you'll be all right by yourself?" asked Archie.

Athena gave him a look. "What, 'cause I'm the girl?"

Archie blushed. "No – I didn't…"

"Just messing with you," said Athena, smiling. "Nah, I'm good here alone. You guys spook too easy."

Chris took the lead, pushing a steady pace towards the distant line of trees. Archie fell behind. There was no trail here, so they were forced to bushwhack through the thick underbrush, the massive stands of fern and the webbed blankets of ivy. Occasionally, Chris would perch on a fallen tree, waiting for his friend to catch up.

A feeling of familiarity bloomed inside Archie as they walked. Here he was, marching through the woods with his best friend, always a few paces behind. They'd been doing this for as long as he could remember – on family outings, as soon as they were old enough to break away from their parents, they'd be off on their own, scouting up the trail or sneaking through the roadside bracken to find the perfect ambush spot. It was familiar; it was comfortable. Somehow this feeling made it easier to simply lose himself in the moment, though the knowledge that Chris would be gone in September hovered over everything like a shadow.

They hadn't spoken about it all morning. Archie guessed that was the unsaid deal between them: *Let's not talk about it. Spare us both the heartbreak.*

After a time, they arrived at a place where the ground levelled off and then began to fall away down a steep slope – they'd come to the highest point of the saddle. To their left and right, the forest floor continued to climb, presumably leading to the low peaks of the two hills.

"How about we split up?" suggested Archie. He pointed

to one of the inclines. "I'll go this way, you go that way. We'll see if we can see each other from the tops."

"Race ya," said Chris. And he was off, jogging through the scrabbly vegetation towards the hilltop.

It was late afternoon, and the sun hung midway across the sky, sending long, refracted rays through the trees. Archie, walking alone, headed up the slope towards where he guessed the hilltop was.

The way confused him; the trees were so dense on the slope that he had a difficult time determining where he was in relation to the other hill. He found himself on a false peak; the ground continued to climb, just beyond where he stood. When, after a time, he looked up and reckoned his surroundings, he realized he was no longer climbing, but had, in fact, begun to descend.

"Ah, man," he said quietly to himself.

He retraced his steps for a while, but he quickly lost track of the route he'd taken. He shouted, "Chris!" but got no response. The wind hissed through the leaves of the trees; the greenery below his feet quaked at his step. The forest suddenly felt very hostile. He mouthed a sort of pep talk to himself and tried to find his bearings. He could see the sun through the trees, lower now on the horizon. He knew that the saddle had been to the east of the meadow, so he began walking towards the sun, hoping that he would eventually catch sight of the camp. He thought that Athena might've started a fire by this point, and that gave him some hope. He would, eventually, be able to see the smoke and follow it to the campsite.

Climbing over a fallen tree, he slipped and fell; he scraped his knee against the bark and a strip of blood appeared on his skin. He lifted himself up and continued walking, his leg throbbing from the fall. The ground began to level out; he had just navigated a thicket of young trees when he found himself on the edge of a small clearing. A creek babbled through the middle of it.

On the bank of the creek stood a woman.

She was facing away from him, towards the far edge of the clearing, and her long grey hair tumbled down from the crown of her head to the middle of her back. She was naked, and her flesh was pearly white in the fading sun.

It was shocking to see someone, a stranger, in these woods. Aside from the logging road that led to the meadow, there were no trails here. What didn't belong to the Novaks was forest-service land, leased long ago to timber companies and left fallow. What's more, the woman's clothing was nowhere to be seen – there was no backpack laid down to suggest that she had hiked all this way and was simply enjoying a midday bath at the creek.

She appeared immobile, statuesque, her hands at her sides in an almost unnatural manner. Archie began to back away, not wanting to appear as some peeping tom. She heard him and turned.

It was Birgitta Woodley, the woman he'd just seen on Friday when he'd delivered the videotape to her door. She was naked, wild-eyed, staring at Archie. He froze in place.

"Birgitta," he said. "I'm sorry. I didn't…"

But then she smiled. It was a weird, lazy smile. "Archie Coomes," she said. "Hello, Archie." She began to walk towards him, stepping carefully over the little mounds of weeds in the clearing.

"I'm sorry," repeated Archie helplessly. She was not reacting in the way he'd expected her to; there was no flash of embarrassment at her nudity or a dive for discarded clothing. Instead, she continued her slow, measured walk towards him. She reached out her arms, her fingers long and spindly.

"Come here, Archie," she said.

"I should really get…" stammered Archie. His heel caught on a fallen branch, and he fell backwards, landing with a thud on his back.

"Please, come here," said Birgitta, now coming closer. Her voice was odd and singsong.

Archie pushed himself up from the ground. "Birgitta," he said. "Are you OK? Are you lost?"

"I'm very well, Archie," responded the woman. She was closer now. He could see the blank stare of her eyes; he could see the drooping white flesh of her body, the channels of wrinkles that crisscrossed her skin. "Come to me," she said.

"I have to go now, Birgitta," said Archie. He was suddenly aware of his own fear; it gripped him like a vice. "I'm sorry. I have to go."

"There's nowhere for you to go, Archie," said Birgitta. She'd begun to walk faster. Her arms were still outstretched, reaching for him. Her voice did not suggest kindness. There was something sinister in it.

Archie turned and began to run.

He didn't look back. He didn't choose a direction. He simply ran.

His throat was choked with terror; tears ran down his cheeks, and his heart throbbed in his chest. He no longer felt the pain in his knee; every cell in his body was firing on adrenaline as he dashed through the thick woods, leaping fallen tree trunks and crashing through bushes. He tripped once, hard, and rolled down a deep ravine into a dry creek bed. Blackberry bushes laced his cheeks with scratches and his shirt was torn, but he picked himself up and kept running. After a time, he allowed himself to look behind him. There was no one there.

The relief fell over him like a cascade; he sobbed a few times before containing himself. He wiped the tears from his cheeks with the sleeve of his shirt; there was blood there, there was snot and dirt.

He walked as if in a trance, his limbs still recovering from the effect of their adrenaline transfusion. His mind raced: What was Birgitta doing all the way out here? Why was she acting so strangely? What had she wanted with him?

This last thought produced an enormous lump in his throat and he fought it back. He tried desperately to assemble some sort of explanation but had a difficult time doing so. Just then, he heard a voice call his name, somewhere distantly. It was Chris.

"Chris!" he shouted back, turning in the direction of the voice. "Chris, I'm here!"

His friend appeared over a small hill; Chris smiled to see him, until he saw what shape Archie was in and his expression shifted to a look of concern and wonder.

"What happened to you?" he asked. "You look like you got mauled or something."

Archie sputtered out an explanation the best he could. "Birgitta. I saw her. She was naked. She came after me."

"Naked lady," said Chris, smirking. "Nice."

"It was Birgitta Woodley, Chris," said Archie, ignoring the remark, "that Swedish lady. She lives near us. She was just out there, in the woods."

"Is she lost?"

"No – no, she's not. I don't think so. She came after me, Chris. She looked crazy." The old fear returned, the lump in his throat.

"Should we get help?" asked Chris, his face now serious.

"I don't know. She said she was fine. I don't know."

"Let's get back to camp," said Chris. He reached up and pulled a blackberry thorn from Archie's wild mop of hair. "You're a mess, Arch."

Chris knew the way back; he'd made it to the top of the hill and had climbed a tree, hoping to see Archie from his lookout. When he hadn't, he'd gone looking for him; he'd managed to retain his bearings and could point them in the direction of the meadow. Before long, they could smell woodsmoke on the air; Athena had made a fire.

The sun had just dropped below the tops of the trees when they arrived back at the camp. As they approached from across the meadow, Archie was surprised to see two figures standing around the fire in the ring of rocks. Coming closer, he recognized the second.

"Oliver," said Archie.

There he was, Oliver Fife, in the flesh. It was striking, having only seen him two days before in a hospital bed. He was the last person Archie had expected to see. His face was flushed and his hair was matted against his forehead; he looked like he'd sprinted to the campsite from town.

"You made it, Ollie," said Chris as they came closer. He looked around. "What's up, guys? You look like someone died."

Oliver looked anxiously at Athena; Athena was staring into the flames of the campfire. A dark cloud seemed to have gathered over them, and it made Archie's heart seize in his chest.

Finally, Athena spoke. "They've started work again," she said. "At the headlands."

"They're digging, Archie," said Oliver. "They're digging."

Gaunt, pale Lugg sits recumbent on the beach. He has his hands pressed down into the sand, his fingers slowly raking the grains. He has noted sand in his book, he has given it two full pages, and yet still it is mysterious to him. At first he thought it was a single, unbroken unit – a surface that extended for miles between the soil and the sea (each with their own entries, one and two pages, respectively) like a kind of barrier. Still unknown: Does the sand keep the soil from sea? Or the sea from the soil? His entry, initially a short paragraph, expands to its current length after his first setting foot on the beach. He discovers, much to his surprise, that what he thought was an unbroken surface was in fact made up of many, many individual grains. Being thus constituted, it gives at the slightest pressure, collapsing in on itself at every footfall. Truly, he has noted, this landscape carries many mysteries. But he has made these discoveries before. He knows this, and yet must continue his notation, his documenting. He is an emerging consciousness, a re-emerging one, waking from a long slumber.

The sun is shining; a bird wheels over the crashing ocean. It dives repeatedly into the spray, sometimes coming up from the water with a small fish in its beak, which it hungrily consumes. Lugg watches it with wonder. He does not hear his companion approach above the roar of the waves.

"Good afternoon, Lugg," says the man.

"Good afternoon, Toff," replies Lugg.

"What is it you are doing?"

"I am regarding the ocean."

"For what reason?"

"For understanding."

Toff considers this response, then sits down next to his companion. They do not speak. The waves continue, as if clocked to some unseen mechanism, to push into the sand and recede. Push and recede. Push and recede.

"'The cold earth slept below,'" speaks Toff, having pulled from the interior pocket of his brown jacket a notepad. "'Above the cold sky shone. And all around, with a chilling sound, from caves of ice and fields of snow the breath of night like death did flow beneath the sinking moon.'" Having read the lines, he returns the book to his pocket and says, "Percy Shelley. English poet."

"And where is our third?" asks Lugg.

"We will wait," says Toff. "He will come."

The sun grows low over the ocean, just above the line that divides the sea from the sky. Two young children and their accompanying adults walk by them; the children gape at the two men, dressed as they are, and are quietly chided by

111

their parents to leave the men alone. Toff and Lugg ignore them. Toff grinds his fingers into the sand; it grows colder the deeper he goes.

"Good afternoon," comes a voice. Toff and Lugg look up. It is their companion, Wart.

"Good afternoon, Wart," says Lugg.

"Good afternoon, Wart," says Toff.

"We are regarding the ocean," says Lugg. He points in the direction of the dark sea, as if Wart needed some indication.

Wart looks out at the ocean. He says, "Ah, yes."

"It is as it was," says Toff, "when last we arrived."

"It is unchanged," says Wart. "I have noted that. And yet the surroundings."

"Are altered," says Toff.

"Indeed, Brother," says Wart. "Much altered. Where there once was a great hummock of earth, there is now only ocean." He is looking northward, up the beach, towards the headlands.

"And where before there was only forest, there is now so much … humanity," says Toff. "Since last we arrived."

"Do you suppose we will be hindered again?" asks Lugg.

Wart stares blankly out at the ocean. "I do not think so."

"He does not think so," says Lugg to Toff. Toff has resumed digging his hands into the dry sand.

"And yet," says Wart.

"And yet?" asks Lugg.

"I believe we may be *suspected*," says Wart.

"Suspected?" asks Toff. He abruptly lifts his fingers from the sand.

"By whom, Brother?" asks Lugg. "By whom?"

"By a child," answers Wart.

There is silence between the three men now. They each consider the words just spoken by Wart. Toff speaks: "A child?"

"Even now, It calls for him," says Wart.

"Well," says Toff, "this child will need to be addressed."

"Undoubtedly," says Wart.

"Undoubtedly," says Toff.

"Shush, now," says Lugg, pointing to the dark horizon, where the sun has dipped and is disappearing beyond the rim of the sky as if it were being swallowed by the far ocean. His two companions look at where he is pointing and they see, the three of them, each from their own position in a kind of parallax, the waves as they push and recede, push and recede. They each pull their notebooks from the interior pockets of their jackets and notate the change.

SUNDAY

Night-time in the hospital was the worst.

Strange, irregular beeps sounded in the dark; the air-conditioning heaved and rattled at odd intervals. Footsteps in the corridor sounded outside the door and then drifted away; voices murmured distantly like conversing ghosts.

Oliver, awake in his bed, listened to it all. Alone.

The stack of *Conan the Barbarian* comics his friends had brought him lay exhausted on the bedside table, all thoroughly read, alongside the completed notepad of *Mad Libs* he'd done with his dad until the nouns *poop* and *barf* had long outlasted their funniness. His glasses were there, too; so was a half-finished cup of orange juice.

The first night, Saturday night, he'd had the benefit of being genuinely ill. His body had counteracted the trauma of the day's experience by knocking him out. He'd slept soundly for nearly ten hours. By the afternoon, he'd felt completely himself and had begun lobbying for his release, but the doctor, after conferring with his parents, had wanted to keep him another night, just to monitor him. "We still want to keep an eye on that concussion," he'd said, and that was that.

His dad remained in the chair in the corner of the room until around ten that night, when he awoke from having dozed off, saying, "Oh, Ollie, I have to get home. Dogs have been in all day. You'll be all right?"

Oliver, wide awake, could only nod. To admit to his growing fear would seem like cowardice in the face of his dad.

"Love you," Andrew said from the foot of the bed.

"Love you too."

The door closed, his dad was gone, and Oliver was left to the beeps and the whirs, the wheezes and the whispers.

He lay for some time with his eyes closed, willing sleep to come on. He shifted from position to position, rolling inside the starchy white bedsheets like a pupa in its cocoon. Finally, he surrendered to wakefulness and peeled his eyes open, glancing at the clock. It was eleven fifteen. He let out a frustrated sigh; he'd been sure more time had passed. Reaching to the side of the bed, he flipped on the nightstand lamp, squinting his eyes at the brightness.

A machine beeped in the corner of the room; the air-conditioning fan kicked back on and rattled the grate near the ceiling. Oliver sat up in bed and put on his glasses. The dim room came into focus.

Here, in the light of the bedside lamp, the strange objects in the room – the mysterious machines, the trolley cart with the television, the faded blue chair in the corner – took on an ominous look, like they were inching towards him and had stopped abruptly when he'd turned on the lamp, in the midst of some terrifying version of red light, green light. He watched them, daring them to make their move.

When they didn't, he rubbed his eyes and yawned. Had he been sleeping? He had the vague recollection of a dream: he was there, back at the cliff face, walking towards the crack in the wall. He could hear his friends calling for him. Something was down there, down in the hole. Something that had spoken to him. What had it said?

It was almost too real to be a dream. It was more like a vivid remembering, like his mind was rewinding and replaying a section of a movie, one that stopped each time just before the most important part.

What had it said?

A noise sounded in the hallway outside the door, and his head snapped to face it. Footsteps. The soles of a pair of tennis shoes squeaking rhythmically against the tile floor. He listened to them surge and fade. He glanced over at the remote at the side of the bed. The blue button in the centre of the device would call a nurse, he was told, if he needed anything. If an emergency should arise.

An emergency has not arisen, thought Oliver. *Yet*.

He shrank into the plush of his pillow. A wave of fear had come over him. He picked up the remote and studied it; he placed it back on the table.

Hold it together, Ollie, he thought. He let out a long breath.

The room quietened; the AC fan stopped, and Oliver felt himself calming, his eyelids growing heavier. The welcome weight of sleep was just beginning to fall over him when he heard something, something coming from the air-conditioning vent.

Oliver, it said.

He felt his pulse quicken. He sat upright in bed, staring at the grate on the wall.

Oliver, it repeated.

His mouth was parched; his tongue hung uselessly in his mouth. But even then, even the prospect of speaking, of acknowledging this disembodied voice, struck him with terror. He glanced at the call button on the remote. He tried to imagine what he would tell a nurse, that there was a voice coming from the air-conditioning grate. It would sound ludicrous. It would sound...

Come, Ollie, said the voice. *I'm waiting for you.*

Crazy.

Screw this, thought Oliver. He grabbed the remote and jammed his thumb against the blue call button. He waited for some sound to indicate that it had worked – perhaps some distant buzz at a nearby desk. But there was only silence. The AC fan rattled on. The machine beeped in the corner. He pressed the button again. Nothing happened.

It's been so long, Oliver. I've waited.

He lowered himself farther into his pillow. He urged his brain to find other sources of noise, to drown out the humming words. Finally, he heard steps approaching. Dragging, slouching steps. They did not sound like the tread of the nurses' white padded shoes. Oliver waited for the knock, for the door to open. He called out, "Hello?"

Silence.

"Hey – who's there?" called Oliver. "Is that a nurse?"

There came no sound, no answer. He waited for the steps to sound again, to move away down the hall and away from his door.

"Go away," said Oliver.

Silence.

The machine in the corner beeped. The AC vent rattled awake. Oliver gritted his teeth. He pushed himself out of bed and walked towards the door. He listened for a sound in the hallway; there was only quiet. Slowly, he pushed open the door and looked out. The hallway was empty. A fluorescent light flickered some ways down the hall. The hospital felt abandoned.

"Hello?" called Oliver.

Come. The voice breathed from inside the cavity of the hallway itself, filling his ears with its hiss.

His attention was suddenly diverted to a shuffling noise that was coming from down the hall. He called out, once more, from the safety of his room. When he received no answer, he ventured out into the hallway.

The row of fluorescent lights suspended from the long ceiling seemed to wave and flicker, as if threatening to extinguish. An alcove opposite the door enclosed an empty desk; a cup of coffee, steaming, sat near a stack of papers illuminated by a project lamp.

"Hello?" called Oliver. "Anyone here?"

The shuffling noise happened again; it seemed to be

coming from around a corner, where the hallway made an abrupt bend.

"I pressed the button – the nurse call button," he said to the emptiness. No one answered. The noise continued. Something heavy being dragged over the slick floor. "Who's there?"

Oliver ventured from the safety of the doorway, inching his way out into the hall. His heart was beating rapidly in his chest. He was wearing the pyjamas his dad had bought at the mall the day he was admitted; they were a size too big and he had to bunch the fabric of the trouser legs in his fists so he wouldn't step on the hems. He followed the sound of the shuffling. He turned the corner. What he saw made him freeze.

Down at the far end of the hall, he saw a zebra, and it was nearly dead.

Oliver called them visions. A paediatric psychologist had called them post-traumatic dissociative experiences.

Oliver liked his term better.

He'd first started experiencing them soon enough after his parents' divorce, so it was easy for Andrew and Agnes to correlate this strange behaviour with the surely destructive effects of watching his parents' marriage crumble before his eyes. He'd undergone a litany of tests at a clinic in Portland; the doctors there had agreed with his parents. The trauma of his familial relationship under stress. Textbook case, they said.

To be honest, though, Oliver didn't remember much about the divorce.

He'd been five years old when it was finalized. His only memories of his parents' discontent were a few vague recollections: his mother sobbing in the beige armchair in the living room, and once coming downstairs early in the morning to find his dad asleep on the pull-out couch. The move from Tempe had followed; suddenly Oliver and his sister were living alone with his mother in a small house on the Oregon coast. Andrew, in an effort to keep the family closer, moved to Harrisburg soon after. The bimonthly activity of changing houses became just a part of reality for Oliver – didn't all kids do the same? It was some surprise to him, then, when he first met Archie and Athena and learned that their parents still lived under the same roofs.

But the memory of his first episode, his first *vision*, was etched deeply in his mind. It happened at a birthday party. It had been a party for someone from his first-grade class. At that age, it seemed, there were no friendship circles or cliques to weed out undesired birthday guests – everyone in the class got an invite. The kid's family had rented out the Seaham Grange Hall for the event, the only place in town that could handle a guest list of that size.

Streamers hung from the hall's rafters; balloons bobbed across the floor, chased by sugar-crazed children. A clown was making balloon animals in the corner; a magician was trying to keep the attention of a dozen six-year-olds while a stereo blared Disney songs from a table on the stage.

Oliver wandered the scene as if he were in some enchanted wonderland. This was his first year at Seaham Elementary; many of the faces at the party were new to him.

And that's when he saw the woman.

He found out later that she'd been someone's babysitter. While most of the parents had dropped their kids and left, this woman was taking in the party as if she, herself, was one of the partygoers, always tagging behind the kids she'd been hired to watch.

As soon as he saw her, he noticed something strange about her.

Oliver had been raised to know that it was rude to stare, but he felt compelled to follow the woman closely, trying to pinpoint what exactly was different about her. After a time, the woman noticed she was being tailed; she began looking at Oliver curiously. Finally, after she'd found the boy standing at her side while the kids were all out in the middle of the floor dancing the hokey cokey, the woman looked down at him and smiled.

"Don't you want to dance?" she asked. She was pretty; she had green eyes and dusky blonde hair that she wore back in a ponytail.

Oliver stared at her. Then he said, "You've got something around your neck."

The woman started. She blinked in confusion; she put her hand to her throat. "Sorry?" she asked.

"There," said Oliver, pointing. "Wrapped around your neck."

"No, I don't," said the woman, reddening. She smiled awkwardly.

But she did, Oliver could see. There was a faint black line, like a cord, that started somewhere around her left ear, inched along the base of her skull, and coiled tightly around her neck. As he looked at it, he could feel his pulse quickening and his forehead beginning to sweat. He became afraid, suddenly, that he might faint.

"Are you OK?" the woman asked, noting his distress.

Overcome, Oliver fled the woman's side and spent the rest of the party huddled near the entrance to the Grange Hall, trying to dispel the image of the black cord from his mind. The cake was revealed, the candles were blown out, and parents began to appear, looking for their children amid the crowd; Agnes arrived and took Oliver home. He didn't say anything to her about the babysitter and the black cord.

The woman was dead nearly four days before the news filtered through the community and reached the younger grades of Seaham Elementary. The siblings the woman had watched, the Ellisons, had been taken out of school for a few days after the incident. It was even longer, though, before the details of the accident began circulating; that the woman had been in a terrible car accident on Highway 101. She'd been vaulted through the windscreen and thrown fifteen feet in the air. When the police arrived at the scene some moments later, they'd found the woman hanging from the electrical cabling that crossed the highway. The force of the accident had caused the wiring to coil tightly around her neck. It took the better part of an hour to get a cherry picker onsite to cut her down.

It was a sixth grader who'd told Oliver; he'd explained the whole thing in morbid detail in the playground to a bunch of the younger kids. Everyone around him had gasped with disgust and horror; Oliver, however, had remained silent.

He had *seen*.

The zebra's hind legs were broken, and it was dragging itself across the hospital floor with its front hooves. It was emaciated; its ribs were clearly visible beneath its matted and dirty hide. Blood was everywhere; wide, red streaks followed the zebra in a gruesome trail along the chequerboard tile. It soaked the animal's fur so that Oliver could barely discern between the black and the white stripes on its body. It turned its awful head and fixed its dead eyes on Oliver. It opened its jaws, and a bilious stream of black blood poured out.

"Come, Oliver," it said, its voice all sputtering and low. "It's waiting for you."

Oliver stumbled backwards; a scream rose in his chest. Just as he was about to let it loose, a bright flash of white light consumed the hallway, and he reflexively squeezed his eyes closed. When he opened them, the zebra was gone. The hallway's fluorescent lights no longer flickered; they shone down on a pristine, unbloodied tile floor.

"Hey there," said a woman from behind Oliver. He turned and saw it was one of the orderlies from the hospital. "What are you doing out of bed?"

"Did you—" stammered Oliver, pointing to the spot on the floor where the zebra had been. "Did you see something there?"

The heavy-set woman in blue scrubs looked at Oliver with her head cocked sideways and her eyebrow arched. "I haven't seen anything," she said. "You know, you got a call button if you need something."

"I pressed it," said Oliver. "I hit the call button. Nothing happened."

"Uh-huh," said the nurse. "Listen, you're all out of sorts. Let's get you back to bed."

Oliver's pulse was still racing as he followed the nurse back down the hall to the door of his room.

"Must've been a bad dream," said the nurse, her voice softening. "You know, it happens."

Oliver could only nod.

"Couldn't count the times a kid your age comes in here for a night or two and he's got bad, bad dreams. Hospital's no place to sleep, that's for sure. C'mon, let me get you tucked in." She laid a comforting hand between his shoulders and ushered him into the room.

Once he was back in the swaddling of his sheets, the nurse switched on the bedside lamp and set the call button near at hand. "Now, I've tested this thing. I know it works," she said. "You just buzz me over the littlest thing; I'll come running. You got that?"

"Yes, ma'am," said Oliver. He was crushing the back of his head into the pillows like some cornered animal searching for protection. His eyes darted across the room.

"Don't worry. Night's gonna be over before you know it. And then your mom and dad'll be here to pick you up." She left the room, keeping the door cracked. A sliver of light from the hall crept into the room. Oliver stared at the bare ceiling.

The machine beeped; the AC fan rattled. The voice from the grate, however, was silent. Oliver, in time, fell asleep. He did not dream.

It was late morning when he woke. His mom was standing over his bed, gently pressing at his shoulder.

"Ollie, hon," she said. "Time to rise. We're going to get you out of here."

The doctor, a brusque older man with a moustache, ran Oliver through a series of observations – taking his blood pressure, measuring his pulse, running a stethoscope across several coordinates on his bare back and chest – punctuating each of these with an inscrutable grunt. When the last test had been done, the doctor scribbled a few notes on a clipboard and said, "OK, Mrs Fife—"

"Gibson," said Agnes, correcting to her maiden name.

"*Ms Gibson*, your son is free to go."

Agnes looked at Oliver and beamed. Oliver smiled back wanly.

On the drive back to Seaham, the radio played the local jazz station. A trumpet wailed over a frenetic backbeat as Oliver stared out the window, watching the trees meld to a blur along the side of the road. Agnes hummed along.

That night, Oliver couldn't sleep. He tried to remind

himself that he was in his own bed, free of the noises and the voices and the

zebra

clinging sheets of the hospital bed, but to no avail. His mind kept flashing to his friends. They were, no doubt, just now settling into their sleeping bags at the fort, trading stories and looking up into the dark, open sky. A feeling of dread fell over him as he imagined them. They were in danger; *he* was in danger. Something was not right – he felt certain that these strange hallucinations he'd experienced were some kind of warning, some kind of message. Even though he'd been given assurances that the hole would be filled, somehow he knew that the saga was far from over.

He looked at his bedside clock; the blue digital face read 12:36 a.m. He pushed himself out of bed and walked down the hall to his mom's room. He found her soundly asleep with her reading light on and a book unfolded across her chest.

"Mom?" he called.

She started awake. "Ollie? That you?"

"I can't sleep."

"Aw, honey," said his mom, dragging herself upright. The book spilled off the bed, landing with a clunk on the hardwood floor. "What time is it?"

"After midnight," Oliver said. It felt strange to be here, in her room, this late at night. He couldn't remember the last time he'd come to her because of sleeplessness. It was possible, he realized, that he hadn't done this since before his parents had split.

Agnes smiled warmly and shifted her weight to the centre of the bed. She held the blanket open. "Come on," she said. "Climb in."

Oliver fell asleep like this, pressed against the warmth of his mother's shoulder, eased by the rhythmic movement of her chest as it rose and fell with her breath. He felt drawn back into his childhood. It was a sensation that was both comforting and alarming, knowing that it was only an illusion. Tomorrow the feeling would be dispelled, and he would be the thirteen-year-old boy again.

Somehow, Oliver knew the phone would ring before it did.

He was sitting at the kitchen table, guardedly spooning cereal into his mouth, when a feeling came over him. He'd later describe it to his friends as a sort of reverse echo, as if the ring of the phone left an impression on the air before it had happened. It was inexplicable, really. He looked up from his bowl and stared at the phone.

It rang.

"I'll get it," said his sister, Jenn. She leaped up from the table and grabbed the phone from the wall. Oliver watched her intently. "It's for you, Mom," she said, disappointed, as she limply held the receiver.

Agnes had been watering a plant in the kitchen sink; she dried her hands quickly before taking the phone from her daughter. Jenn went back to the catalogue she'd been flipping through at the table. Oliver's attention turned to his mother.

Agnes spoke into the phone. "Hello? Oh – hi!"

Despite his mother's tone, which was easy and conversational, a surge of dread rose through Oliver's chest. He dropped his spoon to the table with a clatter. Jenn said something snide to him, but he did not register it.

"Uh-huh. Oh, really? They are? That's surprising." Agnes's eyes were now fixed on Oliver. He met her gaze and held it. He knew that Athena's mom was on the other end of the line. He knew what she was calling about. It was as if he'd been privy to the conversation before it started. Agnes was silent as she listened. Finally, she said, "Well, today's a bit rough, actually. I don't think I'd be able to make it till later this afternoon." Pause. "Yep, he's back. Doing pretty good, I think. Well, I don't know. He just got home – but I'll ask him."

Agnes held the mouthpiece of the receiver to her chest and said, "It's Cynthia. She wants to—"

Oliver interrupted her. "They've started again," he said, "haven't they?"

Agnes looked shocked; Cynthia's garbled voice, just audible through the receiver, recalled her to the phone. "Hmm? Sorry – that was Ollie talking. One sec." She pulled the earpiece down again and said, "They've started work again, on the cliff up at the headlands." She said this as if she hadn't just heard her son say it already. "Anyway, the Quests are going up with a bunch of folks to protest. I can't right now, but they're trying to get a gaggle. Wanted to know if you guys wanted to go."

Jenn noisily flipped a page of her catalogue and said, "Uh, no thanks."

"I want to go," said Oliver. He abruptly stood up from the table and brought his half-finished bowl of cereal to the sink.

"Are you sure?" asked Agnes. "I mean, you just got home."

"I'm fine," said Oliver.

Agnes stared at him momentarily before she spoke again into the phone. "Well, Oliver wants to go. Sure, OK. I'll let him know." She said her cursory goodbyes and hung up the phone. "They're on their way. Pick you up in ten minutes." Her shoulders sagged resignedly as she stood by the phone. "You're sure," she said.

"I'm sure," said Oliver. He walked into the living room. He sat on the couch and began putting on his tennis shoes. He did all this calmly while his mind was racing. The ten minutes passed quickly; it wasn't long before he heard the honk of the Quests' horn out on the street.

"Sorry about the mess," Cynthia said as Oliver crammed into the back seat of the Quests' Rabbit alongside a jumble of poster-board signs stapled to wooden stakes. Cynthia was driving. Jordan, Athena's dad, was sitting in the passenger seat.

"Feel free to pick one out," said Jordan. The car pulled away from the kerb; Oliver could see his mother standing at the front door, watching them go. "We made most of them this morning. Not our best work."

Oliver turned and leafed through the signs. One of them had a mushroom cloud on it, drawn out in red and orange marker. Jordan said, "That one's from the no nukes rally last fall. Figured, what the hell."

"Glad you're coming, Oliver," said Cynthia. "We could really use more kids on the front line. It's your future they're screwing up, after all."

Stirring up his courage, Oliver asked, "Why did they start again?"

"What's that?" asked Cynthia over the hum of the VW's engine.

"He wants to know why they started again," said Jordan, turning to his wife. He craned his neck around to speak to Oliver. "And I can tell you, it's all about greed. That's what it comes down to. Every time. These corporate money-grubbers don't give a rat's ass about ecology, about sustainability. They just want to make money."

"I thought Archie said—" began Oliver, fear rising in his throat. "I thought Archie's dad said it wasn't safe."

Cynthia and Jordan shared a look. "I don't want to say anything bad about Peter," said Jordan. "Nice guy. Good guy. But, you know, these folks tend to go with the corporations on this stuff."

Cynthia turned the car onto a dirt road, the same one that Oliver and his friends had walked only days prior. They drove alongside the iron fence that lined the perimeter of the Langdon property, and Oliver could see, just over the yellow scrub, the broken windows of Langdon House. The mist that had so enveloped the surrounding countryside those few days prior was gone, and the sky was a wide, pale blue above the grey ocean. Other cars appeared before them on the road, parked in the shallow ditch between the pavement and the fence. A couple emerged from a car and waved at Cynthia and Jordan; a woman farther down was removing a large card-stock sign from her hatchback. It read: *KEEP THE HEADLANDS WILD*.

"Oh, wow," said Cynthia. "Good showing. Great activation."

"You better park here, hon," said Jordan. "Doubt we'll find a spot farther down."

Cynthia veered the Rabbit onto the side of the road and parked behind a green camper van. She stuck her head out the window and greeted a foursome who were walking towards the beach. Oliver recognized them – they were the Adlers; they lived a few blocks from him. Katie Adler, Mike and Gina's daughter, had been in art camp with Oliver last summer. She was ten.

"What a turnout, eh?" said Mike, recognizing Cynthia.

"People have the power!" shouted Jordan as he stepped out of the passenger side.

"Where's Athena?" asked Katie, peering into the car.

"She's up camping, but we kidnapped her friend," said Cynthia.

"Oh, hi, Oliver," said Katie.

Oliver was too distracted to reply. He was looking down the road, watching it wind its way towards the ocean, disappearing over the hillside down to the beach below. Finally, he said, "Hi, Katie."

She looked at him queerly. "You OK? You don't look so good."

"C'mon, guys," said Gina. "Let's head down together."

At the bottom of the switchbacks, where the dirt road let out onto the sand of the beach, there were easily a dozen people of all ages gathered in front of the safety fence, many holding handmade protest signs. Seeing the Quests arrive, the crowd quickly clustered around them.

"I made it as fast as I could," said one woman, brandishing an armful of fresh-cut flowers. "Flowers for everyone, in solidarity."

Oliver, by this time, had orbited away from the Quests and moved to the fence. He pressed his fingers into the wires and stared at the scene before him. What had once been a derelict construction site was now humming with activity. A bulldozer was pushing debris away from the cliff while an excavator was clawing into the brittle rock of the cliff face. The hole in the wall was expanding. Oliver felt the urge to vomit. He put his hand to his mouth and willed the feeling away. They had to stop the work. Did they know what they were unearthing?

Did he know?

I'm here, Oliver.

Perhaps ten workers in all were busying themselves around the job site – those not operating the heavy machinery were moving about the area with an air of purpose. They wore bright yellow reflective safety vests and worn white hard hats. A group of men was poised over the hood of an idling truck, inspecting what looked like a sheaf of blueprints. The logo of Coomes Construction was stencilled on the door of the truck. No one seemed to take any notice of the protesters that were gathering on the other side of the fence.

Suddenly, from behind Oliver, a chant erupted from the crowd: "KEEP IT WILD! KEEP IT WILD!" Oliver glanced over his shoulder as the crush surrounded him; he saw Jordan and Cynthia acting as conductors for the chant. Only then did the workers seem to take any note of the protesters.

"KEEP IT WILD!"

Oliver saw the silhouette in the cab of the truck slowly move its head towards the sound of the crowd. Oliver felt a kind of coldness come over him; were it not for the fact that he was surrounded by bodies, he would've assumed it was the air coming off the ocean. It seemed, instead, to be emanating from the landward side. From the cliff.

The door of the truck opened, and out stepped Peter Coomes, Archie's dad. He was wearing a blue work shirt and jeans; his boots were caked in mud. He looked out at the crowd by the fence; he looked directly at Oliver.

He smiled.

Oliver felt himself fall backwards; his shoulders pressed into the chest of a woman who was standing directly behind him. He grabbed the fence to steady himself, staring intently at Peter Coomes, at Peter Coomes's smile. Oliver did not recognize it as the smile of his best friend's dad. It was too long, by some *infinitesimal* amount, for the man's face. It was a subtle change – like something you caught out of the corner of your eye. He walked towards the fence, towards Oliver, with the immovable grin slashed through his features like a toothy, red incision.

"NO MORE DESTRUCTION!" came the new chant from around Oliver, and it seemed to clatter on his ears. The noise was an assault. The front-end loader crashed its bucket into the cliffside, sending another shower of dirt and rock to the beach below. More of the crack was exposed; more darkness pushed forth.

"STOP THE CONSTRUCTION!"

Peter Coomes did not appear as if he were about to engage with the protesters; rather, he seemed intent on Oliver, on walking towards Oliver. The smile remained on his face.

"NO MORE DESTRUCTION!"

Oliver pushed backwards against the crowd, but he felt the surge of the people behind him move forward, pinning him against the fence. Peter kept walking.

"STOP THE CONSTRUCTION!"

Oliver felt tears springing to his eyes. The front-end loader continued to scrape away at the cliffside, scraping jagged stripes

zebra stripes

into the rock, tearing away the dirt, the debris, the sand, and the shake that had, for millennia, been pushed into this spot by the forces of the ocean and the movement of the wind and rain. Forces that had buried whatever was below them, below the headlands.

They shoulda left it hid.

And suddenly, Oliver felt very alone. Despite being jammed between the shoulders of protesters, overwhelmed by the smell of their bodies, the feel of their heat, he felt isolated, abandoned. He saw Archie's dad approaching, the menace on his face; he heard the frenzied cries of the people around him. He felt he had no one to turn to. No one to trust.

No one but his friends.

"NO MORE DESTRUCTION!"

With an explosion of effort, Oliver pushed against the chain links of the fence with all his might, throwing himself backwards into the crowd. He managed to snake into the space between two people, freeing himself from the crush. He felt his balance tip sideward and he fell, momentarily, before he was righted by a steady hand. He looked up – it was Cynthia Quest.

"Oliver," she said, "are you OK?"

"I have to find them," he said breathlessly. "I have to tell them."

"Who?"

"My friends. I have to find them."

And with that, he wrenched his arm free of Cynthia's grasp and pushed through the remaining bodies in the crowd. In the midst of the turmoil, of the grinding noise of the machinery on the beach and the relentless chanting of the protesters, Oliver fled up the road, away from the beach, towards the trees. Towards his friends.

TUESDAY

The fire had died.

A black ribbon of smoke drifted up from the last remaining log inside the circle of stones. A bird sang somewhere from the distant shroud of trees. The three friends surrounded Oliver in a kind of half-moon shape – they were like a shelter, each of them leaning in towards him. When his story finished, no one said anything for a time.

"We have to go back," said Archie finally.

"And do what?" asked Chris.

"We have to stop them," said Oliver. His voice sounded worn down. "They can't keep working. They can't keep digging."

"You think they're going to listen to us?" asked Chris. "And what will we tell them – that a dead zebra told us they should stop working? That'll go over great."

"Chris," said Archie. "Chill for a second."

"Archie, why don't you talk to your dad?" asked Athena. "Maybe you could reason with him."

Oliver looked at Archie, stricken. Archie noted this and said, "I could try. Not sure what good it'll do."

"He's not well," said Oliver. "I swear it. I swear something's not right."

"What, that he smiled weird at you? C'mon, Ollie," said Chris. "All this stuff you're seeing – it's scary, but it's *not real*. You had a seizure. You were in the hospital…"

"I know what I saw," said Oliver quietly.

"You were in the hospital," continued Chris. "They kept you two nights. You probably had a concussion. Don't you think that's the likely story?"

"I don't know, Chris," Archie said. A knot had grown in his stomach. "What about what I saw? What about Birgitta?"

Oliver looked up at his friend. "Wh-who?" he stammered.

"He saw that lady, Birgitta Woodley," said Chris, as if wanting to get the information out before Archie had a chance to, as if that would somehow strip it of its strangeness. "In the woods. She was lost."

"She didn't look lost," said Archie. "She was naked."

"What?" said Athena. "Out there? Does she need help?"

Archie suppressed a shiver. "Something wasn't right. *She* wasn't right."

Oliver started shaking his finger at Archie, saying, "That – that's just what I felt about your dad. He wasn't right. Whatever it is – something's not right with him."

"You guys," said Chris, exasperated. "What's up with everyone all of a sudden? It's like we had one bad night and we're all seeing, like, ghosts and goblins everywhere."

"We need to go back," said Oliver, standing up from the stone circle. "We need to go back now."

"What about Birgitta?" asked Athena.

"I think we need to get away from Birgitta as soon as possible," said Archie. He had crawled into the tent and was busy cramming his sleeping bag into its stuff sack. "I agree with Oliver. I need to see what's going on. I need to see my dad."

"What? Are you for real?" asked Chris, watching his friend packing away his gear. "You guys, we've been planning this camping trip for like a month. We packed in food for three days, and we're just going to head back after one night?"

Athena stood on the edge of the firepit, looking off into the trees. "What if she's hurt? What if she's, y'know, having, like, a mental thing?"

"We can tell someone in town, then," said Archie. "A doctor. Or her husband. Someone who can handle that kind of thing."

"I can't believe this," said Chris. "I seriously can't believe this. So they started work on the cliff again – so what? What are we going to be able to do to stop them?" When this got no response, he said, "And noises in the woods? There are *always* noises in the woods. You guys are acting like a bunch of chickens. This was our big trip – our big thing to end the school year. You guys can't just bag on it like this. Wait – Athena, you too?"

She had joined Archie in the tent and was rolling up her sleeping bag. "I trust Oliver," she said. "This seems serious,

Chris. Besides, I want to check in with Ed Woodley, let him know we saw Birgitta out here. And maybe I can help out my parents at the protest."

"Oh, so you can, like, chain yourself to the fence? Get arrested or something?"

She glared at him. "We have to do *something*, Chris."

"This is it, guys," said Chris. "This is our last summer together, all of us. This is it."

"What?" asked Oliver, squinting at Chris. "What does that mean?"

Athena nodded. "He's moving," said Archie. "Yeah, we just found out too."

"Mom got a job. In Ohio. I'm not thrilled either," said Chris. "So this is all we got. Let the grown-ups deal with all this stuff." He waited for someone to respond; Archie and Athena glanced at one another, then continued packing.

"Well, I'm staying," said Chris, and he sat down on one of the logs that had been pulled up to the firepit. He picked up one of the discarded marshmallow roasting sticks from the night before and began jamming it into the smouldering coals.

"You shouldn't stay," Oliver said to Chris. His voice was flat. "It's not safe for you to stay."

"I'm sure he'll be fine," said Athena.

"I *will* be fine," said Chris. "Gonna have the time of my life." He threw a pile of dried branches onto the fire and began to coax it back to life.

No more than twenty minutes had passed before they

had their packs loaded and on their backs. The sun was still high in the sky. It was two o'clock by Oliver's watch. Archie hung back while Athena and Oliver made their way towards the forest-service road on the edge of the meadow. Chris was gathering firewood from the nearby deadfall and stacking it into a neat pile beside the now-crackling fire.

"Sure you don't want to come?" asked Archie.

"Nah," said Chris. "I'm good. You guys knock yourselves out."

"I'm sorry we're ditching on the trip. We'll just plan another one. Soon."

"Yeah, sure." Chris looked up at his friend. "Why don't you stick around? It could be just us two – like old times. Promise we won't starve this go round."

Archie laughed. "Way to sell it," he said.

"I'm serious."

"I gotta get back, though," said Archie. "I gotta see what's up with my dad. See what's going on at the cliff. I've never seen Oliver like this."

"I've seen Oliver like this," said Chris. "It's just another one of his things he gets; that's all."

"I don't know, man. This feels … realer somehow."

Chris nodded. His gaze wandered, taking in the meadow, the surrounding trees. "Don't worry about me," he said. "Kinda prefer this, actually. A bit of quiet."

They stood for a second, silent. Archie had the urge to hug his friend, but he suppressed it. They hadn't hugged, he didn't think, since they were in kindergarten together. He looped his fingers under his backpack straps and gave Chris a nod. "See ya," he said.

"See ya," said Chris.

Archie walked quickly to meet up with his friends on the forest-service road. He did not turn around until he'd reached Athena and Oliver, but by that time the campsite was no longer in view.

It was almost six when they arrived back in Seaham.

They stopped just past the culvert that ran beneath the highway. Before them was the well-worn neighbourhood trail they'd followed from Chris's house. They all seemed to share a kind of hesitancy, here on the boundary between the town and the wilderness. The trees that hung over the trail had taken on an almost hostile aspect, looming like bent, skeletal giants.

"I'll let you know what I find out," said Archie.

"Be careful," said Oliver.

"I'll be fine. Listen, I've seen my dad in moods before. It'll pass. I'll get to the bottom of all this." Archie hoped he exuded confidence as he spoke; it was not something he was feeling.

Athena wanted to find her parents at the worksite — assuming they were still there, heading up the demonstration. They would know who to speak to about Birgitta. Oliver needed to get home to his mom. She would, no doubt, be getting worried about him. Archie suggested they meet at Movie Mayhem the following day.

"First thing," he said. "Just before Randy opens. Then we can figure out the next step."

They all shook hands grimly and continued down the trail. They parted ways at Duncan Street; Archie walked home alone.

The sun was just setting behind the crown of fir trees when he arrived back at his house. He mounted the stairs warily. Archie peered into one of the windows set into the door and saw an empty house. He opened the door and called out, "Anyone home?"

No one answered.

He dropped his backpack near the coatrack. He walked to the kitchen and called out again.

Archie looked at the clock that hung above the coffee maker. It was getting on seven thirty. Past dinnertime. Maybe they'd gone out for food? He grabbed the bag of sandwich bread from a cupboard and threw two pieces into the toaster.

Minutes later, the door swung open; Archie turned.

"What, you're back already?" It was his brother, Max. "Did you guys wuss out again?"

"Where's Dad?" asked Archie, ignoring him.

"Honey," said his mom, following Max through the door. "You're back so early. We should've waited for you. We went out for burgers." She hung her purse on the coatrack and said, "Is everything OK? I thought you weren't coming back till Thursday."

"Everybody's fine. Everything's fine. I just need to talk to Dad," said Archie.

Liz looked over her shoulder, towards the door. "He's coming," she said. "What's this all about?"

Annabelle and Olivia had filed in and gone straight up the stairs to their room; Max had flopped down on the couch and was turning on the television. "It's nothing," said Archie. "Is Dad OK?"

Liz looked at Archie quizzically. "I mean, he's had a long day. Good news, though – the job started up again at the site. We went out to celebrate. Wish you could've been there."

"Yeah, Disneyland trip's back on," said Max from the couch.

"It's back on? But – but what about...?" Archie stammered. "What about it not being safe and all that? The cliff and stuff?"

Liz shrugged. "I guess it's all worked out. Wasn't long after you'd left, he came home saying they'd figured out how to safely excavate at the site. And that was that."

The front door was still open. The twins had left it ajar when they'd hurried upstairs. Archie could see the family's car parked at the kerb. He saw his father emerge from the driver's side, and for a second he felt a thrill of relief to see him. But as the man approached the house, Archie saw something was different.

He couldn't put his finger on it, exactly. Maybe it was something in the way his father walked; it might've been something in the way his arms swung at his sides – they were somehow held too close to his waist, too stiff.

"Hello, Archie," his father said as he climbed the front

steps to the porch. He'd paused on the threshold, and Archie had a full moment to reckon the change in the way his father stood.

"Hi, Dad," he said. It was as if he was sounding the waters. Testing for something.

"You're back awfully early from your camping trip."

"Yeah. Something came up."

"Can I come in?" Peter asked. His head was suspended on the pedestal of his neck in a way that seemed perhaps too straight, too tall.

Archie, distracted, could think of no reason to delay him. "Yeah," he said, stepping aside.

"Thank you," said Peter as he walked into the house. He then smiled at Archie. And Archie saw.

The smile.

Oliver was right. If a smile was like a fingerprint, an identifiable trait that one person held that was unlike anyone else's, then Peter Coomes's smile had a few lines missing – a change that would perhaps fool a fingerprint scanning tool but not the people closest to him. Certainly not Archie.

He watched his father walk into the living room and stand behind the couch. Max had turned on the TV; some sitcom was playing.

"Dad?" asked Archie, suddenly remembering himself.

"Yes?" Peter's eyes did not leave the TV screen.

"Why is the work at the cliff starting again? I thought you said it wasn't safe."

Peter Coomes did not answer; the laugh track from the

TV show bloomed behind a joke and filled the room with its white noise.

"Dad?" asked Archie.

"We determined it's safe," said his father finally. "We're back to work."

"But you said—"

"I know what I said, but we've determined it's safe," said Peter. He turned away from the TV and looked at Archie. "And now we can go to Disneyland."

"It's not safe," said Archie defiantly. "You can't keep—"

"Shut up, butthole." This came from Max, on the couch. "You heard him. It's safe. LA trip is back on."

"I don't care about LA. I don't care about Disneyland," said Archie. "It's about what you said."

Peter's face went through a series of contortions – a kind of spiteful rage appeared, rippling from his forehead and down the bridge of his nose, which softened into an almost forced expression of sympathy, of understanding. To Archie, it was unconvincing. "I know," said Peter, "that you're concerned about the safety of the work. But I am in a position to say that it is perfectly safe and the work will continue."

Archie began to object again, but his father interrupted him.

"I've had a long day," said Peter. "I'm going upstairs to rest." With that, he turned and walked up the stairs and disappeared. Archie watched him go. He looked back at the television, at Max, in a kind of shock.

"What's up with Dad?" he asked.

Max shrugged. "Seems fine to me," he said.

"You don't think there's anything, like, weird about him?"

Max didn't answer for a moment, then said, "No."

Liz appeared at the doorway to the kitchen; she had witnessed the exchange. "Go easy on your dad, hon," she said. "He's wiped out. The Quests got a bunch of folks down there to protest."

"Yeah," said Archie quietly, "for good reason."

"What's that?"

"I said, for good reason. They shouldn't be digging up there. They should leave it alone."

"You're sounding like one of the Quests now," said Liz, her voice edging towards anger. "Remember whose family you belong to."

"I don't think I even know," said Archie.

"What's that?" asked his mother.

Archie repeated, louder, "I don't even know who my family is." He flew up the stairs, several steps at a time.

"Don't talk back to me, Archie Coomes," came his mother's voice. He walked down the hall and stood in front of his parents' closed bedroom door. He lifted his hand. He knocked.

"Come in," said his dad.

He opened the door and saw his father sitting, still fully dressed, at the edge of his parents' king-sized bed. His back was to the door. He was sitting very rigidly, as if there were a wooden stake wound through his spine and impaled into the mattress.

"Hey, Dad," said Archie.

Peter Coomes's head turned slowly. The motion was so smooth it reminded Archie of a turning globe. From this position, Peter looked sidelong at his son and said, "Hey, Archie."

"Sorry to bug you. I know you've had a long day."

Peter removed his hand from his lap and gently patted the space next to him on the bedspread. "Sit down," he said. When Archie hesitated, his father repeated himself: "Come on. Sit down."

Archie walked to the bed and sat down next to his father. There was a scent that came off Peter that Archie could not, at first, pinpoint. It was not his father's usual scent, which was a heady blend of body odour and Speed Stick. The smell was something altogether more ... organic. It reminded Archie of wet woods, of cold, mossy forest floors.

He cringed to feel the weight of his father's arm over his shoulders. "How ya doing?" said Peter.

"Fine, Dad," said Archie.

Peter smiled. That smile. "Now what can I do you for?" he asked. There was a sweat-like sheen on the man's skin, on the backs of his hands and across his brow. He looked like he was ill, but his touch didn't feel warm.

"I just wanted to say..."

"Uh-huh?"

Archie took a nervous breath and restarted. "I just wanted to say – and I know this is going to sound crazy – but there's been some weird stuff going on. Like, a bunch of things." He looked up at his dad, as if he were sounding out this statement, gauging his dad's response. It was eerie to see his father's expression – smiling – remain unchanged.

"What kind of – *weird things*?" asked Peter, the last two words spoken in a kind of playful monster voice.

"Well, just some things we've noticed. Going on around town."

"Uh-huh. And who's this *we*?"

"You know, Oliver and Athena and Chris. Us. Oliver maybe in particular. And we think that maybe it has something to do with the cliff. I think – I think you should look into what's going on. Like, maybe think about, I don't know, stopping work. Let someone else build that hotel. Some other company." It was a lot for a thirteen-year-old boy to suggest to his grown father, but Archie felt he owed it to his friends to try.

Peter's face grew serious. He locked eyes with his son and said, "Now why would you ask me to do a thing like that?"

"I just thought I'd…"

"Just thought you'd what? Get me to give up this job? Just because of some *feeling* you have?"

"No, I…"

But Peter wouldn't let his son talk. He spoke angrily now. "Do you know how much money it takes to run this household? Do you know how much I have to make just to get things like food and clothes and movie tickets and dinners out? You think your mother contributes a dime to this? No. It's me. It's all me. And if you think I'm going to give up this job just because of your *feelings*…" He paused here and looked away from Archie, towards the wall. He seemed to regain his composure. "This is not for you to decide," he said icily.

Archie looked down into the palms of his hands, chastened. He didn't know what to say. He felt like he wanted to cry. His father had never spoken to him like that. It was alarming.

Finally, Peter spoke again. "Besides, aren't you excited?"

"Excited about what?"

"About going to Dis-a-neyland," said his father, pronouncing the last word in a flat cadence that Archie hadn't heard Peter use before.

"Yeah," he said after a time. "I guess I am."

"You guess you are," said Peter, pulling a chiding, serious face. "You guess you are. What kinda response is that?"

"I am," Archie said, correcting himself. The urge to leave the room became suddenly overwhelming, but he felt captive, crushed against his dad's side by his arm.

"That's right. We're all going. Going to Dis-a-neyland." Again with the strange pronunciation. It was unnerving. "But there's one thing, Archie."

"What's that, Dad?"

"You and your friends. You gotta stay clear of that work site. I don't want you going around there. I don't want your friends going around there. I want you to steer clear." As he spoke, he became more and more serious until the last words came out like little bullets.

"Why?" asked Archie. It took his entire reserve of bravery to ask the question. "Why can't we?"

Peter seemed taken aback, but his steely composure soon returned. "I just don't want anyone to get hurt. That's all. I just don't want anyone to get hurt." He gave Archie's shoulder a squeeze. "Now you get on to bed. It's past your bedtime, isn't it? And I've got a *big* day tomorrow."

Archie was in a state of paralysis as he left the room. He didn't know what to think, how to react. It was as if he'd forgotten why he'd even gone into the room in the first place. He walked to his parents' door in a fog, only pausing once he'd arrived at the hallway. He turned to shut the door and looked back at his father, again sitting on the bed, facing the wall. Upright. Unmoving.

"Dad?" Archie asked.

"Yes?"

"Are you feeling OK?"

"Feeling OK?"

"You just seem a little, I don't know. You seem like you might be sick."

Archie could see his father flinch. "I feel fine, Archie," he said. Peter swivelled his head again, in that same clockwork-like motion, and looked at his son over his shoulder. "In fact," he continued, "I feel better than I have in a long, long time." The man then turned his head to face the wall. "In a very long, long time," he said.

Archie said nothing. He left the room and quietly closed the door behind him.

Olivia was standing in the open doorway to her room. She was watching Archie as he moved down the hall. She caught his eye.

"What's going on?" she asked.

"I don't know," said Archie. "But it's not good. Whatever it is."

He left her and retreated to his room, where he closed the door behind him. He undressed and climbed into bed. He turned on his bedside light and lay there for some time, with his back to the headboard and his knees bunched to his chest beneath his blanket, watching the door.

There was a strange sensation on his fingers, and he brought them up to inspect them. There, on his finger, on the spot where he'd touched his father's skin, was the unmistakable tackiness of tree sap.

WEDNESDAY

Archie woke early but remained in bed, waiting for the sound of activity on the floor below to dissipate. Finally, he heard his father's truck start up and pull away from the kerb. Only then did he climb from his sheets, throw on some clothes, and venture out into the hallway. In the kitchen, he wolfed down a quick breakfast and rode to Movie Mayhem. Oliver and Athena were already there by the time he arrived.

"How'd it go?" asked Oliver intently as Archie approached the counter. Randy was standing at the computer, peering at the green lettering on the black screen from above his spectacles. He seemed oblivious to the fact that the kids were there.

Archie sighed and shook his head. His quick high fives with his friends had a kind of serious, conspiratorial feel to them. "Something's definitely not right," he said. "He's not doing good."

"Not good?" asked Athena.

"I think he's sick or something," said Archie. "He was acting all weird and spaced out. And he had this kind of sweat on him, like he was running a fever or something."

"A virus," said Oliver. "He's got some kind of virus."

Archie shrugged. "I don't know. I've never seen him like this. I mean, I've seen him sick and all – but this was, I don't know, different somehow."

"You think that's what's going on?" asked Athena. "Like, a sickness? Maybe that would explain Birgitta up there in the woods. She's got this sickness."

"It's like that movie – what's it called?" said Oliver. He waved at Randy, drawing the man's attention from his computer screen.

"What's that?" asked Randy, now peering over the top of his glasses at the three kids.

"The movie – the one where the, like, virus or whatever takes over the town," said Oliver.

Randy cracked a smile. "You're going to have to be more specific."

"The one with the plague," said Oliver impatiently. "You know, with the lady from *The Exorcist* in it."

"It's called *Contagion of Fear*, Mr Fife," said Randy. "And it's not the lady from *The Exorcist*; it's Lee Remick." When this name received no recognition, Randy said, "From *The Omen*."

"Whatever," said Oliver. "This town uncovers a box, right? And they don't know what to do with it, but then some government scientists get to it and they open it and it, like, unleashes this ancient virus on the town…"

Archie took up the story, having seen the movie at Oliver's house the summer before. "And they all get infected, becoming these weird super zombies."

"Super zombies?" asked Athena incredulously.

"Something like that," said Archie.

"Flopped at the box office," said Randy.

"That's what we're dealing with here, clearly," said Oliver. "In that hole, that's what's been unleashed. A sickness. A plague."

"That's a movie," said Archie. "My dad's not a super zombie."

"He's got the sickness, doesn't he?"

"I don't know, man," said Archie. "It's probably just a bad cold. Or the flu or something."

Oliver was undeterred. "You have to talk to your dad again, Archie. You have to make him see. They have to stop working – that's why he's sick. It's not good, what they did. It's not good. I can feel it."

Archie's reservoir of patience was quickly draining; he could feel the colour rising in his cheeks. "You can *feel* it. Great. This is, like, my dad's job. This is his work. We're screwed if he doesn't do the job. And he seems really stressed about it."

"He's not stressed," said Oliver. "He's infected."

"Oh, shut up," said Archie.

"Arch," said Athena, "don't be a jerk."

"He called my dad a super zombie. Seriously," said Archie, looking at Oliver. "I'm done with your little acid flashbacks or whatever."

"They're not acid flashbacks," said Oliver. "They're visions."

Archie rolled his eyes. "Oh, *visions*. That's much better."

"You wouldn't understand," Oliver snapped.

"You guys," said Athena, her voice rising, "stop it." The two boys fumed quietly, abashed, while Athena stared at them both. Randy glanced away from the computer screen to eye them, then returned to his work. "We need to stick together on this. We can't be fighting each other. There's some serious stuff going down here and we have to get to the bottom of it. Right?"

"Right," murmured Oliver.

"Right?" asked Athena again, this time looking at Archie.

"Right," said Archie.

"Now – we have to get our heads clear. Figure this out," said Athena. She drummed her fingers against her cheek in thought. She looked at Oliver. "We've all seen enough movies; you're not supposed to ignore the guy with the visions, right? The bad feelings. That's what they all do, in those movies." Here, she gestured towards the horror section. Randy's attention was now won, and he'd turned from the computer monitor to watch the girl speak. "There's one dude who's, like, don't go down into the basement, I've got a bad feeling. And of course, what do they do?"

"They go down in the basement," said Archie, rolling his eyes. Oliver shot him a vindicated look.

"Exactly," said Athena. "And what happens? They get eaten, or whatever. The creature, the murderer, what have you, it gets them. Things are getting so weird right now, I feel like we have to trust the guy with the bad feeling."

"Thank you," said Oliver.

"But we're still on Earth, right?" continued Athena. "We're not in a movie."

"This much is true," put in Randy.

"Thank you," said Archie.

"But still," said Athena, "things have got weird. Real weird. Maybe it's a sickness; maybe it's something more. We need to figure out what it is, what's down in that hole. *Then* maybe we can convince your dad to stop."

"We're not going back there," said Archie. "We're not going back to that hole. I just don't want to go against my dad now. He was so … so serious. Not like before. I don't even want to know what he'd do if we got busted."

"I'm not suggesting that," said Athena. "But there's got to be *something* under that cliff, right? I think we need to believe Oliver here. Something was buried there. Something that shouldn't be found again. Maybe that's a sickness, maybe it's something else. But let's say someone put it there – someone buried it. There's got to be a record of that, somewhere." Athena was staring off at the rows of videotapes as she spoke. "Like, in the movies, they go to the library, right? There's always those … those what do you call them?"

"Microfiche," said Oliver.

"Right, that," said Athena. "There's probably some record of what happened there, at the cliff. Old newspaper articles or something."

That's when Randy spoke up. "Hold on, hold on, hold on," he said, waving his hands at the kids. "I don't think you need to go to the library."

156

Everything was swiftly moved from the surface of the counter – the tape cases, the rolled-up promo posters, the empty Styrofoam coffee cups – to make room for the cardboard box Randy had brought out from his office. He set it down with the ceremony of a priest unveiling a relic. It was a typical file box; the words *SEAHAM ARCHIVE* had been written on the side in black marker. Randy patted the top a few times and then rested his arms on it.

"Adrienne Springer, librarian up there at the public library, brought these over – I don't know how long ago. Been meaning to get to 'em, but I been so busy running the store, it was the furthest thing from my mind. Funny, I don't think she even remembers I have 'em. I think she just had some time on her hands, was trying to organize some of the clutter in the basement of the library."

"What is it?" Archie asked, craning his neck to get a look into the box.

"Photos, old film," said Randy. "Some of the original photo documentation of the town's inhabitants and whatnot, back when film was the newest tech to hit the scene. We come a long way, I can tell you, from this stuff to the prime medium that is Betamax NTSC coded magnetic tape. Anyway, she said she wanted all this stuff to be preserved on video so that it could be viewed at the library on request. Wasn't probably till January, just after the holiday rush, that I finally got around to looking at what's inside."

The three kids had moved close together, their shoulders

touching, as they crowded in towards the box on the counter.

Randy continued, "It's interesting stuff, that's for sure. A bunch of pictures of the old buildings; a lot of 'em aren't around any more. The old drugstore up on Charles. The original library building, the one that burned down. The other Langdon house, downtown, the one that Josephine Langdon asked her daddy to build her because she wanted something more *cosmopolitan* than that big old thing up on the headlands. Wanted to be closer to the nightlife." He laughed a bit here. "That kinda stuff. Historical-society kinda stuff. Pretty basic. Didn't think much of it, except I dug a bit deeper and found a bunch of old tintypes."

"Tintypes?" asked Archie. "What's that?"

"Early photography," said Randy. "We're talking late nineteenth century. Kinda stuff they were using to take pictures of the dead bodies on the battlegrounds of the Civil War. Probably dated to the 1870s, was my guess."

"Wait," said Oliver, "I thought Seaham wasn't even, like, a town till 1900 or whatever."

His friends looked at him, amazed at this sudden flush of knowledge.

Oliver reddened. "What? I did a report on it in sixth grade."

"You're right, Mr Fife," said Randy. "Seaham, as we know it today, incorporated in 1902. But there was a first Seaham, one before the one we got now. A whole town. And one day, that whole town was gone."

Archie stared at Randy; he could feel Athena tense up

next to him. Oliver nodded knowingly. "I did a bit about that in my report," he said. "But there's not a bunch of stuff about it in the history books."

"That's the thing," said Randy. "No one knows much about that first group of settlers. Best guess is most of 'em came by way of the beaver-pelt trade. That's how Charles Langdon ended up here. By all accounts, and there aren't many of 'em, they had a nice little bustling metropolis. A few buildings, a general store. Heck, they even had a school. Little one-room schoolhouse, just over where Dolly Park is now. By the looks of things, a town that was just about to take off. And the next thing you know – *whoosh*. Gone. It's a ghost town."

"How?" asked Athena.

"No one really knows. Some folks said cholera. Smallpox. Others said some of the local Indians didn't take kindly to them, wiped 'em out. You have to understand, this was the frontier for white folk, even back then. Plenty of little fishing or mining communities up and down the coast boomed and busted. Sometimes people just got fed up and left. But not all of 'em. All at once."

Randy took a deep breath. He removed his glasses from the bridge of his nose and gave them a cursory cleaning on his T-shirt.

"Record's all a bit hazy, but next thing you know, Charles Langdon is building his house up on the headlands and naming every godforsaken square inch of the place after his kids and his pets, and suddenly the town just kinda builds up again. Post office showed up in 1897. Incorporated as Seaham in 1902. But I gotta say, I always wondered about that first Seaham. The one that vanished." Having said this, Randy stared wistfully off towards the front door of the store.

"And…?" prompted Athena.

"Right!" said Randy, reminded of his task. "Well, enter this box of old pictures and film. I'm up late, just this last January, poring over this stuff, trying to figure out how I'm going to shoot it and put it on tape, when I find this envelope." Here, he pulled up the lid of the box and reached in; he retrieved a manila envelope, deeply stained with age. Inside were a stack of panes of what appeared to be flattened metal. The three kids moved in to inspect them.

The photos were dark and dingy; the images on the metal seemed shadow-like, grimed with a patina of age. Motes of black dust marred the images; a fog seemed to encroach from the margins of each one. They looked impossibly old, still images from a long-lost time. The first one showed three figures in the central portion of the frame. Two women and one man. They were standing on a beach, staring uncertainly at the camera, as if observing some foreign creature. The man wore a fine black suit and a wide-brimmed hat; the women were dressed in lacy gowns, their faces somewhat obscured by the bonnets they were wearing. Beyond them, two children played, just out of focus.

Randy pointed to an outcropping of rock behind the picture's subjects. "That's where those condos are now. So we know this was taken just up north of here, past where the benches are. These, as far as I can tell, are the only record that

160

exist of that first Seaham." He set the plate off to the side, revealing the one below it.

A group of men stood in the centre of the photograph; a dark streak seemed to wind its way down from the top corner of the plate, distorting some of their faces – but the three kids could see that several of the men appeared to be Indians, dressed as they were in what seemed to be Native garb: handmade leathers adorned with beads and feathers. Five white men stood facing them; these men wore outfits made entirely of animal skins. Wild facial hair bloomed from their faces like moss. The Indians and the white men were posed as if in mid-conversation; the two central figures were shaking hands.

"My best guess is this is some kind of welcome delegation from the Tillamooks – that's the tribe whose land we're on right now. And these guys have to be fur trappers – I mean, look at the getups. This photo's got to be about as old as the state of Oregon, if you can get your mind around that." He studied the photo momentarily before saying, "Shame, really. How those early settlers exploited the Native tribes. Genocide, really."

"What happened to them?" asked Athena.

"What happened to tribes everywhere, all over the country. Those that didn't assimilate, and those that didn't succumb to one of the diseases these white folk brought with them, well, they ended up being shipped off to one of the reservations. It's criminal. Downright criminal. And this kinda stuff – this posed glad-handing? It's a sham, is what it is. Anyhoo – don't get me started." With that, he began flipping through the tintypes at a quicker speed.

"Here's the schoolhouse I was talking about – you can see the sign there says 1874. Look at 'em, all lined up. Five kids in the class – imagine that, huh? Think you're sick of your friends; gotta wonder what it was like for them."

Athena snorted. "What about this one?" asked Oliver, pointing to the metal plate beneath the school picture.

"Huh," said Randy, inspecting the photo. It was a formal portrait; a man with a tidy beard sat centre frame in an ornate chair while a woman with a high bustle and impeccable hair stood above him, her hand on his shoulder. "I believe that is our good town father himself, Charles Langdon. And his wife, Abigail."

"When was this taken?" asked Archie, inspecting the photo.

"Might be around the same time – I'm guessing late 1870s, early 1880s," said Randy. "I mean, guessing from the condition. It's about as worn as the rest of 'em."

"And when did the town, like, disappear?" asked Athena, catching Archie's line of questioning.

Randy nodded knowingly. "Within that time. There's no proper record. But sometime around 1880."

"So the Langdons were there?" asked Athena. "Part of the original settlement?"

Archie glanced at his friends, confused. "How did they survive?"

"Your guess is as good as mine. Maybe they were out of

town for a spell – maybe they just managed to miss whatever came through and wiped out the rest of their townsfolk. Like I said, history's really spotty on this one. No one took the time to record it. Here, here's Abigail with young Dolly." He had skipped to the next tintype; there was the same austere woman from the photograph before, this time holding an infant in white swaddling clothes. The woman looked down at the baby and beamed. It was a marked departure from the expression she'd worn in the previous shot.

"Dolly Park," said Athena.

"The same," said Randy. "Poor thing, didn't see her twelfth birthday. But that was pretty common in those days." He slid the portrait away, revealing the one below it. Here, he froze.

"Now, this is the one," he said, "this is the one that got me real curious."

At first glance, the tintype that Randy had revealed seemed perfectly ordinary for its kind – again, it was a group of men, dressed in period costume, standing in a grove of trees. They were facing the camera. It reminded Archie of the photos he'd seen developed from his dad's trips to hunting camp – a line of weatherworn men standing proudly next to the dead and gutted remains of the beast they'd killed. The strange thing, however, was that in the centre of the frame, the place where that trophy might be, there was only a large dark spot.

Archie initially thought it was a hole in the metal, it was so deeply black. But no: it was there, seared into the tin. Part of the photograph. A spot of pure blackness. For whatever reason, it chilled him.

"What's that?" he heard Athena ask. "Some kind of flub in the picture?"

"That's what I thought," said Randy, "at first. Then I saw this."

He uncovered the photo below the picture of the men; this one was similar, but now it was a larger crowd, and the setting had moved to a more populated area. Men and women stood on an unpaved street; the facades of small wooden buildings could be seen laid out behind them. Children milled nearby; the figure of a dog, blurred in action, chased something within the bounds of the frame. But there was no denying: the focal point of the photo, what everything in the shot seemed to revolve around, was an inky black spot the size of a thumbprint.

"Oh God," Oliver said.

"What is it?" asked Athena, peering closer.

But now Archie's attention was drawn away from the dark spot towards a figure who stood on the edge of the crowd, just behind the first row of people. Archie squinted, trying to will away the blur that obscured the man's face – but still, he could make out the man's dark facial hair, the knot of his tie, the shade of his suit, the shape of his worn cap.

No way, he thought. *It's not possible.*

Just then, Oliver repeated his moan. "Oh God!"

"Oliver!" shouted Athena.

Archie tore his eyes away from the photo and looked at

his friend. His cheeks had taken on a pale greenish hue. His lips trembled. "Ollie," Archie said, "take a deep breath." He grabbed Oliver by the arm and pulled him away from the counter. Oliver's eyes were riveted on the tintypes; Archie could hear the boy's loud, forced breaths. His arm felt warm in Archie's hand. "Oliver," he said intently, "don't do this."

The spell broke. Oliver looked down at the ground, at his feet. "That's what I saw," he said.

"What did you see?" asked Archie.

"That darkness. In the hole. In the cave. That darkness." The words came out in heaves, like he was vomiting them.

At the counter, Randy had pulled away the tintypes; he was holding them against his chest, guarding them from sight. "You OK, Fife?" he asked.

Oliver nodded. He took another long, deep breath. "I'm OK."

"What *was* that in the pictures?" asked Athena.

Randy shook his head. "No idea. Honestly. But those two photos, those are the last known photographs of any of the occupants of the original Seaham."

"That's it?" asked Archie.

"That's all she wrote," said Randy. "Until – well, until this film." Here, the man reached back into the box and retrieved a small metal film canister. It glinted in the low light of the counter's desk lamp.

The film was nearly unwatchable – projected against the bare wall of Randy's back office, the images they saw were blurry and washed out, beset by a moving constellation of spots and scratches. Five figures, cast in starchy black and white, stood briefly in front of the camera, their faces totally erased by the deterioration of the film. When they moved, they moved quickly and jerkily, as if captured in fast-motion.

They were holding shovels.

A few trees could be seen in the distance, but otherwise the men appeared to be standing in a wide clearing. As they moved, the film abruptly flashed and a new scene was set. The men were now digging.

One man stood above a large hole, resting on the haft of his shovel. He occasionally looked up and marked the camera. Several other men were standing hip-deep in the hole. On the ground above them was a large pile of dirt. The film was spliced again here; now the frame of the camera was empty of people. There was only the hole. The pile of dirt, however, took up such a big part of the picture that it disappeared beyond the frame. Now a man appeared pushing a wheelbarrow. He shovelled dirt into the wheelbarrow and, once it was full, turned and looked at the camera.

"Earliest, I can imagine this sort of thing taking place is 1890," said Randy, "The Lumières weren't even up and running till five years later, but the technology was around."

"Who filmed this?" asked Athena.

"No knowing, really," said Randy. "There's nothing on the canister. My guess? It's Charles Langdon. He was into this stuff, this new technology. He was wealthy, too, remember. Practically controlled the fur trade in this part of the territory." He watched the film in silence for a moment before saying, "That's an awfully big hole they're digging. Oh, here we go."

The scene had changed again. Now the foundation of a wooden building was being constructed. A group of men were assembling the frame of a wall; in the foreground, a man was sawing at a long wooden beam laid over a pair of sawhorses. Their movements were comically altered by the film speed; they scurried across the ground as they moved, their arms whipping around as if motorized.

"Where is this?" asked Archie.

"Good question. I didn't know myself what I was looking at," said Randy, watching the footage. "But then this – this was the dead giveaway."

The frame went blank; an abrupt edit now moved the camera to a lonely field. In the centre of the frame, a gravel driveway curved away into the distance. On either side of the path stood two concrete pillars; Archie immediately recognized them.

"Langdon House," he said.

"Exactly," said Randy. "First I saw it, I figured this was just footage of them building the house. For posterity or whatnot. And that's them digging out the foundation. Didn't think much of it. Well, you guys talking about burying something got me thinking about this little spool of film altogether differently."

"Why didn't you say something sooner, Randy?" asked Archie.

"It honestly didn't occur to me till just now," said Randy, his hands at his hips. "I figured all that talk about them finding something under the house was just, y'know, kids talking."

Athena had stood up from her seat and walked towards the image on the wall. She held up a finger, pointing at one of the strange symbols that had been carved into the twin pillars. "Those drawings," she said, "why are they there?"

Suddenly, the screen went blank; the room was flooded with the light of the projector's bulb reflecting against the bare white wall. The film had ended.

"Drawings?" asked Randy.

"Yeah," said Athena. "On the pillars. They're still there. We saw 'em, just the other day, when we were up there."

Randy busily spooled the film back onto the opposing reel; he powered up the projector and manually cranked the film back to where the image had first appeared. There it was again, in ghostly black and white, the two front gate posts of Langdon House. Randy approached the image on the wall.

"Well, I'll be damned," he said. "To think I'd never noticed that."

The film ended again; the film tail began slapping against the metal of the projector. Randy jogged back to turn off the machine.

"Like sand dollars," said Archie, "or something."

"I always thought they were flowers," said Athena.

Randy was silent; he stood at the projector with his hand on his chin. Finally, he said, "Frank Darcy, 1976."

"Huh?" asked Archie.

"*The Witches' Coven*," said Randy. "That's it." He looked at each of the kids in the room in turn and said, "Follow me."

They stood in front of the shelf of tapes as Randy scanned the spines and covers. The sign reading *HORROR* hung on the wall above the shelf, its letters all done up in red marker, made to look like dripping blood.

Finally, Randy pulled a tape from the shelf. He flipped it face-up and studied it; he wiped a bit of dust that had accumulated on the top edge and read the title out loud. "Yep," he said. "*The Witches' Coven*. Seventy-six. Lotsa movies like this came out around that time. Everyone cashing in on the *Exorcist* hype. This is one of the forgotten ones."

Archie stood at Randy's elbow and looked at the cover of the tape. Below the title, which was written in a kind of spiky red typography, a woman in a cowl loomed with her wizened hands curled before her, as if she were poised above a crystal ball. A group of what appeared to be teenagers stood at the bottom of the design in various states of distress and action.

Randy continued, "They must've made three more after this, each one worse than the one before. Anyway, this town gets taken over by a bunch of witches. All these kids go missing; turns out they're being sacrificed for some sort of ritual. Summoning a demon, I think. The only thing that can defeat the witches is this kind of warding spell, something that repels the witches. These teenagers figure it out and eventually, y'know, defeat their plan."

Here, he flipped back to the front image. Below the fingers of the cowled woman there was a symbol:

"That's it," gasped Athena.

Archie could see: it was identical to the symbol that had been carved into each of the pillars on the Langdons' front gate.

"What is it?" asked Oliver.

"It's called a hexafoil," said Randy. "It's a real thing, you know. Goes way back, like medieval times. I guess you see it in churches and barns in Europe. Folks carve it into doors to keep their family safe from evil spirits. Anyway, the kids use it to ward off the witches. Evil spirits can't go past a door with a hexafoil on it. Or, I imagine, a gate." He handed the box to Archie, who continued to study it while his friends gathered in closer to examine the cover. *WHAT YOU DON'T KNOW WILL HAUNT YOU* was the slogan below the title.

"Why would the Langdons carve that on their front gate?" asked Athena.

"Keeping witches away?" ventured Archie.

"Or keeping them inside," said Oliver ominously.

They all stood staring at the illustration on the back of the tape box, each of them lost in their own reverie. Finally, Archie said, "You guys. It's just a movie. There are no witches in Seaham, sacrificing children or whatever."

Randy blinked a few times; he rested against the wall of the shelf. "True," he said. "It is, as you say, just a movie."

"This is creeping me out," said Athena.

Just then the phone rang and Randy walked over to the counter to answer it. This left the three kids alone by the rack of horror movies. Archie placed the tape of *The Witches' Coven* back on the shelf.

"I don't know what to make of it all," said Archie.

"Hexafoil," repeated Oliver. "On the Langdons' gate this whole time."

"Didn't seem to do a very good job," said Athena, "this protecting mark. I mean, think of the Langdon curse – they all go crazy, right?"

"That's just a rumour," said Archie.

"Hey, Athena," called Randy from across the room. He had the phone receiver pressed against his chest. "It's your dad."

Archie and Oliver watched as Athena went to answer the phone. A smile spread over her face as she listened.

"What's up?" asked Archie.

"Papa wants us up at the cliff," she said, holding the receiver away from her mouth. "He says the mayor is coming by. Thinks he's going to shut down the job. Everyone's headed up – they want us to come. Papa says they need as many people as they can get."

"We need to go," Oliver said.

Archie realized that everyone was looking at him, waiting for his response. He finally acquiesced, nodding silently. "OK," he said.

Athena pulled the phone back to her lips and said, "We're on our way."

A headwind blew down the coastline, carrying wisps of clouds and ruffling the high tree crowns; the smell of ocean spray was carried inland. The three cyclists rode high on their pedals, battling the wind. Before long, the wrought-iron fencing of Langdon House came into view. Several cars were parked on the side of the road, up against the fence. Archie pulled his bike up alongside the gate; he climbed off and set his hands on his hips.

"Yep, there they are," he said. "Hexafoils."

Athena and Oliver were soon behind him, and all three of them inspected the worn runes that had been carved into the pillars on either side of the gate. Athena reached up and ran her finger along the lines, tracing them. Archie peered through the bars of the fence at the old house. He tried to imagine it as new, as a freshly built structure, awaiting the arrival of its occupants. Occupants who had somehow survived the eradication of an entire community.

A car drove up alongside them and stopped, some way down the road, on the grassy shoulder near the fence. A long string of parked cars lined the road down to the beach.

"It's like the whole town's here," said Oliver, looking towards the ocean.

The kids dropped their bikes against the fence and walked the rest of the way; they could hear voices being carried up the hillside from the beach below. Archie found himself slowing as he walked, as if forestalling his inevitable arrival at the site. He could see, now, the gathered protesters; there must've been forty people assembled at the fence. Poster-board signs, held aloft, hovered above the heads of the crowd, and the sand of the beach was pitted with their footsteps. There were no shouted slogans now, no organized chants. The crowd seemed to be awaiting some kind of event. The work on the other side of the fence continued unabated, and the sounds of great machinery carving through sand and rock drowned out the casual chatter of the protesters. Archie recognized the shape of his father's truck amid the workers.

"You made it!" came a voice; it was Athena's dad. He was standing at the edge of the crowd. He had Becky riding on his shoulders. He waved the three of them over.

"Thena!" called Becky cheerily.

"Hi, Becks. Hi, Papa," said Athena. "We came as soon as we could."

Jordan Quest was beaming, evidently emboldened by the turn of events. He spoke quickly. "You should see your mother – she barely slept a wink. We think we really got 'em this time. Mayor Kwan's gonna be here any minute. Did you bring signs? Don't worry – we've got a bunch to spare. Miss

Turner — you guys remember her from first grade, right? — she's got a sign-making station set up."

"OK, OK, Papa," said Athena, blushing. "We got it."

When Jordan saw Archie, his face became more serious. "Hey there, Arch," he said. "Appreciate you coming down. I know this is not easy for you."

"See the tractors?" asked Becky from aloft Jordan's shoulders. "They're so big. And yellow."

Archie smiled at the girl. He then asked Jordan, "My dad here?"

Jordan nodded. "He's in there, working. I keep trying to talk to him, y'know, engage with him. But it's like he doesn't even hear me."

"I know," said Archie. "Something's weird."

Jordan rubbed his thumb and finger together. "It's the money, Arch. Makes people deaf as well as blind."

Suddenly, the sound of a car managing the switchbacks down to the beach arrested the attention of the crowd. It was the sheriff's cruiser, and its lights were flashing as it slowly arrived at the hardpack gravel where the road met the sand. When the car idled to a stop, the driver's-side door opened and out stepped Bert Hoagley — or Hoag, as he was known locally — the sheriff for Merwin County. The lights switched off; Hoag surveyed the scene, standing at his open door. Eric Plant, the sheriff's deputy, climbed out of the passenger side of the car. The two men were dressed in nearly identical khaki uniforms: Hoag wore a cowboy hat with a yellow braid around the crown; Plant was in a baseball cap with the words *Deputy Sheriff* printed on the front.

They'd barely emerged when Jordan Quest set Becky down from his shoulders and approached the car, waving warmly. "Welcome, Hoag! Hey there, Eric."

Hoag put a finger to the brim of his hat by way of greeting. "Whatcha got cooking here, Jordan?" he asked. Plant leaned against the cruiser, his thumbs stuck into his belt.

"Well, I believe what we have is a destructive and arguably illegal construction operation happening on what should be federally protected coastal lands, is what we have. And we're trying to do something about it." The crowd had grown quiet as Jordan spoke; everyone moved closer to hear the exchange.

"I believe this has all been properly permitted, Jordan," replied Hoag. "We been over this before. That's all private land, up to the beach. Belongs to the Langdons. It's their *prerogative* what to do with their property."

"I know – but that was before there was a work stoppage. And I have reason to believe it was because of environmental issues. Why did they start again?"

"I'm gonna defer to Coomes Construction on this one, Jordan," said Hoag, his voice sagging with impatience. "But I can't have all this commotion down here – this is a lot of people to be congregating without a permit."

"This is public land, Hoag." This was from Cynthia Quest, who'd come up alongside her husband. "We have as much right as anyone to be here."

"I'm fully aware of that, Cynthia…" began Hoag, and the conversation between the two officers and the Quests continued in a tense, if civil, exchange; in the midst of it, Oliver had grabbed Archie's elbow and begun leading him to the far end of the crowd. From here, they had an unimpeded view of the work site beyond the fence.

"Archie, look," he said gravely.

There was Peter Coomes, standing in the midst of the milling workers, staring at the hole in the cliffside. While the crowd gathered at the fence seemed to elicit looks of curiosity from the workers on the site, Peter appeared unconcerned. His focus was intent on the cliff. An excavator's metal teeth were busy scarring the volcanic rock, sending little avalanches of broken gravel down to the pile on the sand below. The hole in the cliff was growing larger. Archie recognized Emilio standing between two other workers; they were each wearing identical white hard hats. Except for one man – Archie squinted to see him. He was standing on the far side of the job site. He was wearing a brown suit; the wind off the ocean ruffled the brim of his hat.

"Look, Ollie," said Archie, pointing.

"What?"

"Just there, on the other side of the rock. See that man?"

"The one in the suit?"

"Uh-huh. I keep seeing that dude. Or one like him." What he didn't say, however, was that he had thought he'd seen him in the tintype – it was too strange, too unbelievable, to admit.

Just then, they felt a sudden rise in activity from the crowd behind them. What had been hushed chatter became loud talking; someone called: "There he is!" while another said, "He's coming down the hill!"

Archie looked towards the switchbacks and saw a man in a fleece jacket and brown slacks walking as quickly as he could down the uneven surface of the road. Behind him came a woman in a dark trouser suit carrying a thick manila folder. The man was Billy Kwan, the mayor of Seaham; Archie did not recognize the woman. The crowd surged forward to greet these new visitors, and Archie and Oliver found themselves carried along with it.

"Hold on, hold on!" shouted Billy as he rounded the final switchback and walked onto the beach. "Hoag, Eric — everyone, calm down."

Archie glanced back towards his dad. Peter Coomes was still staring at the crack in the cliff; the man in the brown suit was gone.

"Hello, Jordan. Hiya, Cynthia — we got held up for a bit at the office," Billy said as he arrived at the patrol car. He was a man in his mid-fifties; he'd been Seaham's mayor for nearly eight years — he was up for re-election in November. The woman standing at his side looked nervous; she was wearing black leather flats, and she shifted them uncomfortably in the dry sand.

"Mr Kwan," said Hoag. "Didn't expect to see you down here."

"Extreme circumstances, Hoag," said Billy. "This is

Cindy Chavez. She's from the county. We've got some paper-work that I think Mr Coomes will find pretty interesting."

Hoag rolled his eyes. "You coulda called with this kinda info. What you got to come all the way down here for?"

"I must heed the call of my constituents, Hoag," said Billy, quickly flashing a smile at the gathered crowd. As if on cue, a subdued cheer arose from the crowd, and the poster-board signs above their heads gave little individual waves. "Now, if you don't mind," continued the mayor, "I need to speak to Mr Coomes."

With that, he left the side of the patrol car and waded directly into the centre of the crowd of protesters, allowing them to part for his and the woman's approach to the fence line. He took his time getting there, however, pausing to speak to people as he went, shaking hands and sharing hugs.

"Oh, don't worry, Mr Nelson," he said, shaking a man's hand. "We'll have this shut down pronto."

"Thank you for your advocacy, Mr Kwan," said a woman in her seventies. "You're a wonderful man."

"It's the only reasonable action," responded the mayor. He then raised his voice to address the crowd. "Keep the headlands wild!" he shouted.

Everyone cheered; Billy and the woman continued towards the fence. When they arrived there, Billy turned and spoke to the crowd. "This is Cindy Chavez," he said loudly. He brought the woman in the trouser suit up alongside him. She appeared uncomfortable being the object of the crowd's attention. "She's from county permitting. We heard, up at town hall, that this work was continuing. Well, we did a little digging – no pun intended – to see what it was that held it up in the first place. And you'll be surprised at what we found."

There was a pause here as Billy looked over at Cindy Chavez. She apparently hadn't received the cue, because she was still staring uncomfortably at the crowd before her. He gave her a little nudge and said, "Go on. Tell them what you told me."

"Uh … yes," said the woman, surprised. "This property, currently being developed by … uh…" She opened up the manila folder in her arms and read, "Halcyon Properties LLC has been flagged by county and state services for further inspection based on geological data found in the permitting process."

The mayor, evidently dissatisfied with the woman's performance, took up the announcement, saying, "And so we have determined that until we have a full review – *plus input from the community*" – he emphasized these last words, to the delight of the crowd, who tittered in approval – "that this development cannot – and will not – continue."

The crowd made a happy noise for the mayor; Cindy Chavez smiled, and Billy Kwan turned to the fence and gave it a shake. "Hello there – Peter!" he shouted through the wires in the fence. "You're going to want to let me in. I've got some paperwork you'll need to see."

Archie shrank back, letting the crowd overtake him as it pushed forward to watch the exchange. He felt a body press into his elbow; it was Athena.

"You OK?" she asked.

"Yeah," said Archie. "Just don't want my dad to see me."
He peeked out from the side of the crowd; through the fence,
he saw Billy Kwan, his dad, and the woman from the county
walking towards a small trailer some ways up the beach. The
protesters had quietened as they all watched the three figures
disappear into the building; the colourful signs, once held
high, had now disappeared, resting against bodies with their
wooden stakes planted in the ground. Idle chatter broke out
as everyone began to pass the time, their objective having
been briefly paused.

The three friends reunited in the crowd.

"Well, maybe that's it," said Athena.

"I wouldn't bet on it," said Archie.

The machines continued unabated, tearing away at the
cliffside. As they spoke, more rock spilled down from the
mouth of the hole. Oliver was watching it intently. Finally,
he said, "I'm worried about Chris."

The sentiment was unexpected. Archie had been so
consumed by thoughts of his dad and the job site, about the
photos and the films they'd seen at Movie Mayhem, that he'd
neglected to consider his oldest friend, who was still – as far
as they knew – camped out up at the meadow. "Yeah," he said
absently. "Me too."

The crowd around them suddenly became agitated, and
the kids' attention returned to the activity at the job site.
Archie saw Mayor Kwan and the woman approaching the
fence; the mayor was smiling. As he came closer, he began
waving his hands dismissively.

"All done," he was saying. "All done. No more to see here. This work is stopping now."

Archie glanced back at the trailer; he could see his father standing at the door, watching the proceedings dispassionately. The machines had stopped digging. The workers now idled, watching the mayor as he was let out of the gate.

"All done," he repeated. "Pending review. Environmental impact statements. Et cetera. And that's *after* we hear from the community! And so I've called an emergency town hall meeting. Tonight, at the Grange Hall. We need everyone there. We're going to have the developer there, members of city council. We want to hear from you. Should this continue? What are the greater ramifications for the Seaham community and environment? I say: enough is enough!"

Again, the crowd hollered their support, and the mayor passed back through as a saviour, receiving hearty slaps on the back, handshakes and hugs. The woman, Cindy, seemed enamoured of her newfound fame and was on the receiving end of several embraces herself. She beamed appreciatively, her face beetroot red. Athena's parents cornered the mayor and began talking with him closely, their eyes lit with excitement.

Athena was staring past the fence into the work site. Archie looked and saw his father walking down from the trailer and approaching someone in a hard hat. Archie recognized the figure as Emilio. The two men spoke for a few moments before Emilio walked over to the front-end loader and hailed the driver. The machine stopped its work, its toothy bucket coming to rest in the sand. Within moments, word had spread among the workers, and they began gathering around Emilio as he addressed them. Archie's father stood wordlessly off to the side. He then glanced over at the fence, and he and Archie locked eyes.

Archie's heart lurched, and he fell backwards out of Peter's line of sight. "Guys," he hissed. "I have to go. I have to go now."

Oliver and Athena huddled around Archie and conveyed him from the milling crowd, as if their presence would somehow protect him from his father's wrath. They left the protesters and walked past Sheriff Hoagley's patrol car up the gravel road. Only once they'd reached their overturned bicycles at the top of the hill did Archie feel like he could breathe again.

"I'm toast, you guys," he said.

"I mean, what's he gonna do," said Oliver helpfully, "kill you?" He then felt moved to qualify, "He's not going to kill you."

"You shouldn't go home," said Athena. "Not till this is all settled."

"Where am I going to go?" asked Archie. "I'll have to face the music sometime."

Cars had begun driving slowly by them, navigating away from their roadside parking spaces. The protesters were leaving, their efforts having temporarily won the day, and Archie and his friends watched the line of cars as they departed. They saw the mayor drive by, piloting a brown Mercedes.

Just then they heard a car horn sound from behind. They turned and saw the Quests' VW making its way towards

182

them. Jordan, in the driver's seat, slowed to a stop and rolled down the window. He waved for the line of cars behind him to pass. "Hey," he shouted to the kids. "What do you say to that, huh? I mean, what do you say to *that*?"

Athena's mom, in the passenger seat, leaned over the centre console and shouted, "He means the protest." She was smiling. Becky was waving at them through the window.

"Of course I mean the protest, honey," said Jordan, giddy as he spoke. "But what did I say – we needed *everyone* there. So glad you guys came out." He pumped his fist excitedly a few times. "I mean, this is just the beginning. Development up and down the coast is going to hear about this. We're only starting."

"You guys coming to the meeting tonight?" asked Cynthia.

Athena glanced at her friends before answering, "Yeah, we'll be there."

"We need you there," said Jordan. "Just like this – we need a real showing. All generations. Remember..."

Athena had heard the refrain many times. "This is *our* future," she answered.

Jordan seemed nonplussed by his daughter's less than enthusiastic response. Cynthia said, "Exactly, honey. See you guys tonight." She tapped Jordan on the shoulder. "C'mon, let's leave them be."

The Quests waved cheerily, and the Rabbit puttered away, leading a line of cars up the dirt road and away from the beach.

"Maybe this is it," said Athena. "Maybe this is just what we needed to do. To shut it all down."

Archie nodded. "Maybe so."

"I should get home," said Oliver. "My mom thinks I'm on my deathbed still."

"Let's meet up at the Grange Hall," said Athena. "Tonight. Be part of the — what do my parents call it? — *critical mass*. Then we can stop this for good."

They all shook hands gravely, agreeing on the plan. They yanked their bikes up from the scrabble of weeds on the roadside; Oliver and Athena began riding away towards town. Only Archie remained, as if forestalling his return home. He glanced over at Langdon House; just then, something arrested his attention. There was a movement — he swore there was — in the topmost window of the house, the window set into the house's tower. It had been a person — someone standing at the window, staring out. He squinted against the sun, trying to get a better view. But the window was now empty. He shook his head; he closed his eyes tightly and opened them again.

An empty window; a long-deserted house.

He was seeing things, he decided. Oliver's weirdness was wearing off on him finally.

"Wait up!" he shouted at his friends, and he pedalled off down the road to catch up with them.

"Hello?" Archie called out as he opened the door. There was no answer. He turned briefly and looked back at his mom's car, still parked at the front kerb of the house. He moved into the house and called again: "Mom?"

Still no answer.

The television was on and was playing the title sequence of *Super Mario Bros*. Mario was now on autopilot, running across the horizontal landscape under no control but his own. The music played cheerily.

"Max?" called Archie. "Annabelle? Olivia?" Receiving no call back, Archie felt compelled to say, "Anyone?"

He went into the kitchen and opened the fridge. His mother, ever the frugal one, had saved the leftovers from their dinner out the night before. They were there on the top shelf, in two neatly stacked Styrofoam containers. Archie pulled them out and set them on the counter, diving into their contents indiscriminately. The sound from the television was still playing in the other room, and it bothered him. Stuffing several cold Tater Tots into his mouth, Archie walked into the living room and switched off the TV. The sudden silence was unnerving; he paused in his chewing and listened to the house. A car drove by. The neighbour's wind chime sounded.

There was a knot in Archie's stomach that felt, at this point, very familiar to him. It had started so small – imperceptible, almost – days before. Now it felt like it was tying in on itself, one loop after another. The first knot had been tied when he saw the homeless woman laid out on the street; another had been tied on the first when he'd encountered Birgitta in the woods near the camp. Seeing his father last night – another knot tied on top of the first two. And now it lived in him, this knotted chain, as an unrelenting feeling of dread. He was suddenly very aware of it, aware of its birth and growth. Here, in his silent house.

But now: three swift creaks sounded in the floorboards above his head. He looked up.

"Mom?" he called out.

No answer came. He swallowed his mouthful of Tater Tots and ventured to the bottom of the stairs, calling her name again. As if in response, he heard a few distinct sounds suggesting movement from a room above him. He began walking upstairs.

At this moment, Oliver, some ten blocks away, had just arrived at home. An electrician's van was parked outside; his mother was standing at the side of the house, talking to a man in coveralls. She waved to her son as he walked by.

"Hey," she called. "You were out early. How you feeling?"

"Fine," said Oliver wanly.

The response seemed to satisfy Agnes's parental curiosity; she continued talking to the man in coveralls. He appeared to be giving her some kind of lecture about the electrical panel. Oliver walked into the house. His sister, Jenn, was sitting at the kitchen bar, reading a magazine and talking on the phone. A wave of tiredness hit him and he threw himself down on the couch in the living room. He closed his eyes; he listened to the one-sided conversation of his sister's telephone call – lots of "oh my Gods" and "uh-huhs" punctuated what sounded like a captivating monologue from whoever was on the other end of the line. They lulled him, word by word, into a kind of sleep that was as thin as a sheer veil.

In his dream, he saw Archie, climbing the stairs in the Coomeses' house.

"Mom?" Archie called, taking each step slowly, waiting to hear a response. Still none came.

There were photos on the wall of the staircase, photos of the four Coomes children in various stages of life – kindergarten portraits of all four of them, Max's freshman-year soccer photo, a picture of Annabelle ice-skating for the first time; Olivia as Frenchy in the middle school's production of *Grease*. They acted as a kind of time-lapse slideshow of the siblings as Archie ascended the stairs. Oliver saw them all.

At the top of the stairs, Archie turned down the hall towards his parents' room. There was another noise, and then: what could only be described as a humming groan. It sounded like Archie's mom. It came, muffled, through the closed door.

"Mom?" he called again.

The noise stopped abruptly. But now he was at the door. He held up his hand to knock. He paused. Listened. No sound. He tried the door handle. It was unlocked. He pushed open the door and saw his parents' room, awash in daylight. There was always something strange to Archie about bedrooms during the day. They always felt abandoned, unused. Their time was night-time, when their occupants would be snuggled up, the room lit by the singular glow of a bedside lamp. But now, with light flooding in from two skylights in the ceiling, his parents' bedroom felt more forbidding than it would in total darkness. His eyes scoured the room – the bed, the twin bureaus on the far wall, the door to the bathroom, slightly ajar.

Archie called out again – this time, inexplicably, he used her name. "Elizabeth?"

He saw a shadow pass across the gap in the bathroom door. He put his hand on the door and pushed.

His mother was standing in her nightgown in front of the mirror, staring at her reflection in the glass. Her eyes were unblinking, her face was pallid. Her mouth was set in a grim line.

"Mom?" asked Archie.

The woman suddenly smiled. "Hi, honey," she said, "I didn't hear you come in." She did not turn when she addressed him.

"Hi," said Archie uncertainly. "I didn't know you were home." He studied her momentarily and said, "Are you OK?"

Again, the smile. A manufactured, plastic smile. She continued to speak to him through the reflection of the mirror. "I'm right as rain, honey," she said.

In the closeness of the bathroom, Archie's senses were struck by a pervasive smell. It was not his mother's typical smell. It was not the smell of her perfume, the smell of whatever product she put in her hair.

"Can I get you a snack?" asked Elizabeth Coomes. Slowly, inch by inch, the woman turned, as if being cranked on a swivel. She locked eyes with her son and said, "You hungry, kiddo?"

Moss. Lichen. The woods. His mom smelled like the woods.

"N-no thank you," said Archie, stammering. He backed

away from the door; he was stopped by the corner of the bed. "I'm sorry. I'm sorry to bother you. I'll just… I'll just leave you alone."

"It's no trouble, darling," said his mother. She was advancing towards him now, her arms stiffly at her sides. "You must be famished." Her expression changed then, and she was frowning again. She fixed him with a concerned look. Her brow glinted in the sunlight; it was damp with perspiration. "You weren't up there at the work site, were you?"

"Huh?" asked Archie. His legs were pressed against the edge of the bed; he placed his hands on the duvet, feeling his way around the corner of the bed frame. "N-no," he said. "What makes you say that?"

"Why, you have sand on your shoes," she said.

"Oh," said Archie. He glanced down; the toes of his trainers were freckled with white sand. "Right – well, we were there. Just for a second."

"Didn't you hear your dad?" Elizabeth asked. "Didn't he tell you not to go near that place?"

Archie's heart rate was quickening. "There's something not right up there, Mom," he said. "They buried something there. A long time ago. I don't know what, but it's not good."

The woman froze. "What kind of talk is that?" she asked. "Who told you that?"

"R-Randy did," he said, and then immediately regretted it. "He showed us these old photos. And a movie. From a long time ago. They found something, and they had to get rid of it. I'm afraid…"

"What are you afraid of?"

"I'm afraid that Dad, well, uncovered it. Accidentally."

The smile returned to Elizabeth's face, the wild smile. "What nonsense," she said. "Sounds like someone has watched *too many movies*. That Randy Dean. He's watched *too many movies*. And you know what happens when you watch *too many movies*?"

She reached out and placed her hand on Archie's cheek; Archie felt a tackiness to her touch. Archie said, "What?" He'd said it mostly to fill the vacuum, the silence that had followed her question.

"You start to lose your mind," she said.

"I don't know about that," said Archie. He flinched from his mother's touch; he could feel the resistance on his skin as her finger left his cheek. He reached up and touched the spot. The flesh there was sticky. Sticky like sap.

"Come on, you must be famished," said his mother. "Let me fix you something."

"No thanks, Mom," said Archie. He'd found his way to the other side of the bed. He backed towards the door; he felt his hand on the doorknob. "I gotta go, Mom," he said. "I'll talk to you later, OK? I'll talk to you later."

"Suit yourself, honey," said his mother. She then turned and walked back into the bathroom, where she resumed her pose in front of the mirror.

In the silence that followed, Archie retreated from the room.

That's when Oliver's dream changed. In the dream, he was descending a wooden stairway, the air close and damp around him. Time passed as in a dream: it was elastic. He did not know how long he'd been walking when, finally, he reached a cold, stone floor. The dampness here was pervasive; it chilled him to his bones. There was no light in this new, subterranean place and yet he knew the way forward. He'd been here before in his dreams.

In time, he arrived at a stone wall. He felt compelled to hold his hands up to the cold stones. He fished his fingernails into the mortar between the rocks and began to prise them away, exposing a hole in the wall. As he did so, light began to flood into the room and his eyes became blinded. Having torn away enough of the rock, he stepped through the hole and found himself suddenly standing in the culvert that ran below Highway 101. It was a bright day and the sun seemed to hang high in the sky, but the cement culvert was shrouded in darkness. There, silhouetted by the light from the far side of the overpass, a shambling figure appeared to be struggling to move.

Oliver walked closer, into the patch of shade thrown by the culvert. His eyes adjusted. He saw the zebra, the half-eaten thing he'd seen in the hospital corridor, pushing itself up on its legs. It looked back at him, its eyes streaked red, as it slowly steadied itself on its feet.

It began walking away. It paused as it crossed into the light on the far side of the culvert; Oliver could see the animal's pink, bloody viscera hanging from the gash torn in its belly.

It looked back at him again briefly before continuing along the trail towards the forest-service road. It clearly wanted Oliver to follow. And so Oliver did.

He felt calmed, strangely. He would not expect to feel this way, but there was something about the zebra that instilled comfort. It was familiar to him somehow, but in the fog of the dream, Oliver could not place this feeling of recognition. He'd been uncertain before, but he now knew that the zebra was good. It did not mean him or his friends ill will. In a way, he understood instinctively that the zebra was somehow existing in opposition to whatever evil had been unleashed on Seaham through the hole in the cliff. And so he followed.

They came up the track that led onto the gravel of the forest-service road; the zebra waited at the juncture for Oliver to catch up. Oliver found he could only walk at a single speed, as if his dream were slowing him, and the zebra would stop occasionally to wait for Oliver. After the first mile or so, Oliver hazarded a question to the animal.

"Where are we going?" he asked.

The zebra stopped and looked at him with his sad, red eyes, and only continued walking. He left a dark trail of blood behind him.

The sun seemed to hang unmoving in the sky. The day did not progress; the air felt still.

After a time, they arrived at a spot where the ground levelled out at a clear-cut section of woods; the road ran straight through the flat towards a line of trees at the far side of the clearing. Oliver recognized it, of course – he'd walked this road a handful of times since he'd fallen in with Chris and Archie. But now, here, something stopped him.

The zebra kept walking.

"Where are you going?" called Oliver. "Wait for me!"

It stopped once briefly at the line of trees and looked back at him. Those hopeless eyes, red eyes. But then the animal was gone, lost in the briar of trees at the far side of the clearing.

Suddenly, Oliver felt two hands grasp his shoulders, hard. He let out a scream as he was violently swung around to face his captor. It was a woman of indeterminate age, her face grimed with dirt. She wore dirty, ill-fitting clothes and she smelled of campfire smoke and cigarettes.

"Where are the bodies?" shouted the woman. She gave Oliver a desperate shake. She repeated loudly, "WHERE ARE THE BODIES?"

That was when Oliver woke.

It was quiet in the house. He pushed himself up on his elbows and looked around the room. His sister's voice was no longer drifting from the kitchen; out the front window, the electrician's van had driven away. He looked at the clock above the gas fireplace in the corner of the room – it was already five o'clock. How long had he been sleeping? Rubbing his eyes, he reviewed his dream in his mind, piecing together the disparate components, those little shades of images that his unconscious – or whatever – had put in front of him.

A flash of recognition surged through Oliver. It was more than just a bolt of déjà vu. He knew this zebra. He knew where it came from. It came from his memory.

A family road trip, five years ago, when Oliver was eight. A long drive down to Los Angeles, post-divorce, to see his mother's family. A wildlife safari on the way home, a kind of open-air zoo in the scrubby hills of northern California. It was a shoddy operation, that much was clear from the hand-painted, sun-bleached advertisements on the roadside. Oliver in the back seat; his sister, Jenn, in the front – they both wanted to make the stop, to see the animals. They drove ten miles off the interstate to a ramshackle gate on a dirt road. They bought tickets at the gift store, a small dilapidated mobile home, and proceeded to navigate the one-lane road through the enclosure. An emu followed them for several yards; a hippopotamus bathed in a muddy pond just off the road. The animals they saw looked wan and bone-thin. Oliver stared at them through the protection of his closed window. They looked like they didn't belong here. The animals disinterestedly watched the car pass them, more silent witnesses to their captivity. Then Oliver saw the zebra.

It was lying on the ground, surrounded by a small pride of lions. They came upon it suddenly, having just rounded a hill. Jenn covered her mouth and muffled a scream; Agnes slammed on the brakes and yelled at Oliver to close his eyes. The lions dispersed, settling in at a distance to watch the family with a casual curiosity. Ignoring his mother's command, Oliver craned his head over the front seats and gaped at the animal. Still alive, it was dragging its half-eaten carcass across the dry grass, a dark stain of blood soaking into the dirt.

Four men on ATVs came roaring past them, scattering the pride of lions. They appeared to be employees of the park. They were armed with scoped rifles; two of them raced off after the lions on an ATV while the remaining two walked up to the zebra. Having observed it for a moment, they then turned and approached the car. Agnes warily rolled her window down.

"Gonna have to ask you to move on, ma'am," the man said.

Agnes heeded the man's request, and within fifteen minutes they were back on the interstate, speeding northward towards Oregon. No one spoke. The image of the zebra remained seared in Oliver's mind's eye.

And here it was again, five years later. In a hospital corridor in Harrisburg; in his dream, on the far side of the culvert beneath Highway 101. Trying to pull its way to safety as its blood fled from its body in slow, pooling spurts.

"Archie," he said suddenly, forcefully.

"What's that, hon?" It was his mom, who had just walked in the door.

"N-nothing," he said. He now vividly recalled the section of the dream where Archie had encountered Liz Coomes in the bathroom. He looked at his mother, wide-eyed.

"What is it?" asked Agnes.

"How…" he began, "how are you feeling?"

"Me? I'm fine, sweetie. I mean, a little put out by the estimate that guy gave me. Two hundred dollars for an outlet? Give me a break." She paused, looking at her son. "Are you OK?"

Oliver's gaze drifted; he stared at the floor in silence. "I don't know," he said.

Agnes sat down on the couch next to Oliver. She placed the back of her hand on his brow and frowned. "Doctor said it might be a few days before you're back to your old self," she said. Her hand drifted down from his forehead to his cheek. "No fever or anything. But you just let me know if you feel the littlest bit out of whack, OK?"

His mother's touch against his skin was immediately calming. Oliver took a deep breath and let it out slowly. "Will do," he said. "I'm OK. Just a little… I'm sure it's just left over from the accident."

Agnes smiled and stood up. "Well, I'm going to the store – any requests for dinner tonight?"

"Mom?" asked Oliver, ignoring the question.

"Huh?"

"Be careful," he said.

Agnes looked at her son, her head cocked as if she were observing some strange and mysterious creature. "Always," she said, smiling. "Always."

Athena came home to an empty house.

Her parents' car was there in the driveway, but no one answered her calls as she walked through the front door. There was still half a carafe of coffee in the coffee maker; her mother's half-drunk cup of tea was still on the dining room table. She turned on the radio in the living room; it was set to the classical station. Biting her lip, she carefully dialled the spindle on the receiver to 105.5, the rock station that broadcast out of Astoria. She caught a song mid-chorus – "Rhythm is Gonna Get You" – which sounded strangely threatening to her at that moment. Rather than give in to her own paranoia, she turned up the volume and let the song soundtrack her way through the house: rifling through the cupboard for snacks, pouring herself a glass of orange juice. She found herself fighting back waves of dread that would flood over her from moment to moment. The dark spot in the old tintypes seemed etched in her imagination, much as it had on the metal of the photograph.

The phone rang. She answered it.

"No, they're not here right now," she said to the caller, a woman.

The woman said Athena's dad had asked her to call that afternoon – surely they must be somewhere on the property.

"No," replied Athena. She craned her neck around a corner and searched what parts of the house she could see. "The car's here, but no one's home. Yeah, I'm good. Sure. I'll tell them."

She hung up. The song on the radio had changed; it was now a slow ballad, but the ominousness remained. She walked quickly over to the radio and switched it off, listening to the silence in the house.

"Mom? Papa?" she called. "Becky?" She could hear traffic hum by on Highway 101, just up the road. The wind hissed through the boughs of the trees outside.

"Come on," she said. "Where are you guys?"

She ventured beyond the living room and the kitchen into a small nook walled in by bookshelves. On the far side of the room was a ladder that led up to her parents' bedroom loft. She craned her neck and looked up, calling their names, but no one answered. Crossing a room that Cynthia mostly used for craft projects, she peered into Becky's room – empty. Arriving at her own room, she saw it remained as she'd left it this morning: slightly messy, unmade bed, low, full bookshelf, posters on the wall – *Lord of the Rings*, a large moon chart, and a portrait of Corey Hart; he was peering at the room over lowered sunglasses.

There was some relief in an empty house. She'd been afraid of what she might find. Still, the worry remained. She walked out the back door into the garden.

"Mom?" she called. "Papa?"

That's when she heard the sound. It was coming from the pottery, the ramshackle studio that her father had built out of reclaimed wood and cinder blocks in the back garden. She recognized the sound; it was the humming whir of the pottery wheel. But now it was whining, its motor seemingly pushed to its limit. "Papa?" she called as she approached the door. She looked inside.

No one was at the wheel. And yet it spun relentlessly. There was an object on the wheel, but it was rendered indistinguishable by the spinning. Athena ventured forward and put her foot down on the pedal, bringing the wheel to an abrupt stop. She stared at what she saw. It was a piece of mangled clay, the grotesque approximation of a large bowl

– its sides bent and deformed by the potter's hands.

She called her dad's name again weakly. There was no answer. Athena bit her lip in thought.

She walked back to the house and picked up the phone. She dialled Archie's number from memory and nervously twisted the phone cord between her fingers as the buzz of the ring sounded in the receiver. After five rings, she heard a pause on the line and then the telltale sound of an answering machine kicking on.

"Hey there," came Max Coomes's recorded voice. "You've reached the Coomes residence. We can't come to the phone right now, but if you'd like to leave a message, do it after the beep. Bye." There was a click, then a long beep, and Athena began to talk. "Archie. Call me. I'm home. I..."

She stopped, suddenly remembering Oliver's and Archie's warnings about how Peter Coomes had *changed*. But before she had a chance to hang up or amend her message to one that sounded less worried, she heard a voice come over the phone line.

"Athena?"

It was Liz, Archie's mom. "Hi, Liz," Athena said, feeling relief flood over her. "Is Archie there?"

There was quiet on the line and then Liz said, "Well, no. He's not. What's the matter, Athena? Is something wrong?"

"It's just that... I think that..." She felt a tremendous temptation to blurt out all her worries, right there on the phone, to Archie's mom. But there was something in the way Liz responded that made her pause.

"*What* do you think, Athena?" asked Liz pointedly. "What is it?"

"N-nothing, Liz," Athena finally stammered.

"There are no secrets here, Athena," said Liz. There was a kind of buzzing static on the line now. It seemed to pulse with Liz's every word. "You can tell me. C'mon. No one likes to hold a secret back. It can be so … so lonely."

Athena's heart was racing. This was not the woman she knew, who'd answered this phone so many times before when she'd called her friend. Something was broken. "I have to go now, Liz," said Athena. "I'm sorry."

"Don't go," said Liz. The buzzing had grown louder. It was as if Liz's voice was causing some kind of interference on the line. "Archie'll be back any moment now. Can't think where he's got to. Are you calling from home, sweetheart? I can…"

Athena slammed the receiver down on the cradle; the bell inside gave a little jingle on impact. She stepped backwards away from the phone, like it was some dangerous creature intent on doing her harm. Keeping the phone in her sight, she continued to back away until she reached the front door. She twisted the handle with one hand behind her back, threw open the door, and ran out of the house.

She did not see the penny that had been laid on the worn wooden boards of the front porch.

Randy Dean's eyes were going.

These were the words he was thinking as he screwed up his face and peered through the lenses of his glasses at the dark computer screen. Experimentally, he lifted the frames from the bridge of his nose and let them hang at the top of his brow, now looking at the screen with his naked eye. That was worse still. He sighed and let the glasses fall back into place. Slightly blurry would just have to be the standard. He hit the enter button on the keyboard and turned to the printer, waiting.

Nothing happened.

It had been six months since he'd installed this computer system at the store, replacing the pen-and-paper method he'd been using since he'd opened, and he still hadn't got used to it. It was his cousin's suggestion, his cousin who owned a movie-rental shop in Salem. Easier way to keep a tally of inventory, he'd said. Better bookkeeping. So far, it had only given Randy Dean headaches. Headaches and paper jams. Which was what he guessed was happening now. He pulled the plastic cover off the top of the dot-matrix printer and peered into the guts of the machine. Sure enough, he saw a mash of paper accordioned into the space below the roller.

"Blast it," he said. "Stupid thing."

He loosened the wheel and pulled the paper from the printer. The paper tore as he did so and he cursed again, loud enough that he had to announce a polite apology to the only customers in the shop, a father and son browsing the kids and family section together. Having finally freed the paper, Randy ended up with a kind of rats' nest of crumpled dot-matrix-printer paper in his arms; he imagined he must've looked very foolish when the father and son approached the counter with a copy of *The Secret of NIMH* to rent.

"Sorry," Randy said through the eruption of paper. "Still working out the kinks."

It was another twenty minutes of tinkering before he'd managed to load the printer again, and another fifteen before the computer was printing the late-fee notices he'd meant to start making that morning. Feeling somewhat accomplished, Randy picked up the wad of paper from the floor and headed out to the rubbish bins.

It was a sunny day, and Randy briefly paused to take in the weather. He'd lived in Seaham for nearly ten years now, and the feel of the summer coastal air affected him as much as it had the first day he'd arrived. The ocean still held a kind of magic to him, a man who'd spent most of his life in landlocked Wisconsin. With a new spring in his step, Randy continued around the side of the building to the back alley, where lived the large green dumpsters he shared with the nail salon next door.

He'd just emptied his arms of his load of printer paper, hissed a quiet "good riddance" to the maw of the dumpster, and was about to return to the store when he heard someone say his name. He turned and saw Archie Coomes.

"Hey there, Arch," said Randy. "Loitering in alleyways these days?"

"Is there anyone in the store?" asked Archie.

"Well, there was a kid and his dad in there just a minute ago." Randy studied the boy briefly. He'd never seen him look so serious. "Thought you guys were up at the headlands. What's up?"

"Let's go inside," said Archie.

Randy closed the door behind them and locked it, flipping the sign hanging in the window to his boilerplate temporary-closure sign: *Swallowed by aliens! Back in fifteen!* written below a drawing Oliver had done of the rental-shop owner being attacked by a xenomorph. Randy watched as Archie scanned the store for any other occupants.

"We're alone," said Randy reassuringly. "You mind telling me what's going on?"

They made their way to the front counter, where Randy slid the bucket of Red Vines towards the boy. "Here," he said. "Have a liquorice. Get your mind straight. Tell me what's up."

Archie accepted the Red Vine and, chewing thoughtfully on one end, said, "I think my mom…" And here he stopped, suddenly overcome with emotion.

"What about your mom?"

"I think – I think she's changed. Like my dad."

"Now, what makes you think that?"

Archie shrugged. "Something's weird. I saw her. I can't put my finger on it."

"Where was she?"

"Just at home, like, staring at herself in the mirror. Still in her nightgown. In the afternoon." Archie paused to chew on the liquorice. He swallowed hard. "I didn't know where to go. I had to get out of the house."

"So you came here," said Randy.

"It was the only place I figured was safe."

Randy prised the top off the Red Vines bucket and pulled out a rope for himself. He offered another to Archie, who took it. Randy sucked on the end of the candy rope for a second before he said, "Well, Arch, like I said before, your parents are under a lot of strain. Gotta think it's taking a toll."

Archie was about to respond when he heard a knock at the door. He turned and saw Athena, her hands cupped at her brow as she peered into the glass. Seeing them, she knocked again.

Randy gave Archie a look before jogging over to the front door and undoing the deadbolt. Athena rushed by him as soon as he opened the door.

"Archie," she said breathlessly. "There you are."

"What's up?" asked Archie.

"My parents – they're gone."

"Gone?"

"You saw them, on the road. They should've been home. But the house was empty when I got there. The car was there, but the house was empty. No one's home."

Randy had returned to the counter in time to hear the girl's story. "Hold up," he said, raising his palms. "Both of you. What's got into you?"

"The pottery wheel – it was spinning."

"The what now?" asked Randy.

"The pottery wheel. In my dad's studio. It was just – running. Spinning. With this big lump of, like, warped clay on it."

Archie looked at Randy, his eyebrows raised, as if to say, *See?* Randy ignored the look. "Lots of explanations," said the store owner. "Plenty of 'em. They went for a walk, they were out in the garden – I don't know! Lots of reasons why folks wouldn't be at home."

"I called your house, Arch," said Athena, ignoring Randy's words of reassurance. "It went to the machine, but then your mom picked up."

Archie stared at Athena. "And?"

"And something wasn't right."

Randy began rubbing his eyes.

"I swear it," continued Athena. "Something weird. In her voice."

Archie had become agitated. "I told you," he said, looking at Randy. He turned back to Athena. "I went home. I saw her. She was acting all – I don't know – all weird."

"Like your dad," said Athena.

205

"Who is under a lot of stress," interjected Randy.

"I was looking everywhere for you," said Athena to Archie. "Figured you'd be here. What do I do?"

"Maybe Randy's right," said Archie. "Maybe your mom and dad are out. Maybe they dropped the car and then went somewhere."

"Voice of reason," said Randy. Then, "Jeez, what is this, community hour?"

Archie looked up at him; Randy was looking towards the door. Archie followed his line of sight and saw, standing at the glass door, a woman. It was Birgitta Woodley.

"Don't let her in," said Archie suddenly.

But Randy was already walking towards the door. He spoke to the woman through the glass. "We're closed for the moment, Birgitta, if you wouldn't mind coming back in a bit."

Birgitta's eyes were looking past him; they were intent on Archie and Athena, standing by the counter. She held up something in her hand; it was a tape box.

"I've brought this back," she said, her voice muffled through the door.

Randy glanced back at Archie and Athena; he undid the deadbolt and let Birgitta into the store.

"Thank you, Mr Dean," she said, smiling.

She was dressed in a floral skirt and a yellow tank top. Her long grey hair cascaded over her bare shoulders, and her arms were white and puckered with wrinkles. She approached the counter and laid the tape on the countertop.

"That was a wonderful film," she said. "A truly *wonderful* film."

"Glad you enjoyed it," said Randy, walking back from the door.

"Are you OK, Birgitta?" asked Athena, staring at her.

"Why, yes, Ms Quest," said the woman stiffly. "Why wouldn't I be?"

"We – well, Archie – he saw you," said Athena. "Out in the woods."

Archie could feel himself begin to blush. He flashed on her naked body, her pale, sagging skin. "Don't you remember?" he asked.

Birgitta blinked rapidly several times before saying, "It was a *wonderful* film. John and I enjoyed it *so* much."

Then the smell hit Archie again. The smell of wet wood – the same scent that had exuded from his mother's skin, there in the closeness of her bathroom. He recoiled from it.

"Anyway, I've come back to return it," said Birgitta, her voice lilting in its brittle Scandinavian accent. "On time. As I always do. On time. I've even rewound it, Mr Dean. You know, this *Bee Kind, Rewind*. As you say." She smiled a wide grin; her teeth were gappy and stained.

"Thanks very much," said Randy. "Now if you'll excuse us, we are closed for the moment."

"Closed?" asked Birgitta. "On a Wednesday afternoon?"

"Just for a moment. We were…" Here Randy paused, looking at Athena and Archie. "Just having a little confab."

Birgitta smiled again. "Ooh," she said, "a *confab*. A little secret meeting? What about, pray tell?"

"Nothing that would interest you," said Archie quickly.

"I don't know about that, Archie Coomes. I don't know about that." Birgitta reached her hand out as if to touch Archie's cheek. Archie stepped backwards.

Randy said, "If you wouldn't mind, Birgitta. We are closed. You can come back later if you'd like."

Birgitta was staring at Archie; the smile had drained from her face. "Very well," she said. "I'll leave you all to your — what did you call it? — *confab*."

Athena stepped aside to let the woman by as she walked back towards the door. Just before she left, though, she turned and spoke. "I expect I'll see you at the town hall tonight," she said. "The whole city council is assembling, don't you know. We're discussing the project up at the headlands. I think it's going to be very interesting."

"Interesting?" asked Athena.

"Very interesting," said Birgitta. "I don't think you'll want to miss it. No, you will not want to miss this." The woman then turned, swung open the door, and left the shop.

Randy walked quickly to the door and threw the deadbolt. He paused for a moment, staring out the glass.

"What was that all about?" Randy asked, as if to himself.

"See?" said Archie. "She's not right — they're all not right. And did you smell that? It was like…"

"Wet grass," said Athena, finishing for him.

"Exactly. That's what my mom smelled like – I swear to God. And my dad. I don't get it."

Randy was still at the door, staring out into the empty street. He shook his head and returned to the counter.

"See?" repeated Archie. "That's what we're talking about."

"Strange, I'll admit it. Something not right about Birgitta. She's been coming here since we opened. Never seen her act that way. And her on the city council, no less. Very odd." Randy stroked the red stubble on his chin. After a moment, he said, "Y'know, if I didn't know better, I'd be inclined to think…" Randy's voice trailed off.

Archie prompted him, "Think what?"

"Swaplings," said Randy. "I'll be, I think it's swaplings."

"Swaplings?" Athena grimaced at Randy as she spoke. "Is this from another movie?"

"No, it isn't," said Randy. He arched his back and crossed his arms before saying, "I mean, it is. *Vacant Souls*. 1981. Richard Bruno, director. But before that – before *that*, it was a real thing. I mean, a real thing from folktales and such. Some evil spirit goes out snatching folks from their houses and swapping them, y'know, with fake versions. In order to do their bidding. Swaplings."

"H-how do we know?" asked Athena.

"Gotta catch 'em when they think no one's watching. Then they reveal theirselves, their true selves. They become strange. That's how the folktale goes, anyway."

"This is not a movie, Randy," said Archie. "This is real.

Something is happening."

"Listen, you come to me for advice, this is what I got. I got movies." Randy had stiffened, defending himself. "And where do those movies come from? They come from real people. Real people's stories. There's always something to learn in 'em."

Athena had been listening, her brow furrowed; finally she spoke up. "Birgitta – on the city council. Your dad, running the job up there. There's a connection there."

"Pennies," said Archie suddenly.

"What?" asked Athena.

Randy raised an eyebrow at the boy.

"Pennies," repeated Archie. "I saw one. On my doorstep. The day before my dad went all weird. That same day, there was a penny on Birgitta's doorstep too."

"Why didn't you mention this earlier?" asked Athena, looking at Archie sharply.

"I don't know – it sounded nuts."

"Uh, we're way past that now," said Athena.

"It does sound a bit wild, admittedly," added Randy. "Pennies on doorsteps. Must be a kind of marking."

"Have you seen any?" Archie asked Athena. "Pennies? They'd be, like, dropped on your porch, right in front of your door."

Athena shook her head. "No – no. I haven't seen... I mean, I haven't really looked." She began cradling her head in her hands. "Mom, Papa – Becky. I have to find them. I have to know they're OK."

"Well, they'll be at that meeting tonight; you can be sure of it," said Randy.

Athena nodded; she looked at Archie. "We have to go to the meeting."

"Seems like it," said Archie. "Like Birgitta said…"

Randy finished for him, "Sounds like it's going to be *interesting*."

It was six thirty in the evening when Athena, Oliver and Archie met at the Seaham Grange Hall. The old clapboard building had served many purposes over the years – it was a home for seasonal craft fairs and charity bake sales; it hosted twice-yearly community theatre productions by the Seaham Grange Players and was the Sunday sanctuary for a small group of local Methodists without a church to call their own. And now, it was hosting a town hall meeting called by the mayor and the city council to discuss the dangers of the building project currently underway up at the cliffs below Langdon House.

"It's that smell," said Athena as soon as they'd entered the room.

"Smells like … like mushrooms. Or something," said Oliver in a whisper.

"Like dirt," said Archie. "Wet dirt."

There were perhaps fifty people in the room; white plastic folding chairs had been arrayed on the wooden floor of the hall, all pointing towards the stage. On one side of the room a long table had been laid with cookies and muffins. A coffee urn burbled on the table, and several people gathered around it, cradling small white mugs and chatting to one another. On the low stage at the front of the room was a podium. Five chairs had been unfolded alongside it. An elderly volunteer was standing at the podium, gently patting the shroud of the microphone while another volunteer stooped over a mixing board, perplexed.

Archie glanced at Athena; he could see she was scanning the room for her parents.

"I don't see them," she said.

"They'll be here," Archie said, attempting assurance.

Just then, Mayor Kwan mounted the steps to the stage and walked to the podium. He dismissed the man at the microphone, who shrugged and walked from the stage. Billy turned to the audience and said, unassisted by the microphone, "I guess we'll get this started, then. Can you hear me?"

The audience grumbled assent. The room, while long, was small enough to carry the mayor's voice to the back rows of chairs. He cleared his throat, tucked his thumbs into the pockets of his fleece sweater, and began to speak. "Thanks so much everyone for coming out," he said. "It's unfortunate that it's moments like this, moments of divisiveness, that bring us all together."

"Speak up!" shouted someone from the back.

"Bring us all together like this," repeated the mayor loudly. "How's that?"

The speaker mumbled with begrudging satisfaction, and the room quietened again to listen.

The mayor continued, "I'd like to welcome a few people to the stage, and we can get this underway. Our three city councillors, Betty Suttcliff, Jeremy Bryce and Elliott Sager." Two men and a woman, each in what Archie guessed to be their seventies, came up onto the stage and waved at the audience. He recognized one of them, Elliott, as the man who ran the post office. "Thank you," said Billy, greeting them each with a perfunctory nod. "And our esteemed council president, Birgitta Woodley. Come on up, Birgitta."

Archie's eyes laser-focused on Birgitta as she mounted the steps to the stage. She wore a wide smile and stared eerily out at the crowd as she moved to shake the mayor's hand. Even from the back of the room, Archie could see the same sheen of sweat clinging to the woman's brow that he'd seen on his dad and mom. Billy didn't seem thrown by her appearance, and instead kept speaking. "Then I'd like to call Candace Rockwell – some of you may know her – she's been responsible for the development of several properties around town and is, as you know, heading up the development of the Langdon property north of town for this hotel project."

A woman arose from the front row of chairs dressed in a black skirt and suit coat. She made her way to the stage gingerly, her feet wedged into heels that seemed precariously tall. Archie saw that she'd been sitting next to his father; he recognized the little bald patch on the back of his father's head.

Candace shook the mayor's hand politely and sat down in one of the chairs on the stage, next to Birgitta. She ironed out the front of her skirt with her hands and regarded the crowd. Birgitta stared out into the room as if she'd been set there, still as a statue. The mayor had begun to speak again, a kind of introduction about how the evening would go, how questions would be received, when someone from the centre of the room interrupted him, exclaiming, "Where are Jordan and Cynthia?"

"Quest?" asked the mayor, peering out at the room. "Good question. No idea. Jordan? Cynthia? You out there?"

No one responded; there was a cascade effect of swivelling heads as each person began their own search for the absent Quests; the room became awash in the collective murmur of the crowd. Someone saw Athena and said, "Have you seen your parents, honey?"

Athena shook her head, frozen in the spotlight of the entire room's attention. Archie's father, still seated in the front row, turned around in his chair and fixed his son with an icy stare.

The mayor seemed bewildered, the outcome of the event suddenly more uncertain than it had seemed that morning. He stammered a few words before saying, "Well, I suppose we can continue without them. Ms Rockwell, did you want to say a few words?"

The woman in the black skirt stood up and smiled warmly at the crowd. Mayor Kwan relinquished his spot at the podium as she approached. She began to speak, but Archie barely marked her words – there was some introductory patter about her connection to Oregon, to Seaham, to the coast in general. Some words were spared in description of a humble upbringing in far Southeast Portland, followed by a long monologue about her desire to introduce the Oregon coast to the world, to be a kind of ambassador for the region – that this, somehow, had been her mission since her very first days as a real estate developer; Archie hardly listened. He was instead trying to keep his eyes from his father's stare.

Peter Coomes had not moved since he'd first looked back at his son. He remained swivelled in his chair, his gaze fixed on the children in the back of the room.

"We need to go," hissed Archie.

But now Birgitta Woodley had stood up from her seat on the stage. She walked to the podium and placed her hand on Candace's arm. Candace stopped abruptly mid-sentence to look over at Birgitta.

"Dear," said Birgitta, "I'd like to take it from here."

As if chastened, Candace stepped away from the podium and gestured for Birgitta to take her place. Birgitta smiled courteously and stood at the podium, gripping the sides with her bony hands. "Hello, everyone," she said.

"Hello," came a unison response from several of the attendees. The uniformity gave Archie a start. He felt Oliver shudder and gasp at his side. He glanced over at his friend; he looked pale, worried.

"Oliver," whispered Archie. "You OK?"

Oliver only nodded, his eyes intent on the action on the stage.

Birgitta was continuing. "I understand that the Quests

cannot make it this evening, which is unfortunate. I believe they are not feeling well. They have passed on their blessings to you all. I have spoken with them and know that I have their full support when I say, 'the work must continue'." Birgitta's smile widened here, and Archie could see the yellowish gleam of her teeth from the back of the building. Several people gasped at what she'd said; he felt Athena grip his arm.

"She's lying – she must be lying," said Athena.

"This work is about so much more than a hotel," continued Birgitta, becoming serious. "It is so much more than that. I appreciate Ms Rockwell's enthusiasm for our community, but simply *enticing* travellers to our town is such a small part of this project. Believe me, there are blessings far beyond money in store with this work. Yes, it must continue. The digging must go on. They must go deeper. They have so much to uncover."

Archie looked at Mayor Kwan, standing against the proscenium of the stage, his arms crossed tightly against his chest. He wore a look of shock; his mouth hung slightly agape. More surprising, there seemed to be little opposition in the room to Birgitta's sudden declaration; the few murmurs of dissent that came were quickly hushed down by neighbours.

"Let her speak," someone said loudly.

"And dear Peter," said Birgitta, her arms now outstretched to Archie's dad in the front row. Hearing his name, he turned back towards the stage, abandoning his relentless glare at Archie. Birgitta continued, "Dear Peter. Your labours will not be in vain. You are destined for great things. This will be a crowning achievement. A moment of glory for you and your family."

A cascade of applause suddenly erupted from the room; those who were not clapping, perhaps a dozen attendees, stared at their neighbours, bewildered. Someone shouted, "Keep the headlands wild!" but it was a half-throated call, one that died out quickly when no one else repeated it. Following this, several people stood up from their chairs and walked out of the room, murmuring to each other in dismayed tones. Two of them, a couple Archie did not recognize, shook their heads at Athena as they walked out the doors. "What a fiasco," someone said to Archie.

"This town should be ashamed of itself," said another.

Now the room grew quiet again as Birgitta continued to address the crowd. "Those who leave now will regret their decision."

Mayor Kwan seemed to pull himself out of his state of shock; he approached the lectern and spoke quietly to Birgitta. Birgitta, pausing in her speech, listened to the mayor's words politely, a smile still carved on her face, before ushering him away. "This is not a concern of yours, Mayor Kwan. You will see the light soon enough." She turned back to the crowd and said, "Let us join together, now, in our blessing of this great project. Let's dig! Dig! Dig!"

One by one, the remaining members of the audience in the Grange Hall stood up from their chairs and began applauding in time, chanting the words "Dig! Dig! Dig!" in an eerily uniform monotone. Even the city councillors had risen from their chairs on the stage and were grinning as they clapped and chanted the words. Archie found that he'd stopped breathing, that his breath was somehow caught in his chest. The chanting of "DIG!" grew louder and louder in his ears until it was as if he were standing next to a jet engine. Unable to move, he stared across the crowd at this sea of people, some of whom he recognized from school or through his parents or from businesses around town, all seeming to have thrown themselves into the chant with a kind of wild abandon that bordered on mania. Birgitta, from the stage, was the conductor; she'd stepped beyond the podium and was standing at the lip of the stage, waving her arms ecstatically above her head like she was in the midst of some great rapture.

"Dig!" she shouted, exhorting the crowd. "Dig! Dig! Dig!"

The chanting could still be heard roaring through the windows of the Grange Hall as Athena, Archie and Oliver raced down the steps to the pavement. Oliver was nearly insensible. His eyes darted about in his head, and he was wringing his hands like he was trying to wipe some indelible stain from them.

"Oh," he moaned. "Oh, oh, oh."

"Keep it together, Ollie," said Archie.

"It's there – it's everywhere," he said. "The smell. They're changed, Archie. Changed."

"It's like this sickness," said Athena, stricken. "It's catching – it's contagious."

"They're swaplings," said Archie.

"Swaplings?" asked Oliver, now massaging his temples.

"You believed that?" asked Athena. "From Randy's movie?"

"It wasn't just from the movie, though. He said it was from, like…"

"Folklore," said Athena. "Yeah. Like, fairy tales."

"What are swaplings, guys?" asked Oliver.

"A thing Randy told us about," explained Archie. "People who have been kidnapped and replaced by fake versions of themselves."

"Like Birgitta," said Oliver. "In the woods."

Archie nodded. He saw Athena look over his shoulders, towards the low roar of the highway and, beyond it, the densely treed hills of the coastal range. "Chris," she said, almost absently, her voice sounding choked in her throat.

"I know," said Archie.

"What are we going to do?" asked Athena. "Someone should tell him. He's not safe up there."

"I'm sure he's OK," said Archie, as if those words were solace enough, as if they had the power to clamp down on the fear welling in his stomach and make it go away. "Who knows, maybe it's safer there, out of town."

The noise from the hall continued unabated – frenzied, howling calls to "Dig! Dig! Dig!"

"We have to get out of here," said Archie.

"Let's go to my place," said Oliver. "We'll be safe there. Try to figure out what to do next."

"I have to find my parents," said Athena. She was already unchaining her bike from the stop-sign pole.

"Athena," said Oliver. "I've got a bad feeling. You shouldn't go. Come with me. You'll be safe at my place."

"Oliver," said Athena firmly. "I love you, you're weird, and I believe you. But I can't just not go home. Birgitta said they were home sick. I have to go find them."

"Wait," said Archie. "I'll go with you. You'll be safer with two."

"Not you too," said Oliver.

"Suit yourself," said Athena, and she was off, pedalling down the shoulder of the frontage road that ran along the highway.

Archie looked at Oliver and shrugged. "I'll be OK," he said. "We'll be OK. We'll find you later."

Oliver was left standing on the corner of the road while the frenzy of cheering voices continued to echo from the windows of the Grange Hall.

"Don't go," he said quietly to the shapes of his friends as they disappeared into the night. "It's not safe."

Archie and Athena wove through a warren of side roads and driveways. This was an unincorporated part of Seaham, and as such, the layout of the neighbourhood was wilder, more maze-like. Athena, having lived here all her life, knew it well. It wasn't long before she'd skidded to a stop at the beginning of her driveway.

"Look," said Athena, her voice cheered. "They're here."

Light emanated from the windows of the house. Athena dropped her bike where she stopped and began walking towards the front porch. Archie accompanied her warily.

Towering fir trees surrounded the small, wooden building, casting the property in a dark shadow. Music was playing from the stereo inside. They could hear it burbling through the screen door. Suddenly, there was movement through one of the windows as a figure stood up from a chair in the corner of the living room and walked to the large windows looking out on the driveway. It was Jordan Quest.

Archie and Athena both stopped walking, witnesses to the scene playing out through the window. Athena glanced at Archie; she looked back at her father.

They could see the top of the man's head, illuminated by the lamp in the corner. Cynthia Quest walked out of the darkness of the kitchen. She was carrying two mugs in her hand. She handed one to her husband, smiled, and sat down in the chair opposite the window. It was the perfect picture of a tranquil domestic scene – a man and wife sitting down to their evening tea. Athena gave a relieved sigh and resumed walking towards the front steps.

Just then, something very strange happened.

Cynthia had frozen with the brim of her cup to her lips, as if she were waiting for the liquid to cool. She remained that way for an inordinate amount of time. Then, suddenly, she dropped the cup. It fell to the hardwood floor with a clatter that was audible even out in the driveway. A crooked grin spread across her face, and her eyes went wide. Her head jerked back on her neck and she was staring at the ceiling with her mouth agape.

Jordan, opposite his wife in the chair in the corner, was unmoved. He sipped at his tea.

Violently, Cynthia's arms whipped backwards over her head and she gripped the top of the chair with her palms. Her pelvis shot into the air and she arched her back so unnaturally that it looked as though she were about to snap her own spine with the movement. The chair tipped backwards under the strain and Archie lost sight of the woman. Athena suppressed a cry, her hand across her mouth.

Then they saw Cynthia again, emerging from behind the toppled chair. Her body was contorted into a bizarre backwards crabwalk as she began crawling, somehow, first up the bookcase behind the chair and then up the far wall of the Quests' living room. When she arrived at the place where the wall met the ceiling, the woman's head began to slowly rotate until it was staring down at the room, a twisted version of a human being.

Archie heard Athena choke a scream, her hand cupped across her mouth.

Together, Athena and Archie stumbled back on the dirt of the driveway. They pushed themselves up from the ground and ran for their bikes, which lay on their sides only a few yards from the car. Just as Archie knelt to lift his bike from the ground, he felt a sudden presence; a smell of soil and bramble filled the air, and a feeling of deep terror overcame him. He looked up and saw that there was a man standing in front of him. He resembled the man he'd seen from his bedroom window so many nights before – but he seemed older now, his mutton chops flecked with white whiskers. Archie gulped back a cry of fear as the man gripped him hard by the shoulder.

"Do not cry. Do not struggle," said the man. "This will all be painless."

The statement did not instil confidence; Archie yanked himself free of the man's hand and tried to mount his bike. He heard Athena scream. Another pair of hands suddenly gripped the centre of Archie's handlebars, freezing his progress.

"Struggle will make it worse," said another voice. Archie saw he was now standing between two identically dressed men. This second man wore a moustache; his hands were black with dirt. A third man had appeared and was holding Athena captive, her arms pinioned back while she straddled her bicycle. Archie had never seen her look so fearful.

Oliver wanted to get as far from the Grange Hall as possible – he was repelled by it, by the crowd that had gathered inside. By their inhuman chanting. He feared the worst for Archie and Athena but knew he must get to safety. Get to his home. Quickly. Hopefully, his friends would heed his advice and make their way there as soon as possible. He didn't have much hope for Athena's parents.

These were the thoughts that consumed him as he rode his bike up the shoulder of Langdon Road towards the centre of town.

The sun still hung obstinately over the western horizon, casting the world in long shadows. As he made his way into Seaham proper, the streets began to change – they became more populated with houses and cars. A few people strolled by on the pavement, walking dogs, idly chatting, and Oliver eyed them with a new suspicion. He passed a driveway where a boy, perhaps seven, was standing, dribbling a basketball.

The boy watched Oliver intently, slowly bouncing the ball in his hand off the pavement.

The staring eyes of the boy unnerved him. The rhythmic striking of the basketball on the ground. Oliver gripped the brakes on his bike and came to a stop. He stared at the boy.

The boy stopped dribbling the ball. He held it to his chest.

"They're coming for you," said the boy.

White light flashed; Oliver's vision was obliterated.

There was no immediate explanation as to why the man had let go of Archie. It was as if his captor had received some kind of shock, so abruptly did the hands lift from Archie's shoulders. It took a moment for Archie to register that he'd been freed. He immediately began to push away from the three men, letting his bike carry him down the sloping driveway away from the house. He looked over at Athena. He noticed that she'd been let go as well. The man who had been holding her in a kind of bear hug had dropped his hands to his sides and was staring at the ground, dumbfounded.

"Archie!" shouted Athena. "Let's go!"

It might have been her shout, or it might have been some other trigger, but the three men's paralysis came to an abrupt end. They swung their arms out into the open air, as if they'd not noticed their captives were standing several feet away from them, and were presently pedalling as fast as they could down the gravel driveway.

"What's going on?" asked Athena, looking over her shoulder at Archie.

"Keep riding!" was Archie's response.

Archie and Athena flew through the maze of roads and

driveways of the wooded neighbourhood until they reached the incline towards Highway 101. The light against the trees on the far side of the highway had gone hazy and pink as the sun began to dip towards the horizon. Cars blew by on the road, and Archie was amazed to see Athena whip out into the northbound lane without hesitation. A car came around a blind corner just as Archie approached the shoulder and Archie was forced to jam on the brakes; his rear tyre skidded and the driver in the car reflexively swerved away when he saw Archie coming. The car horn blared and warped as the vehicle sped away down the highway; Archie breathed a silent oath and pulled onto the road. He caught sight of Athena just as she disappeared around the bend in the highway. He stood up from his seat and began to lean into the pedals, trying to catch up.

The first exit to Seaham appeared, a gentle sloping road that led down the right side of the highway, into the trees. Athena took it; Archie followed. Athena came to a skidding halt at the stop sign at the end of the road, at the intersection of Charles Avenue. Archie came up alongside her.

"What did they do?" asked Athena. "What did they do to my parents?"

"I don't know. I've seen those guys before. They're the ones doing all of this. I'm sure of it." Archie was panting from the ride, coughing out the words in little spurts.

"What do they want with us?"

"I don't know. To swap us."

"Did they – did they do *that* to my family?" Athena's face was red with exertion.

226

"I don't know!" shouted Archie. "I don't know anything."

"Where do we go? What do we do?"

"We can't go to my place – we can't go anywhere."

"Oliver's – let's find him," said Athena. And then she screamed.

Archie looked up. One of the brown-suited men was standing in the middle of the street. He was walking towards them. Archie glanced around him; there was no car, no vehicle, no conveyance that might have carried this man so quickly to this spot in the street. It was as if he'd teleported himself. As the man approached, Archie heard a voice behind him.

"Children," said the voice. "Please don't make this any harder than it needs to be." Archie turned; it was the man with the mutton chops, the hair sprouting from his cheeks all wiry and grey. He had emerged from the streetside bracken and was wiping pine needles from the sleeve of his jacket. The third man, the one with the moustache, had emerged from the shadows along the avenue.

"Go!" shouted Archie. "To Ollie's!" And they were both riding, fast, towards the man in the middle of the street. To Archie's surprise, the man seemed to let them fly past, a look of resignation pasted across his face. After Archie had travelled a few yards past the man, he hazarded a glance behind him.

The man they'd passed – the one with the grey beard – had suddenly adopted a very strange posture. He seemed to contort, there on the pavement, into the posture of some terrible grotesque animal, his hands on the ground before him. The man began galloping after them, transformed as he was, at a tremendous speed.

"Faster!" shouted Archie. "They're after us!"

Through the brightness, Oliver saw the zebra.

It was standing in the middle of the street. Around him, the town seemed abandoned, swept clean in this strange, sterile vision. Wide tracks of smeared blood led to the body of the zebra as it struggled along, still dragging itself forward by its forelegs. The gash in its stomach produced a fountain now; the blood poured from its exposed insides in steady jets and pooled into the gutters on either side of the street. The zebra paused briefly in its movement to crane its neck backwards and look at Oliver.

Come, the animal said. *It's been waiting for you.*

"Where?" asked Oliver. "Where are you taking me?"

The zebra didn't answer. It turned away from Oliver and continued dragging itself along the street. Oliver watched it for a moment before following.

The creature soon arrived at the end of the street, where a gravel road replaced the pavement. The road began to climb, and Oliver, in this skewed version of Seaham, recognized where they were headed.

"Why are you taking me here?" called Oliver.

Come, replied the zebra. *Come and see. Find the bodies.*

Oliver approached the animal, reaching out to it, when there was a loud *clunk*. Something had fallen from the sky to his feet. He looked down; it was a rust-red brick. Soon, another one fell and landed alongside the first, as if it had been set by a bricklayer. Then, in quick, violent succession, more and more bricks tumbled from the air around Oliver and a wall began to take shape in front of him. He stumbled backwards, alarmed, but found that he was stopped by a hard surface. A brick wall had been built behind him as well; to each side of him, a brick wall assembled itself as if built by an unseen hand. Before long, Oliver found he was encased in a box, a cold, musty box of brick, old brick. He screamed, but the sound was muted by the enclosure.

And Oliver woke.

He was lying on the ground beside his bike. His jeans were badly ripped where his knee had made contact with the pavement. The boy with the basketball was still dribbling in the driveway of his house, staring at Oliver vacantly.

"Home," murmured Oliver, his head suddenly feeling as if it were a television switched to an off-the-air channel, all static and dust. It roared in his ears as he picked up his bike and began pedalling for his house. He did not look behind him.

When he arrived, he dropped his bike in the grass of the yard and ran in the front door. He nearly collided with his sister as he made his way up the stairs towards his room.

"What happened to you?" asked Jenn, staring at his torn jeans, his tangled hair.

He didn't answer. He made his way past her and into his room. He began searching his desk, rifling through the drawers until he found what he was looking for: the hunting knife his dad had bought him on his twelfth birthday. He unfolded the blade and tested the sharpness against his thumb. Oliver had never used it. He'd had no reason to use it – until now. He began to work.

Now Archie was riding his bike as fast as he ever had. He was upright on the pedals, frantically cranking through the gears. His heart pounded in his chest; he could feel it in his throat. He and Athena were neck and neck, flying along the empty street. They were on the edge of Seaham now, and the houses that lined this street were sporadic and set apart by large stands of fir trees. The light was fading; a blanket of clouds had emerged in the pink sky, turning the shadows to darkness.

The man was just behind them; Archie saw him, this bizarre galloping thing, each time he glanced over his shoulder. "Faster!" he heard Athena shout.

"I can't!" Archie yelled.

He could hear the man pounding against the pavement. He could hear his rasping breaths.

They were only a few blocks from Oliver's house now. The realization gave Archie a surge of energy, and he laid into his pedals with all the strength he could muster. He could feel Athena at his side, but his eyes remained fixed on the street before him.

Just then, a car pulled out in front of them. The driver slammed on the brakes, and the car screeched to a halt in the centre of a four-way intersection. Archie swerved just in time to avoid hitting it, but Athena ran headlong into the car's front panel. She was sent flying over the hood; the bike crumpled beneath the car. Archie dumped his bike and ran to where Athena lay. She was on all fours on the street, pushing herself up.

"We're close!" shouted Archie, reaching down to help her. "Run!"

With Archie's assistance, she pulled herself from the ground, and they began running up the street. Archie could see Oliver's porch now; a light near the door glowed dimly. The windows were illuminated. Someone was home.

Athena was limping; her jeans were torn at the knees, and spatters of blood flecked the skin beneath. Archie looked behind him; the man was standing now, walking towards them calmly. They reached the front door and Archie threw it open without bothering to knock; he hustled Athena towards the stairs to Oliver's room. He called out, "Ollie!"

Oliver was at the top of the stairs. His fear was written on his face. "Quick!" he shouted. "In my room!"

Carrying Athena's weight, Archie tripped on the stairs and fell. Pain seared his shins as he made contact with the hard wood of the step. He could feel the man behind them; he was close. Athena was pulling him up, shouting: "C'mon, Archie!" and they were both stumbling up the stairs as quickly as they could manage, while Oliver harangued them from his bedroom door, shouting, "Fast! Hurry! He's behind you!"

They threw themselves over the threshold into Oliver's room. Archie saw Oliver holding some kind of hunting knife;

he was carving a circular sigil into the wood of the door. He was finishing the last arc of a hexafoil.

The man was bounding down the hallway now, close to the bedroom. Archie and Athena collapsed on the floor. The three of them began pushing themselves deeper into the room, away from the approaching thing.

"What are you doing, Oliver?" shouted Athena. "Shut the door!"

Oliver didn't answer; he carved one more half arc into the wood and leaped into the room. The man in the brown suit came bounding forward, and Oliver slammed the door shut.

Stillness.

The three children froze in the bedroom, listening. They heard their breaths, rapid, heaving like three pumps working madly in a machine room. They heard their hearts beating.

They listened.

The man had stopped at the door. They could hear him. He prowled on the other side like an animal momentarily separated from its prey. A loud thud sounded as he threw his weight against the door; the door shook on its hinges.

Archie could feel his friends seize up; they huddled together, their backs against Oliver's bed frame.

And then: nothing. The thud didn't come again. The sound of the man suddenly stopped.

Archie glanced at Athena; she returned the look questioningly. Oliver, near the door, stared at his friends. "Is he ... gone?" ventured Archie.

The door swung open.

The kids, reflexively, all screamed.

"Oh my God," shouted Jenn Fife, leaping back from the doorway, having just casually opened her brother's door to check on the commotion. "What is your guys' *damage*?"

There was a pause, and then Archie began to laugh, so great was the relief that suddenly overcame him. The laugh was contagious; soon Oliver and Athena were laughing with him till tears flowed down their faces.

"You guys are freaks," said Jenn, glowering. She went to shut the door, but then said to her brother, "Mom's gonna kill you for carving this thing in your door."

The suggestion only made Oliver laugh harder.

They spoke quietly, nearly at a whisper, gathered around the glow of Oliver's bedside lamp. They were like some kind of resistance movement in an old black-and-white movie, always glancing towards the door, towards the window, afraid that someone might be listening. Afraid that the door, at any moment, could come crashing in and expose their conference.

"You really think this, Ollie?"

"I do. The zebra showed me."

"You're sure it was the road. That's where he was going."

"Uh-huh."

Athena was fidgeting with an old puzzle toy, a series of flat wooden blocks attached together by nylon ribbons, something she'd found on Oliver's bedroom floor. "Well, I guess the zebra is good, huh?"

"I think so," said Oliver.

"It wants us to find Chris," said Archie. "Right?"

"Seems like it," said Athena. "I mean, what else would he be leading you to, other than the campsite?"

"I don't know," said Oliver. "But there's more. It said *find the bodies*. That's what it said. That's what the hobo lady said, too, the last time."

Archie gave a low whistle. "This is really weird," he said.

"And you guys don't think we go to the cops?" Athena twisted the top block of the puzzle; it clattered down to the bottom of the toy, still attached by the ribbons.

"No way," said Archie. "They're probably swapped."

Oliver nodded. "I think they're starting from the top, getting all the important people."

"The grown-ups," said Athena.

"Well, that answers it," said Archie. "We go to the woods. We follow that zebra. We follow your vision."

Oliver smiled wanly. "Thanks, Archie."

"How, though?" asked Athena. "My bike is trashed. God, if only we had a car. We could just drive up there."

Archie thought for a moment. "I think I know someone who can give us a ride."

Oliver's sister and mother were still sleeping soundly when the kids walked out onto the quiet streets of Seaham the next morning. Someone, in the night, had dragged Archie's and Athena's bikes from the middle of the street and laid them in the grassy median next to the pavement. Athena's front wheel was crumpled, as if someone had taken a hammer to it. She gave it an investigatory twirl; the wheel wouldn't turn. She looked at Archie helplessly.

"That's all right," said Archie. "We can walk."

There was a loose board in the fence that separated the Coomeses' backyard from the pavement – it had been that way as long as Archie could remember. It was a shared secret among the siblings; despite the fact that their father was a very capable carpenter, it remained loose, and the Coomes kids wanted to keep it that way. It was the perfect escape route. Today, however, as the sun rose higher in the sky and the day grew warmer, Archie used it to sneak into his backyard, unseen by the house's residents.

He held the board aside as Athena and Oliver both crawled through. They found themselves in the blackcurrant bushes, looking up at the darkened window on the second floor of the house. Max's window.

Archie grabbed a handful of pea gravel from the ground, near the garden bed. He threw it at the window; the small stones clattered against the glass.

The three kids waited.

"Is he unconscious or something?" asked Oliver.

"He's a heavy sleeper," said Archie. He looked at his watch. It was nine thirty. Way too early for Max Coomes to be up.

"Try again," whispered Athena.

Another handful of gravel; another clatter against the glass. This time, Max appeared at the window and threw up the sash. His hair was wildly dishevelled and his eyes were barely open. He wasn't wearing a shirt. He stared out into the morning like a maddened sailor looking for the first sight of land.

"Max!" hissed Archie. "Down here, in the bushes!"

"Is that you, bug?" he called, peering into the magnolias.

"Come down! We need to talk to you."

Max rubbed his eyes. "It's like, what, it's like – it's too early."

"Just *come down*," said Athena.

"Moonbeam's down there too?" asked Max. His voice was sounding less groggy. "Must be serious. Hold tight." He backed away from the window and slid it back in place. Before long, Max Coomes, clad in a fleece robe, was standing before them in the backyard.

"This better be pretty freaking important," he said.

"Come in here," hissed Archie.

"What, into the bushes?"

"Yes – so no one can see you."

Soon, Max was crowded into the leafy branches of the magnolia with them. "So what's this all about? Dude, what are you doing?"

Oliver had stepped in close and was in the process of taking large, performative inhalations around Max's neck and shoulders.

"Smell check negative," said Oliver.

"You better tell me what's going on," said Max, shooting Oliver a repellent look.

"We need a ride," said Archie.

"Oh, now you want me to drive you somewhere?" asked Max.

"This is serious, Max," said Archie. "We need you to take us up to the woods, to our camping spot."

"What, up those old roads? You're out of your mind."

"Come on, dude," pleaded Archie.

"Find your own way. I've got plans, anyway."

"You're not gonna have any plans if you don't help us out," said Oliver.

"What's that supposed to mean?"

Archie screwed up his eyes and took a deep breath. "Listen. Max. There's stuff happening. Serious stuff. In the town. *To* the town."

Max eyed each of them in turn.

Athena said, "Listen to him, Max."

Archie continued, "Mom and Dad – they're changed. We think they've been, like, switched out. For fakes. I don't know how. It's just happening. Someone's doing it, person by person, through the whole town. They started with Dad. Then some people on the city council."

"Then my parents," said Athena. "I don't know where my sister is. I think they have her."

"Something's buried beneath the Langdon place," said Oliver. "Something really bad. And they're trying to uncover it. We have to go to the woods, to where Chris is. I saw a vision, Max, a real vision. I saw a—"

Archie interrupted him. "Maybe lose the bit about the zebra," he suggested.

"We need to get to the woods, to Chris," said Athena. "He's still up there. And we think he's in danger. Serious danger."

A long silence followed as Max stared intently at his brother's friend. His eyes then briefly met Oliver's and Athena's intent gazes before he burst into spontaneous laughter. "You guys are nuts," he said. "Totally freaking out of your minds. No, I'm not going to spend half my day driving up those roads to save your friend from evil body snatchers. You guys are on your own."

"Max," said Archie. "You have to believe us. It's true."

"Do not tell Mom and Dad about all this stuff," said Max. "They'll have you committed. I swear to God. Then nobody's going to Los Angeles." His face had grown drawn and serious. "For real – are you, like, *trying* to mess up our whole family's summer? Is this some kind of game to you?"

Archie didn't have a chance to answer; his brother was already walking away, back towards the house. He could hear Athena and Oliver breathing loudly next to him; he could feel their tension. After Max had disappeared around the side of the house, Archie turned to his friends and said, "I guess we're walking."

The sun was just cresting the tops of the firs now, casting its sharp, golden rays of light down onto the gravel of the road. They walked in silence, mostly, up the neighbourhood trail behind Chris's house, through the culvert beneath the highway, up the first patches of gravel that led onto the forest-service road into the woods.

There was a marked change in them, compared to the last time they'd travelled up this road towards the campsite. The cheeriness was gone, replaced by a kind of weary determination that bonded the three friends.

And then, just as they reached the spot where the road opened into a clearing and Archie could see the dense shroud of trees on the far side marking the boundary of the deep forest, Oliver stopped.

"What's up?" asked Athena, coming up behind him.

Oliver didn't answer; he was staring at the line of trees.

Archie came up alongside Oliver; they stood, all three of them, in a straight line in the middle of the road.

Archie stared ahead. The spires of the tall fir trees pierced the low blue sky above them. He felt strange; he did not know what lay beyond the line of trees before them, he just knew it was dangerous. He looked over at Oliver. "You OK?" he asked.

But Oliver was staring at the trees.

Just then, there was an eruption of noise in the forest. A frantic flurry of birdsong, followed by the sudden yips and cries of numberless, faceless animals. A rustle began that grew to a terrible clamour of branches and bushes, as if a great gale were blowing through the forest.

And then the animals came.

First were the birds – a carnival of colours and sounds – spilling out from the crowns of the firs. They darkened the sky above the kids, there were so many. Crows, kestrels, jays and robins poured forth in a wild migration out of the woods. Archie craned his neck back to see them fly, holding his hand above his brow to shadow the sun. But then a noise called his attention back to the trees. One by one, emerging from beneath the boughs, from among the green vegetation surrounding the tree trunks, came a menagerie of forest animals. They did not run, but moved very quickly, as if they knew a long journey lay before them and they must conserve energy. A doe urged two fawns along while a pair of bucks leaped ahead, jumping the scrub before them with a kind of desperate agility. A black bear rumbled out of the trees and followed the path of several dog-looking animals – Archie guessed them to be coyotes – while a whole warren of rabbits darted out into the clearing.

The animals paid no attention to the children. It was as if they knew that whatever they were fleeing was so great a danger that three children, stopped in the middle of the road, were the least of their concerns. Archie had seen footage on television of animals escaping a forest fire, terrified moose and deer running pell-mell away from a plume of dark smoke that enveloped the sky. The scene playing out before him was hauntingly similar, except the sky was a pristine blue, and the only thing Archie could smell was pine needles and a hint of ocean air.

Archie heard Athena gasp loudly as the sea of animals moved close to where they were standing – though it was clear they would no sooner bother the kids than if they'd been trees or bushes themselves. They passed them by, refugees fleeing a war zone. The sound of wings above them continued to hum, the vegetation crackling with the footsteps of a mass of travellers.

And then they were gone. Fled.

Oliver moved forward. Athena followed. Archie took up the rear, and together, the three kids began walking across the clearing and into the place where the road became lost in the dark of the trees.

THURSDAY

Toff is standing in the sand of the beach. He is staring down into the hole in the cliff. The machines around him are silent, their operators having not yet arrived. It is early morning. The sun is still shrouded by the hills to the east.

"Good morning, Brother," says a voice over his shoulder.

"Good morning," says Toff. He does not need to look to see that it is Lugg speaking to him. Lugg stands next to him, and together they stare down into the blackness of the hole.

They stand in silence for some time. Toff looks at Lugg and says, "Do you see anything?"

Lugg thinks and says, "No."

Toff nods and looks down in the hole. "I do not either."

"Is it funny," says Lugg suddenly, "that if you look for some time, things form? I see now, Brother, an umbrella. Just there." He points.

"There is no umbrella in the hole, Brother," says Toff.

"I'm aware there is no umbrella, but there is a trick one can play on one's eyes," explains Lugg. "And when I look long enough, I see an umbrella. But now a frog."

"This is a pointless conversation," says Toff.

Lugg looks away from the hole; he looks at his companion and says, "Why, you've grown old, Toff."

Toff looks up from the hole. He looks at Lugg. Lugg, too, has grown old. His beard is grey, and there are cracked lines at his eyes and at his mouth. "We are running out of time," says Toff.

"Have I, too, grown old?" asks Lugg, perplexed.

Toff nods, affirming.

"I did not think it could be so," says Lugg, and he places his hand on the whiskers of his face. He feels the dryness of his skin, the gentle creases on a surface that was once so smooth.

"We are running out of time," says Wart, who has just arrived. He stands some ways off, on the hard, wet sand of the beach, watching his companions. He has been watching them for some time. They did not notice, so engrossed were they in the object of their attention: the hole.

"What's to become of us, Wart?" asks Lugg.

"We will perish, Lugg," says Toff, "if we do not hasten. It is the children who waylay us."

Lugg steps away from the hole, kneading the skin of his forehead with a club-like hand. "We have tried, Wart. How we have tried."

"You yourself know this," says Toff. "For you were present."

"They are children," says Wart. "Human children. How can they be an obstacle?"

243

Lugg and Toff exchange a glance. "Look," says Lugg. "For you, too, have grown old."

"Nonsense," repeats Wart loudly, but his companions cannot know whether he denies the power of the children or his very obvious increase in age. "We will not be thwarted by children."

"They knew the symbol," says Toff. "How did they learn the symbol?"

"They have assistance," says Lugg.

"Someone has told them," says Wart. "They have been taught."

"By whom?" asks Toff.

"There is a teacher." Wart looks at his brothers with something close to contempt.

"Not the man from the video-tape shop," says Toff.

"I suspect it is the same," says Wart.

"Is he from before?" asks Toff.

"No," says Wart. "He is not from before."

Toff has removed his notepad from the inner pocket of his jacket and is thumbing through the pages. He arrives at a new page; he writes on it with the stub of his pencil. "Not from before," he repeats. He looks at Wart. "He should be addressed," he says.

Wart looks at Lugg and laughs. He looks back at Toff. "Yes, Brother," he says. "He should be addressed. He should have been addressed long ago. Our days are short and growing shorter."

"What of the children?" asks Lugg.

"We will address the children in time," says Wart. "But first, the teacher."

"Is he to be stolen?" asks Toff.

"No," says Wart. "He is to be killed. Send the stolen ones."

The three men, standing now in a triangle in which each of them holds the corners, look at one another and nod. "It is agreed, then," says Toff.

"It is agreed," says Lugg.

"It is agreed," says Wart.

The campsite was abandoned.

The ash in the firepit had burned down to a fine dust. Archie kicked at it with his shoe. The few chunks of blackened wood he uncovered showed no sign of smoke or ember. A stack of firewood by the stone circle suggested it had been intended to burn much longer.

"Guys," came Oliver's voice from inside the lean-to. "Look."

There was Chris's backpack. It was not the backpack of a camper who had gone out for a day hike or a search for more firewood. The top of the bag had been left unclipped, and they could see Chris's clothing stuffed haphazardly within.

"Maybe he's coming back for it," suggested Athena. Her voice was thin, uncertain.

Archie fought an impulse to yell his friend's name, to holler it out to every corner of the clearing. He had the feeling they needed to stay undetected for as long as possible. Still, the urge ate at him as he searched the area around the campsite. He could feel frustration welling in his chest. He looked at Oliver. "What now?" he asked.

"What do you mean, what now?" asked Oliver.

"You're the one with the visions. You're the one who led us up here. What does your zebra say now?"

Oliver looked abashed. Athena said, "Archie, chill out."

Archie raised his hands in the air. "He's not here! He's gone! He's probably been swapped!"

"You don't know that," said Athena. "He could've escaped, like us."

"He wasn't there for the hexafoil," said Archie, shaking his head. "He doesn't know about that. He's just up here camping, minding his own business. He doesn't know all that's gone on. They probably swooped in and grabbed him." He snapped his fingers. "Easy as that."

"I know what I saw," said Oliver quietly.

"I should've stayed with him," said Archie. "I knew it. I knew it then, before we left. I should've stuck it out with him. But I left him. I abandoned him."

"That's not true," said Athena. "If you'd stayed here with him, you'd probably both be missing, and it would be me and Oliver up here, searching for you guys."

Archie fought the urge to cry; Oliver was staring at the empty campsite in disbelief, as if he'd been let down.

"I know what I saw," repeated Oliver.

"So what do we do now?" asked Archie. He looked at Oliver; Oliver was unresponsive. "Athena," he said. "What do we do now?"

"I don't know," said Athena, her face now drawn with worry. "I don't know! Why do you think I know? I'm just a kid. My parents are — my parents are not my parents. I don't know who to go to." She wandered off towards the edge of the campsite, her back to the fire circle.

"I know it, I know what I saw," said Oliver. "The zebra showed me. He came here. He wanted us here. We need to find him. We need to find Chris. We need to find the bodies." As he spoke, he became increasingly agitated.

Archie watched Oliver blankly. "Oh God," he said. "Don't do this. Don't do this here."

"They should've left it hid," said Oliver, now pacing a small circle in the dirt. "They should've left it alone. They should've…"

"Oliver," said Athena, walking over to him. She grabbed him by the arm. "Oliver, listen to me. Get ahold of yourself."

That's when the noise began.

It was the sound of chopping. The sound of an axe falling onto wood, repeatedly.

"Oh no," said Athena.

Tchok.

"Where is it coming from?" asked Archie, staring out into the distant trees.

The noise seemed to shake Oliver from his stupor. "What is it?" he asked.

"It's the noise — from the night we were out here," said Archie.

Tchok.

"It's coming from over there," said Athena, pointing towards the tree line.

"We shouldn't go," said Oliver. "We shouldn't go there."

But Archie was already walking away from the campsite towards the edge of the clearing. Athena glanced at Oliver briefly before following Archie. The noise continued uninterrupted from within the trees. It echoed against the distant hills. Oliver swallowed hard and ran to catch up with his friends.

Holding his glazed doughnut in his teeth and his cup of coffee in the crook of his elbow, Randy Dean managed the unlocking of Movie Mayhem's front door like a seasoned pro – until the walls of the Styrofoam cup succumbed and a small tidal wave of black coffee lapped onto the sleeve of his shirt, causing him to curse, which then propelled the doughnut from his mouth to the pavement; the keys remained resolutely in the lock.

"Christ on a pogo stick," he muttered, picking the doughnut up from the ground. He studied it briefly before determining that a little bit of grit wasn't going to hurt him. He shook a few drops of coffee from his sleeve, sipped at the uncovered cup, and finished opening the door to his shop. The bell jangled as he entered. He looked at the clock above the counter – it read ten fifteen. He was early. The store didn't open till eleven. He still had time to finish setting up the printer – again. He turned and closed the door, throwing the deadbolt.

He walked to the front counter and turned on the lamp next to the computer monitor. He took another sip from his coffee and set the cup down, wiping his sodden hand on his jeans. He sighed. He didn't like how the day was shaping up.

The basket beneath the overnight return slot only had a few tapes in it. He picked them up and studied the little plastic windows between the reels – not rewound, of course. He walked back to the counter and began his daily process of doing that most simple of jobs, one that seemed entirely elusive to his customers: the act of rewinding. He turned on the TV behind the counter as he did this; he pressed play on the tape machine. On the screen, Connor MacLeod, cursed with immortality, mourned the death of his elderly wife. Randy found himself humming along to the song that accompanied the scene – *who wants to live forever?*

Just then, there was a knock at the front door. Randy peered through the gloom of the darkened store and saw it was a man he didn't recognize. The man rapped at the glass of the door again.

"We open at eleven!" shouted Randy.

The man continued to knock at the glass.

Jesus, thought Randy, *don't break the door down*. He walked around the side of the counter and approached the door. He repeated himself: "We open at eleven," he said, tapping at his wrist. "That's in half an hour."

The man didn't seem to hear him. He kept knocking on the door, now more intently. Randy then realized he knew the man; it was the guy who worked at the reception at the

Seaview Motel. He didn't know his name, but he'd seen him in the shop before. What was his problem? "Eleven," said Randy. "We open at eleven."

But now a second person appeared at the door. It was Lucía Cruz, the woman who ran the floral shop on Abigail Street. She came up and stood directly next to the man from the Seaview and began knocking on the door. Their faces were expressionless; their fists hammered against the glass like two drummers, beating out opposing rhythms.

"Closed, Lucía," said Randy quietly, as horror began sinking into his chest. For now here was a third person, standing alongside the first two. An old man in a bathrobe, of all things. He, too, began knocking on the glass. Randy began to back away.

Another sound of knocking drew his attention to the small window on the far side of the building. A woman's face was pressed to the glass; her hand was repeatedly slapping against the pane. Suddenly, he saw the small wooden door that covered the after-hours return slot flap open; an arm appeared through the hole, grabbing at the air.

Aghast, Randy continued backing away until he hit the corner of the counter. Keeping his face to the door, he moved around the counter and withdrew to his office. He slammed the door shut.

"What in God's name?" muttered Randy. He could feel his heart pounding through his chest. The knocking, dulled by the cover of the office door, continued unabated. He heard something crack, followed by a cascade of shattering glass. He gasped. *They've broken the door.* Thinking quick, he grabbed his desk chair and leaned it against the office door, setting the back below the handle. He then dashed for the door that led out onto the alley.

A face appeared at the office window, just above Randy's desk. It was Sam Gibbs, the bartender at the Sea Hag. His face looked sullen, lifeless, as he stared at Randy. He raised his fist and began pounding it against the window. Randy quickly checked the lock on the door; it was fast. But now a second person had appeared at the window, pounding on the glass. Randy was surrounded.

"You're all – you're all sick!" shouted Randy, his voice breaking from the strain. "You're not well, Sam! I've done nothing wrong. You got to leave me be here."

Sam did not reply. He hammered his fist against the glass; a crack erupted across the pane.

Randy Dean was not a violent person. He had spent his life assiduously avoiding conflict. In school, he had always been one to shy away from any kind of violent confrontation. But now something in him was changing. His altar, his citadel, his haven was being breached by an unruly mob of – of who-knew-what. What had he told the kids? Swaplings. The strange automatons that were now laying siege to his beloved store had all the markings of a people possessed. He had to defend himself. He had to defend his store.

Sam Gibbs's fist struck the window above his desk a final time and it shattered, sending shards of glass into the office. Seemingly unaffected by the remaining glass that stuck from the windowpane like teeth, Sam began to climb through the window. A second figure followed, waiting its turn to clamber into the room.

Randy's eyes darted across the office. He'd never given much thought to self-defence. Seaham had always been a peaceable town. He'd never felt the need to keep something like a baseball bat in the store, much less a gun. How would he fight back against this sudden invasion?

Then – just then: he remembered.

On the far side of the room, above an ancient, overfilled filing cabinet, was the item that was to be the beginning of Randy's dreamed homage to the history of film, the Movie Mayhem History of Motion Picture Museum (admittedly, destined for the corner of the store that now housed the budget tape resale section). It was the Cimmerian sword – Conan the Barbarian's broadsword from the second film, *Conan the Destroyer*. Not the *actual* sword, Randy would be forced to point out, when pressed, but a backup replica that had been made in case the first one became damaged during filming. It was one of five, in fact. He'd had it there, on the wall above the filing cabinet, for years. He had the certificate of authenticity somewhere.

Just as Sam Gibbs crossed over the windowsill and gained entry into Movie Mayhem's back office, Randy dived across the room and grabbed the sword from the wall. It had been clumsily attached to a cheap wooden plaque by some tacks that gave as soon as Randy grabbed the hilt. He swung it once in front of his face, feeling its heft. *They didn't skimp on this one,* he thought. He could imagine Arnold Schwarzenegger – or Conan himself, in fact – heaving the blade upright to face his enemy.

"Stand back, Sam," said Randy. "Don't make me do this."

Sam seemed not to hear him. He began walking towards Randy.

And so Randy swung.

He couldn't bring himself to go for the neck – he'd known Sam since the guy had been a dishdog at the Sea Hag. But he thought a clean strike to the arm would probably teach the man a lesson. To Randy's great surprise, the blade made contact with Sam's forearm not with a fleshy *shnk*, as one might expect, but with all the resistance of an axe falling into wood. Sam faltered; the blade stuck. Randy grunted and prised the sword from the man's arm. As he did this, Sam's arm broke. It broke in two, like a tree limb. That's when Randy realized that Sam Gibbs – or, at least this version of Sam Gibbs – was made of wood.

Sam stumbled backwards, and Randy took the initiative to swing the blade across the joint of his knee. Again, the blade sank into the man's leg as if into a green tree bough. The momentum of the swing, however, caused Sam to pitch sideways, and his head smashed into the edge of Randy's desk. With a loud crack, Sam's head broke away from his neck and rolled to the floor. Randy was so aghast at this spectacle, he did not see the woman who had followed Sam through the window. She leaped from her place at the sill and threw herself on Randy's back, her arms around his neck, her legs wrapped around his torso. Randy felt her teeth sink into his neck, and he gave a strangled yelp. He bucked forward and sent the woman flying across the room. She lay on the ground, suddenly seized with wild spasms. Randy hefted the sword and brought it down on the woman, every blow sending wooden splinters into the air. Soon she had been reduced to a broken heap of kindling.

"Good lord almighty," said Randy, his arms shaking from the effort.

He looked towards the door to the rest of the shop. He could hear footsteps on the other side; he could hear their flailing knocking on the locked door. He took a deep breath, steadied himself, and kicked as hard as he could against the door, sending it flying open.

There, in the midst of his videotape-rental shop, his prize jewel, owned and operated independently since 1983, was a horde of swaplings. Neighbours, peers, members of the community. Some of them were familiar, others not. They were all, he knew, made of wood. He stepped forward through the door, his sword hefted above his head in his best impression of Conan, facing an onslaught of his enemies.

Connor MacLeod spoke from the tinny speaker of the television above the counter. "There can be only one," he said. And Randy Dean started chopping.

It was easy to follow the sound – it was persistent; it was loud. If anything, it was the sort of sound that demanded running away from. But here they were, making their way towards it – the three of them, crouched behind whatever cover they could find: stands of sticker bush and hazel bramble, trunks of trees. They tried to keep the vegetation between themselves and the sound. The chopping grew louder as they approached it. Then, when it seemed like it couldn't get any louder, Athena stopped behind the rotted trunk of a fallen oak.

She pressed her palm against Archie's chest.

"Look," said Athena quietly.

Archie pushed himself up to peer over the top of the tree trunk. He saw a small clearing, surrounded by several ramshackle structures. Piles of felled trees lay about the clearing, and Archie could see a man laying into one of the trees with a large axe, removing its branches. In the centre of the clearing was a chopping block, and on that chopping block sat a nude woman.

Archie thought he recognized the woman, though her features seemed strangely blank. From this perspective, sidelong, he had a hard time making out exactly who she was. She was sitting very upright, as if she were attending some important function. Just as he was searching his memory for who the woman might be, he saw a naked man approach. The man, too, was no one Archie recognized. He was middle-aged, tall and pale. A ponderous gut hung out over his hips. The man was holding an axe and was looking at the woman as if she were some sort of specimen, his head cocked sideways. Suddenly, he raised the axe over his head. Archie expected to see the woman flinch, but she did not move. She did not seem remotely threatened by the man and his axe. And then, just as quickly as it had been raised, the axe came down squarely into the woman's shoulder.

Tchok.

Archie gasped; he threw his hand to his face to stop the scream that he felt rushing out of him. He heard his friends seize up next to him; Athena gripped his arm.

The woman did not move. Her face remained placid, her eyes fixed on the air in front of her. Then the naked man calmly removed the axe from the woman's shoulder and brought it back above his head. Down it came again, back into her shoulder.

Tchok.

Archie waited for the woman to scream, to fall away from the blow. She didn't move. He expected blood to spatter out from the fall of the axe, but none came. The axe fell again; still, no blood, no scream, no movement. It was then that Archie realized that the noise he was hearing was not that of an axe making contact with flesh and bone; rather, it was the sound of wood being split. He blinked twice, hard. He tried to refocus; he could feel tears welling up in his eyes. He heard Athena speak next to him.

"She's ... she's made of wood?" she asked in a whisper.

But still the blows came raining down; the man's axe fell several more times until a hunk of something – her flesh? – fell from the woman's side. The man then paused; he reached out his hand and placed it on the spot where the axe had been removed. Then, with a kind of artisan's care, the man began landing a series of quick blows on the area he had inspected.

Once this was done, the figure set down the axe and proceeded to shift the woman's body on the chopping block. She was now no longer in profile to the kids; they could see her head-on. The side of her head and upper torso that had been obscured to them became clear – it was not part of a human, but rather a block of marbled, rust-coloured wood. She was half completed; the right side of her body looked perfectly humanoid, while the left side was only beginning to take shape. The lower part of her body was still as much tree as it was human, with scaly bark and moss clinging to it.

And then the woman saw them; she saw them behind the tree trunk and, with her one human eye, she winked.

Oliver screamed. "I'm sorry," he said loudly, his hand covering his mouth. "I'm sorry. I want to go home. I want to go home."

But the man was now turned towards them; he stared at them and let out an ear-piercing shriek, like a wounded animal crying. The man did not move; he just screamed. Archie screamed too. And then he was falling backwards into the scrub behind them, and he could feel the thorny bushes scratching his skin. He was only vaguely aware of the struggles of his friends as they tried to run away from the clearing. Then he felt himself fall against something hard, and he looked up and saw Brody Tyke.

Brody was standing above him, dressed in his typical outfit – black baseball cap and black T-shirt. He looked down at Archie, bemused; a smile widened across his face, revealing his tobacco-stained teeth.

"Hello, Archie Coomes," Brody said. "What are you doing here?" There was something otherworldly about Brody, the way he spoke. The way he held himself. The smell of wet wood exuding from his skin, from the cotton of his shirt. Brody Tyke had been swapped.

But just as Brody reached down to grab him, Archie gave the man a swift kick to the shins. Brody lost balance and stumbled backwards; in the moment, Archie scrambled to his feet and dashed into the trees.

As he ran, Archie could see the shadowy figures of people around them, loping through the woods alongside them. It appeared he was surrounded, followed by an army of these strange figures. He'd lost Athena and Oliver in the confusion. His breath was rattled and heavy from running, and he couldn't muster the strength to call their names.

He burst through a thicket to find himself standing before a mouldering structure. He immediately recognized it as the old warehouse on Lee Novak's property, the one they'd passed on their way to the campsite. He made a split-second decision and ran for the door of the building. The door was heavy, made of thick beams, and it grated noisily against the concrete floor of the building as he pushed against it. A small opening appeared; he was suddenly assaulted by the air of the room. He did not take the time to contemplate the smell – a mealy, musty stench – and squeezed through the door into the warehouse.

Inside, he pushed his shoulder back against the door and managed to heave it closed. An iron latch on the inside clanged against its clasp, and Archie had to shove the door hard against the jamb to make it fall into place. Once it did, he stepped back and listened.

There was quiet.

He let out a sigh of relief. He had eluded them. If only for a moment. He then took a deep breath and the smell hit him again. This time, he was able to pinpoint the sense memory it evoked – there was something dark and visceral about the smell. It was the smell, he realized, of meat.

Once a year, around October, his father would go out on a hunting trip with a few old friends. They'd be gone for a few days, somewhere in the coastal range. But Archie now remembered greeting his father when he'd come home from such a trip, when he'd pulled up to the kerb in his truck and emerged from the cab smelling of beer and grit and campfire smoke. He'd brought Archie around to the back of the truck and opened the canopy to show him his kill – an adult elk, laid out, lifeless against the black plastic of the truck bed. The smell was powerful – animalistic and organic. It was what he smelled now.

He stood with his face to the door, terrified to turn around.

He heard someone's movements outside, the sound of rustling vegetation. He took a step backwards, still facing the door. His breath was caught in his chest; his heart was pounding. Slowly, he turned.

He saw the bodies.

The building was perhaps thirty feet wide and twice as

long. Clouds of dust played in the light that descended from the holes in the roof and through the foggy, cracked windows. Wooden racks lined both sides of the long walls, racks that reached to the hip of the vaulted roof. On the racks, arranged neatly, were several dozen human bodies.

Archie noticed their feet first – an array of naked feet, their toes pointing directly to the ceiling. They belonged to the bodies that were lying, face-up, on pallets, like children in bunk beds. Some were clothed; many were naked. There were about five pallets to each rack, and on each of the pallets Archie counted three bodies laid alongside one another. There were dozens of bodies here – perhaps a hundred.

Archie walked down the centre of the long warehouse with his hands frozen at his sides, breathing in the dusty, warm air in small gulps as he tried to keep the smell of the room from assaulting his senses. He recognized the balding head of one body. He walked towards the rack as if under someone else's power, and he saw his father there, lying flat on his back, stripped of his clothes. Archie's hand went instinctively to his mouth, covering what would've been a holler of anguish. He stepped backwards, repelled, and ran into the rack behind him. The rickety wooden thing creaked noisily, and he flipped around; he saw the crowns of two heads, combed parts in their hair. He immediately recognized them as Bert Hoagley and Eric Plant – the sheriff and his deputy. Their eyes were staring at the air above them. They did not look pale or hallowed like corpses; rather, they looked like they were sleeping with their eyes open. Fighting his fear, Archie rounded the rack and stared at the profile of Peter Coomes. His face, too, seemed composed in sleep. There was colour in his cheeks. And then, looking closer, Archie saw that his father's chest was rising and falling. He was breathing.

"Dad," said Archie loudly. He grabbed the man's arm, felt the warmth of his skin. "Dad," he repeated. "Wake up!" The man did not move or respond. It was like he was in some kind of stasis.

Just then, the door to the building broke open with a loud crack. Archie heard footsteps rush onto the cement slab of the warehouse floor.

Thinking quickly, Archie climbed into the rack opposite the one in which Peter Coomes lay; there was an open spot beside one of the bodies, and he slid himself alongside it, positioning himself so he was staring up at the shelf above him. He stayed quiet. He waited.

The footsteps slowed; Archie couldn't determine how many people they belonged to. He could hear the skidding of their shoes against the cement floor. They were searching between the racks. He held his breath.

"Where's he gone, Toff?" asked a voice.

"He's here, Wart," said the other. A pair of footsteps scuffled, turned, walked towards the place where Archie lay. "He's here somewhere. He can't have gone far. I saw him come in here."

"Suppose he's hidden with the meatbags," said the man named Wart. Archie heard one of the wooden racks creak as the man shook it.

"How should we find him, then?"

The two men were quiet for a moment, as if contemplating their options.

"Hello, child," said one of the men. "We know you are in this building."

Archie squeezed his eyes closed, willed himself silent.

"Please make yourself known. We do not wish to make this unpleasant."

Heart racing. Quiet, slow breaths. *Archie, you can do this.*

"We might not know which is you among the meatbags, but there is an easy way to find out."

Eyes wide, staring at the top shelf of the rack. What could he mean? Just then he heard something metallic – a knife? – being drawn in an almost performative way. One of the racks across the room rattled noisily, and Archie heard the dull sound of flesh being punctured, followed by a phlegmy gasp. Something liquid hit the cement ground in short little splashes.

Archie squeezed his eyes closed again. Felt his body tingle all over. Heart about to leap from his chest.

"Is it not against protocol?" asked one of the voices quietly.

"Hush, Toff," said the other. "We can sacrifice a few meatbags."

Again, the sound: a thick, rubber bladder being punctured. Air escaping; liquid bubbling, falling to the ground. *Splat. Sputter. Splat.*

Archie's neighbours. His parents' friends. His teachers.

All lined up here, stacked like cordwood in a storage shed. His own father and, somewhere, his mom. It was too much. He grabbed the edge of the shelf above him and pulled himself out of the rack, not caring how much noise he made.

"There he is!" shouted one of the men.

"Tender meatbag," said the other. "Couldn't take a little murder." The man laughed, and Archie, rounding the corner of the rack, caught sight of the two of them briefly. Blood had spattered across the white shirt of the one who was holding a knife that dripped black from its blade. Archie's was a momentary glance, barely a breath, and then he was running as fast as he could down the warehouse floor, away from the men.

The men didn't shout or raise an alarm at Archie's retreat; he did not hear them running after him. He quickly realized why they were in no rush to catch him – there was no other door in the warehouse. Once Archie had reached the end of the racks, he saw only a blank wall. He threw his hands up against it; he felt slivers from the rough wood prick his skin. He turned around. He saw the men approaching him, slowly, from the end of the warehouse. He stared at them; they were the same men he'd seen before, but they were somehow much older. The hair on their faces, the hair that sprouted from beneath their warped hats – it was thin and grey. Wrinkles lined their faces and puckered their eyelids and the corners of their mouths.

"Nowhere to go, child," said one of the men.

"We'll make this as painless as possible," said the other. He was brandishing his knife, wiping it clean on the dark fabric of his trouser leg.

Archie pressed his back up against the wall, willing it to dissolve, to fall away. The men grew closer. His breath was rattling in his chest now, coming in wild waves.

"Please," he managed. "Please, don't."

The men did not slow or stop; they continued their march towards him.

Slam. The noise was jarring; it drew Archie's attention to the window to his left, high up on the wall. Something was being slammed against it from the outside. The rotted wood of the sash quickly gave way, and the bottom of the window flew open like a clamshell. Through the opening, Archie saw Chris Pedersen.

"Archie!" the boy shouted. "Quick!"

He had no time to register the shock of seeing his friend. He ran to the wall and threw his arms up; the window was perhaps six or seven feet from the floor. Chris reached in and grabbed hold of his hands, and Archie was able to scramble up the wall with his help. Just as Archie gripped the apron of the window, he felt a hand grasp his ankle and pull.

Chris grabbed his friend's arms at the elbow. "Hold on," he shouted.

"He's got me!" Archie yelled. He flailed his legs and managed to shake loose of the man's grasp. He kicked against his assailant. The man gave a pained howl and fell backwards, but not before another pair of hands grabbed his other leg.

"Pull!" Archie shouted to Chris. "They've got me! They've got me!"

Chris, his face beetroot red, was pulling at Archie with all his body weight; Archie was stretched between Chris and the man, his chest riding the sill of the window so hard he could feel his sternum flex. Archie gave another hard kick and he was free; he let go of Chris and pushed himself through the window, falling to the ground below. His left foot landed on a heap of broken bricks. He let out a yelp and dropped into a crouch, his hands around his ankle.

"Let's go, dude," Chris said, grabbing his arm. "We've got to go."

Archie stood, trying his ankle. It throbbed with pain. "My ankle," he said helplessly.

Chris threw his arm around his friend's shoulder; together they began rushing away from the side of the building. From here, the ground rose in a steep, brushy incline.

"Up here!" Oliver was standing at the top of the hill; Athena was by his side. "The road's up here!"

It was difficult making it up the slope towards the road; the ground was uneven and covered with thorny weeds. Archie's ankle throbbed with every step he took.

"Faster!" hissed Athena.

"We're trying!" shouted Chris angrily.

Archie dared not look back, he was so intent on making it to the top of the incline. He fixed his eyes on Oliver's nervous form, standing where the ground flattened out, waving them forward. Oliver must've seen something because all of a sudden his eyes flared and both he and Athena were running down the hill towards them, reaching out their hands to help.

"They're behind you!" Athena cried. "They're coming!"

Chris grasped Athena's hand; Archie grabbed Oliver. Together, they hauled Archie up to where the gravel road led into the forest.

Archie, his arm still firmly around Chris's shoulder, looked down the incline. The two men were halfway up the ravine. "Run," said Archie.

Athena threw her arm around Archie's shoulder; the three of them, Archie, Chris and Athena, began to move down the gravel road. Oliver sprinted ahead.

Darting a look over his shoulder, Archie saw three men break from the vegetation along the side of the road and begin walking after them. The sight filled Archie with revulsion, and again he fought the urge to sob tears of fright. He could feel the desperation of his friends, the realization that they could sprint away if only they were unburdened of him.

"Go," he said, trying to extricate himself from Chris's and Athena's arms.

They held tight. "We won't leave you," said Athena.

"Children," said one of the men. "Relent."

"You have nowhere to go," said another.

The men walked slowly towards them. At the speed the three kids were going, their pursuers didn't even need to run. Archie felt his will sapping. He began to slow. He began to give in. The pain was too much.

But then: the sound of wheels on gravel, an engine pushed to its limit. Around the corner of the forest-service road came the Coomes family's Dodge Omni. It skidded to a halt just feet away from the four kids. The passenger door was thrown open; Megan Pedersen, Chris's sister, was in the passenger seat. Max Coomes was at the wheel.

"Get in!" shouted Megan.

Before the three men could react, Oliver, Chris, Archie and Athena had vaulted themselves into the back seat. The rear door was still open when Max jammed the car into reverse and managed a deft Y-turn in the middle of the gravel road. The rear wheels sent up a rooster tail of gravel and dirt as the Omni sped down the forest-service road, away from the pursuing men.

Max lay back on his pillow, willing sleep to return. The clock by his bedside read 9:48. His mind was racing: Why on earth would his brother have woken him at that ungodly hour – just to give him some cockamamie story about possessed people and buried evil? He'd always known Archie had a weird streak in him, but he hadn't known it ran so deep. It was his friends, no doubt, who had driven him to this. Each of them weirder than the next.

The light from the sun glowed against his drawn drapes, and he covered his head with his sheets to keep it from his closed eyes. No use. He threw aside his comforter and clambered out of bed. The day would have to begin.

In the bathroom he shared with his sisters and brother, he brushed his teeth and gave his face a thorough wiping with a gauze Clearasil pad. He smiled at his reflection; he ruffled his wavy hair.

The phone rang downstairs; he heard someone answer it. Moments later, Annabelle called up the stairs, "Max, it's for you."

He jogged downstairs into the kitchen. Annabelle had left the receiver on the counter. She was eating cereal at the kitchen table, leafing through the pages of a magazine. "It's Megan," she said in a whiny, singsong voice.

Max rolled his eyes at her. He picked up the phone and held it to his chest. "Where's Mom and Dad?" he asked.

Annabelle shrugged. "Out, I guess," she said.

He lifted the receiver to his ear. "Hey, Megs," he said.

"Hi, Max," said the voice on the other end. The sound sent a little jolt through Max. He'd known Megan Pedersen since they were in homeroom together in seventh grade. He'd harboured a crush on her these past several years. "Are we still on?"

"Uh, yeah," said Max. "Short Sands? I've got beach towels in my car. I think Jerry and Lisa are going to be there."

"I'm up for whatever."

"Cool, how about I pick you up in forty-five minutes? Like, quarter to eleven?"

"Sounds cool," said Megan.

"Cool. See you then." He hung up the phone and took a deep breath, steadying himself. He looked over at the key hooks. The one for the Dodge Omni was there, with its worn yellow key chain advertising some tyre shop in Portland. He glanced at Annabelle. "Where's Mom?"

"I don't know," was his sister's annoyed reply.

"If you see her, tell her I've got the Omni. She said it was OK."

"Whatever," said Annabelle. She flipped the page of her

magazine. "Oh," she said suddenly. "Since you're going out, will you return the movie? I was supposed to do it, but if you're on your way…"

"Yeah, sure," said Max. He grabbed the plastic videotape case from the counter and left the house.

The sky was bright blue as Max hopped down the front steps towards the car, the key chain swinging casually around his middle finger. As he approached the Omni, he glanced down the road and saw their next-door neighbour, Paul Graham, standing in his front yard, watering the well of a newly planted tree. He was wearing a navy blue bathrobe. "Hey, Paul," said Max.

Paul Graham looked up at Max silently and grinned. There was something unsettling in the way the man lifted his head, moving his attention from the water pouring from the hose into the base of the tree, but Max could not quite identify it. Something weird about the man's smile. The water was saturating the ground beneath the man's feet, and Max was disturbed to see that it was soaking the fleecy slippers the man was wearing. Paul did not seem to take notice of this.

Max gave his head a quick shake and climbed into the Omni. He started the car and noisily ground the transmission into gear. The engine stuttered as Max pulled away from the kerb – first gear was always the toughest.

He turned on the stereo. The tape he'd bought earlier in the week was still in the deck; he spun the volume knob till the speakers jumped. The music seemed to drown out his brief feeling of unease. As he drove the backstreets towards the Pedersen house, he glanced out the window at the few pedestrians he saw – he could not help but see them through a new veil of distrust. He shook his head and rolled his eyes. He couldn't let his brother's weird friends' stories trip him out. He was sixteen. He wasn't a kid any more.

Megan was waiting on her porch when he pulled up. She was wearing a loose white sweatshirt with its collar and sleeves torn away and a pair of yellow shorts. She leaped down the walk to the car and threw herself into the passenger seat.

"Thank God," she said. "I gotta get out of that house."

"What's up?" asked Max.

"My parents. They're being so *weird*." She turned sideways in her seat and looked at him. "You know what?"

"What?"

"They said they're going up to the place where your dad is building that hotel, up at the Langdon place. They said they're going to volunteer to help."

"What? For real?" This sounded ludicrous to Max. He didn't know much about the construction business, despite his dad owning one of the most prominent firms in town, but he knew that they didn't take volunteers on a job site.

"Yeah, and like two days ago, they were all against it. Grown-ups. They are *so* weird." She reached into the beach bag she'd brought and pulled out a pair of oversized sunglasses. She put them on and smiled at Max. "Let's hit it," she said. "The farther away from them, the better."

He managed the transition to first gear this time, and

the Omni moved out into the street. He was still affected by what she'd said; he couldn't shake the image of Paul Graham in his yard, the people he'd passed on the street.

"It's funny…" Max began, then stopped.

"What?"

"I don't know. My brother. This morning. He woke me up. Said he needed a ride up to that place where they camp out, up that forest-service road."

"Uh-huh."

"He said something about your brother, how he was up there and they needed to get to him. I don't know, they were acting kind of strange. Saying some weird stuff."

Megan let out a guffaw. "You think?" she asked archly. "Those nerds? I can't deal with Chris sometimes. I blame it on your brother. Nerd influence."

"I had nothing to do with it," said Max, somewhat re-lieved that the conversation was back in familiar territory. "I tried my best. What can I say? He's a hopeless case." He turned onto Charles Avenue, heading towards the ocean. "Hold up," he said. "I gotta do this one thing. Take me a second."

There, just a few blocks down, was the squat rectangular building that housed Movie Mayhem. Max reached back behind Megan's seat and grabbed the plastic tape case. He'd forgotten to rewind the tape, but that was OK. It's not like you got fined or anything. He was just about to pull up to the after-hours drop-off slot when he noticed something very alarming about the video-rental store: the glass on the front door was shattered.

"Whoa," said Megan, registering it at the same time he did.

Max could see that the only other window, the one facing Charles Avenue, had been broken too. He pulled up at the kerb and said, "Stay here. I'm gonna check it out."

Megan said, "Screw that. I'm coming with you." They both climbed out of the car and approached the building.

The front door had been completely destroyed; glass was everywhere. Inside the store, several shelves had been toppled, and videotape boxes littered the floor. Max peered through the broken frame of the door and gasped. Amid the destruction, scattered throughout the store, there appeared to be human appendages. Arms, legs and heads – everywhere. It was horrific. But something strange registered in Max's mind – there was no blood to be seen. He looked down at his feet, recoiling from the sight of a severed hand that lay just inside the perimeter of the building. He bent down and studied the hand. It was made of wood.

He looked up just in time to see Randy Dean, the proprietor of Movie Mayhem, walk towards them with what appeared to be a very real broadsword. The man stopped in the middle of the wreckage of the store, his eyes wild, his hair ragged and matted with sweat. His eyes met Max's.

Megan screamed; Max fell backwards. Randy let out what might be called a battle cry as he raised the sword above his head.

"Randy!" shouted Max. "It's Max! Max Coomes!"

Randy paused, the sword suspended in the air. "Is it?" he asked.

"Yes — yes! Dude — I just came to return the movie."

"What's your proof?"

"Proof? Here — here's the movie." Max tossed the tape case onto the carpeted floor. "*Fletch*. Archie picked it out a couple days ago. It's not *that* late."

Max's words seemed to mollify Randy, and he brought the sword down to his side. A look of concern flooded his face. "Your brother," said Randy. "Where is he?"

"He's up in the woods, at their camping spot," said Max.

"You have to find him," said the video-store owner, his voice shot through with desperation. "You have to warn him. Now."

The four kids were squeezed haphazardly in the back of the car; Chris, Oliver and Athena squirmed to fit themselves on the velour seat between the two doors, while Archie had crawled into the space behind them. He was staring at the road through the hatchback window. Megan looked over her shoulder at the four of them and said, "Do you mind telling us what in God's name is going on?"

"Watch it!" shouted Athena. Max had briefly looked away from the road to stare at the back-seat passengers in the rearview mirror; he nearly ran off the side of the road. He swore and cranked the steering wheel, righting the car.

Archie studied the road behind them intently; he could see the three men standing in the centre of the road, their brown suits hazy in the cloud of dust thrown up by the car's wheels.

"Why aren't they coming after us?" asked Chris, looking over his shoulder at the scene in the rear window.

"They will," said Archie.

"You guys," said Megan. *"What is going on?"*

"We told you," said Oliver. "There's something buried in the cliff below the Langdon place, and there are these three dudes going after it and they're, like, infecting the town, replacing people with what we know now to be wooden versions of them, and I had a vision – a zebra told me to come here, to the campsite."

Megan gaped at Oliver; Max looked at him squarely through the rearview.

"I saw them," said Archie softly. "I saw them all, stacked up in the warehouse."

"Huh?" asked Athena.

"Everyone. All of the people from town." He paused, remembering the wet thud of the knife, the incision of flesh. "I saw Dad."

"Dad's at the job, up at the headlands," said Max.

Archie shook his head. "That's not Dad. Dad's in that warehouse."

"What about my parents?" asked Athena, craning her neck over the back of the seat. "Did you see them? Are they OK?"

"It was like they were all sleeping," said Archie numbly.

"Did you see them?" pressed Athena.

"I didn't have a chance to look around. Those men came after me."

"We have to go back and save them," said Athena.

"No way," said Chris. Everyone's attention was diverted to him. "I'm not going back there. Not ever."

"What happened to you?" asked Archie. "We were so worried…"

"I just want to get out of here." Chris's voice quavered as he spoke. "They were everywhere, all these … these infected people. Or whatever they were. And the chopping – it never stopped. I ended up ditching the campsite and hiding out in the trees. I was afraid they'd find me. Spent last night huddled up in the hills there. Freezing my butt off. Till I heard you guys shouting and I made a break for it."

"Oh God," said Megan. "What is going on?"

"Where do we go?" asked Max, his hands gripping the wheel of the Omni.

"How do I know?" asked Chris. "Seattle? Canada? As far away from Seaham as we can get."

"But what about the people back there?" asked Athena. "What about our parents?"

Just then, Oliver shouted, "Behind us!"

Archie swung around and looked out the hatchback window. They were being chased by the three men in brown suits, their bodies contorted into animalistic postures as they tore down the gravel road on all fours.

Max, seeing them in the rearview, let out a scream.

"Can you go faster?" shouted Athena.

"Oh no," said Oliver, moaning. "Oh no."

Archie could feel the Omni jerk forward as Max laid on the gas; his head cracked against the glass of the rear window.

He looked up in time to see one of the men come up close to the bumper and leap. A tremendous crash sounded as the man landed on the top of the Omni. Everyone in the car screamed. Max jerked the steering wheel, and the car began to fishtail wildly.

The rear of the car careered along the bank on the side of the road, carving a gash in the hillside with its bumper. The man on the roof started hammering on one of the windows; the glass began to crack under the pressure. Just then, Max cranked the wheel and they went sliding sideways. The man was thrown from the top. Archie could see him rolling over the side of the road and down the embankment below.

Archie looked through the front windscreen; he recognized this part of the road. They weren't far from the place where the forest-service road met the highway. If only they could get to civilization, he thought briefly, before it occurred to him that he did not know what civilization was any more.

Bang.

The sound startled him. He looked behind him, through the hatchback window. One of the other men, the one with the beard, had grabbed their bumper and was being dragged along behind it.

"Max!" he shouted. "There's one on the back!"

Again, Max swung the steering wheel erratically, driving the car back and forth across the road. This did not deter the man on the bumper, who began clambering forward, along the passenger side of the car. He had just reached the rear passenger door when Athena threw it open.

"Leave us alone!" she shouted. The man tried valiantly to keep a grip on the car door. His fingers grasped at the handle. But Athena kept jerking it open and closed until the man was pitched off. He rolled several times across the gravel and into the ditch on the side of the road.

Only one man remained – the man with the bushy sideburns. His brown suit was now caked with dust from the road, but he continued galloping after the car, bent over on all fours as he ran. He came up alongside the car and, lowering his head, passed in front of it. He then turned and leaped onto the hood.

Max screamed. Everyone else gave their own version of the howl, as if it were some kind of transmissible disease. The man blinked at them, frowning, before he began crawling towards the windscreen. Once there, he raised his fist and brought it down, hard, against the glass. The windscreen cracked.

Max slammed on the brakes.

The car went skidding sideways. Archie was thrown into the laps of his three friends in the back seat. The man flew off the front of the car and tumbled several times before coming to a stop in the middle of the road.

There was a pause, a silence, as the car was enveloped in dust. And then Max put the car into gear. The man stood as the car approached. His face was unmoved as the front of the Dodge Omni rammed directly into his midsection and he was vaulted over the top of the car, shattering the windscreen as he went. Archie looked behind him and saw the man land in the road as the car sped away.

"Did you…" stammered Megan. "Did you *kill* him?"

"I freaking hope so," said Max.

They were closer to town now; they had passed the spot where Archie, Athena and Oliver had seen the animals escaping the forest. Through breaks in the hills, they could see the vast blue horizon of the ocean. Archie felt his breath returning to him; he could feel his heart rate slowing to normal. He climbed into the back space again and resumed his position as rear lookout.

"They coming back?" asked Max.

"Can't tell," said Archie. "There's so much dust."

"Maybe we lost 'em," said Chris.

"So what do we do now?" asked Megan.

"Get out of town, that's what we do," said Chris.

"How much cash you guys have?" asked Max.

There was a collective silence. Megan said, "I've got ten bucks in my purse."

"Yeah," said Max. "Maybe I've got twenty. We're not going to make it very far. I've got a quarter tank of gas. That's it. And the windscreen is totalled."

"We get as far as we can," said Archie. "As far away from Seaham as possible."

Oliver had remained silent; he occasionally stole looks over the back of his seat towards the rear windscreen. Finally, Archie asked, "What's up?"

"Why aren't they following us?" asked Oliver. "I don't like it."

But now the car had hit the place where the road met the

highway, and Max navigated the Omni down the final few curves. He was about to head north, merging into the sparse traffic of the afternoon, when the sounds of sirens abruptly broke the stillness.

Archie looked behind them; he saw two police cruisers pull away from the shoulder in a spray of dirt, their lights flashing.

"Don't stop!" shouted Archie. "Keep going!"

"It's the cops, dude. I can't outrun them. They'll get me for resisting arrest," replied his brother. Max was looking petrified.

"Just go!"

The Omni's engine wailed as Max laid on the gas, speeding north up the highway. They hadn't got far, however, before they saw two cruisers roll out to block both lanes of the road, their lights blaring, their sirens squawking. One of the cars was white with a blue stripe, a typical county police cruiser. The other was gold and emblazoned with the word SHERIFF in tall blue letters. As they drew closer, they could see Hoag step out from the driver's seat, his hands on his belt.

"He's swapped," yelled Archie. "You have to keep going!"

"How do you know?" yelled Max.

"I saw him in the warehouse! Just go!"

"There!" shouted Megan, jabbing her finger at the windscreen.

Just beyond the patrol cars, over a weedy patch of Scotch broom and blackberry bushes, they could see the dirt road that led to the headlands. Max cranked the wheel and careered the Omni off the road and into the vegetation, the car jumping on the uneven ground. Archie saw Hoag watch them with disbelief before climbing back into the driver's seat of his cruiser. By the time the Omni hit the dirt of the road, long tendrils of blackberry bramble clinging to the windscreen wipers, they had four patrol cars, sirens howling, racing after them.

"Oh my God," said Max, "I'm totally gonna lose my licence."

"Faster!" shouted Athena. "You've got to go faster."

"They're in cop cars!" Max retorted. "I'm in a Dodge Omni!"

Now they were up against the wrought-iron bars of the Langdon property, and Archie saw where they were headed. "Max!" he called from the hatchback. "This is a dead end!" But before he could get the words out, the car jumped as an explosive sound erupted from beneath Archie and the Omni began to judder and slow.

"What happened?" cried Athena.

"I think you blew a tyre," yelled Chris.

Now Max was wrestling with the steering wheel; the car was not following its direction. There was a final, wide fishtail, and the car drove headlong into the ditch, burying its front end with a loud crash into the weedy berm. Archie didn't have time to look through the window; he scrambled with the rest of the car's occupants out of the car and into the road. The Omni was toast, high centred on the side of the gravel road with its hood nosed into the ground, just below one of the concrete pillars that stood between the stretches of fence around Langdon House. In the distance, the central spire of the house could be seen, its windows dark and shuttered. Archie looked down the road. He saw the squad cars approaching through the cloud of dust kicked up by the Omni.

Then Oliver shouted, "The hexafoils!" Archie looked over; his friend was pointing at the gate pillars, each of them etched with the strange insignia.

"Over the fence!" shouted Archie. "To the house!"

Max ran to the edge of the fence and began offering his hands, webbed together, as a foothold for the kids. He was the last to clamber over the wrought-iron fence, just as Hoag's cruiser arrived.

The six kids – Athena, Max, Megan, Chris, Oliver and Archie – were now running for the front porch of the Langdon House, each of them oblivious to the novelty of this moment, that they had breached the perimeter of this storied place. Archie alone paused, momentarily, to look behind him. Hoag and his deputies had exited their cars and were standing at the fence, but they were not attempting to cross it. They had begun pacing angrily in front of the iron bars, like animals in a cage. It did not escape Archie, however, that he was the imprisoned one, caught within the bounds of the fence. He suppressed the thought and turned back to the house as he ran.

The wooden steps leading to the porch were bent and rotted from decades of abandonment. As he ascended them,

Archie could not help but notice the symbols that graced the posts on either side of the steps – hexafoils, those perfect circles and their interior petals, had been neatly carved there, like simple decorative patterns. Another one had been carved into the lower panel of the front door, just below a windowpane that was glazed in dust and cracked from corner to corner.

"It's unlocked," said Chris, trying the brass handle.

The door wheezed open on its ancient hinges. The air of the house's interior issued out like a breath long held in. It smelled like age and dust, like an attic that had long been shut to the world. Archie glanced briefly back at the Seaham police, who were still hovering at the fence line, before he followed his friends inside Langdon House.

The dust has settled. The wind has calmed. Wart has removed himself from the side of the road; he is busily wiping the smears of dirt from the lap of his trousers. He shakes his head; there is a bit of bramble caught in his hair, and it falls to the ground. And now he is joined by Toff, who has arrived, looking very much like Wart himself: that is to say, filthy. His brown suit is stained with dirt and grime; his tie is askew. Wart glares at him. Toff reads the expression correctly and begins wiping away the stains, brushing the bracken from his hair.

"They have escaped us again," says Toff.

"Yes," says Wart. "Yes, they have."

"Our powers grow weaker," says Toff.

There is a noise. The two men look off to the side of the road. They see their compatriot, Lugg, still lying face-up in the roadside bracken.

"Brother," says Wart.

"Brother," says Toff.

Lugg does not respond.

"Has he perished?" asks Toff.

"No," says Wart.

They look again. Lugg has now stretched his arms out to either side of him. He is lying amid a forest of ferns. He is clutching a long vine of ivy.

"The sky," says Lugg finally, "is wondrous, Brothers."

Wart and Toff exchange glances.

"Do you not think so?" asks Lugg.

Wart and Toff look to the sky. It is blue, bright blue, and the many treetops are like the spindly tops of towers reaching towards it. An aeroplane, distantly, leaves a cottony vapour trail like a line drawn across a page.

"It has not occurred to me," says Toff.

But now a noise is heard. It is a vehicle, a motorized vehicle, coming up the road. Toff and Wart turn to face the noise. Soon the vehicle arrives. It is a gold car, emblazoned with a star. It is the conveyance of the notional authority in this area. The car stops in the middle of the road; a man steps out from the driver's seat.

"Have they been caught?" asks Wart.

The man shakes his head.

"Where have they got to?" asks Toff.

"The house," says the man.

Toff and Wart look at one another. Wart says, "Then they are trapped. They can do no further harm there."

The man nods, then says, "Come to the beach."

"What has happened?" asks Wart.

"They've broken through," says the man. "They've found the way."

Wart smiles; Toff smiles. Lugg remains supine in the bracken by the side of the road, looking up at the sky.

"It is wondrous," he says quietly. But no one hears him.

There, by the ocean, piles of limestone and shale slag torn from the cliff face, once small hills, have grown enormous. They now dot the beach, north and south, like massive anthills. The cliff face is unrecognizable from its former self; the coastline has been irretrievably changed by the clawing of the machines.

Now Toff, Lugg and Wart have arrived. They have been driven past the front gate of Langdon House, where the meddling children have been interned, down to the beach in the nominal authority's golden starred vehicle. When they arrive, they are greeted with the sight of so much activity, so much smoke and dirt and sand. The hole is larger. They can see that even before they've crossed the threshold of the chain-link fence.

The car pulls to a halt on the beach. The door is opened for them by a woman in a floral housedress. "They've broken through," she says flatly as they step out of the car and onto the sand.

"Where?" asks Wart. "Show us where."

There is a veritable army of people crowding the beach, operating the machinery, managing the massive piles of rubble that litter the sand. The breach in the cliffside has grown larger; the three men can see that immediately. It is towering, a massive rift in the rock. Metal supports have been put in place to keep the opening intact as hordes of workers come and go from its mouth, pushing wheelbarrows full of rock and debris to dump in an awaiting pile.

The three men, Wart, Toff and Lugg, make their way to the hole; they stand at the edge. Scaffolding has been installed, down in the cavity; klieg lamps blare radiant white light on the depths. Silent workers armed with pickaxes and drills carve away at the rock, far down below. The three men descend the metal ladders; they are greeted on a platform by the man known as Coomes.

"We've broken through," the man says.

"Very good," says Wart. "Show us."

They follow the man down more ladders, down more scaffolding, until they arrive at a small footprint of space that has been carved out of the rock. There, just at the men's feet, is a small hole. The rock has broken away here, and Wart, as he kneels, can feel stale, cold air issuing from the hole.

He looks up at his comrades. He smiles. "Brothers," he says. "We are close. We are very close."

The house was silent, save for the sound of the floorboards creaking under the six kids' feet as they walked into a wide foyer. Someone sneezed; motes of dust scattered in the rays of light sent down from the few visible windows. Archie felt something brush against his arm, and he started at the touch.

"It's just me," he heard Athena say.

"Is there a light switch somewhere?" came Max's voice.

"There's no way this place has electricity," said Megan.

Their eyes were quickly adjusting to the dark of the house; many of the windows, having been assaulted by the town's children over the years, were boarded up with plywood.

"I'm looking – ouch!" said Chris. Archie glanced over at him. He was sucking on his finger. "Splinter," he mumbled.

"Here it is," said Oliver, and suddenly the room was flooded with light.

"Whoa," said Megan. "Guess I was wrong."

The six of them stood quiet as they took in the scene before them. A grand staircase led up from a floor covered in a mouldering burgundy carpet; stacks of newspapers and magazines made little skyscrapers across the floor, a city of junk and debris from a forgotten life. Here was an old television set; there was a stack of wooden chairs, haphazardly balanced on one another like an acrobatic act frozen in time. The stairs themselves served as a kind of shelving unit, with each tread supporting a collapsed stack of old, weather-beaten books. Dust was everywhere – every surface, every corner was blanketed in a thick layer of dust. Cobwebs that could've been spun by a giant spider clung to every corner, spilling from the walls to the broken furniture on the floor.

"They must just keep the power running," said Archie. "I heard all the Langdons – the last of 'em – live in New York or something."

Megan dragged her finger across a section of the wall, next to the door. A layer of mould had accumulated there, marring the floral print of the wallpaper. Archie watched her inspect the black smudge on her finger before she wiped it hastily on her jeans. "Disgusting," she said.

"How long has it been like this?" asked Athena. "I mean, no one's lived here for, like, eons."

Max had walked to one of the windows that looked out over the weedy yard; he cupped his hand against the glass and said, "They're gone. They didn't come after us."

"They're kept out by the hexafoil," said Oliver. "It's a kind of charm. A sigil."

"Why didn't it stop us?" asked Max.

"We're not one of them," said Chris. "Duh."

Max ignored him. "Mom's gonna kill me when she sees the car. It's totalled."

"Mom's got other things to worry about," said Archie.

"How long are we going to be in here?" asked Megan.

"I don't know," said Archie. "Maybe we can sneak out tonight."

"And then where?" asked Athena.

Nobody answered this question. They began to spread out, each of them, drawn to some collection of junk, to some cluttered corner of the large foyer. The air smelled musty and close; clouds of dust swirled around at each footfall, as if they were stepping onto a lunar landscape.

"Guys," said Chris, "over here." A new room – a kind of parlour – was revealed in the glow of a single light bulb hanging from a chandelier. Archie followed the rest of the kids into the room, marvelling at the decaying wallpaper, the strips of paint hanging from the weather-warped ceiling. An old record player sat on a table, surrounded by stacks of ancient LPs. Archie thumbed through them: Brahms, Schubert, Liszt. The sleeves were so warped and faded it was hard to make out the titles. Nearby on a sideboard, a china vase stood between several file boxes. Only the stalks of a long-disintegrated bouquet remained; grey petals lay strewn in the dust at its base.

Megan had sidled up to Max; Max had put a protective arm over her shoulders. "Ugh," said Megan. "I do *not* want to be here when the sun goes down."

"You'd rather be out there?" said Chris, gesturing towards the door.

Megan glared at her brother but said nothing.

"Look in here," said Oliver. He'd passed through the parlour and was in what appeared to be a kitchen area. Archie followed him, feeling along the side of the doorjamb for the light. He found it: a vintage button switch that turned on the bulb in a dirty ceiling fixture. The kitchen was strangely intact: a cupboard next to the sink held neat rows of delicate cordial glasses on one shelf. Below it was a row of identical teacups. Everything was coated in a fine layer of dust.

Tattered drapes hung down over a pair of windows above the sink; two pieces of plywood had been nailed into the frames, blocking out the sun completely. The shadows in the room were cold and sickly in the dim light.

"This place is nuts," came Athena's voice from the parlour. She was looking in at the kitchen. Max and Megan were behind her. It was as if the frantic car chase from the campsite was a distant memory, superseded by the fact that they were *inside* Langdon House, a place that had existed only in myth their entire lives.

"Toxic, more like," said Megan, looking down at the dirt- and mould-stained linoleum floor.

Archie made his way towards the door on the other side of the room. Through an open doorway, the light from the kitchen illuminated a wooden wainscoted study. "What's in here?" he mused aloud.

The floor was strewn with bits of plaster; the walls were lined with shelving. Books filled the shelves, but other bric-a-brac too: old phones, coffee tins and newspapers. Piles of books lay on the floor like mole hills. In one of the walls, between the shelves, was an open fireplace. A high-backed chair was set in front of it, its cushion threadbare. Tufts of horsehair peeked through cracks in the upholstery.

"This is *wild*," said Megan.

"Check these out," said Max, standing by the bookcases. He began reading titles from the book spines. "*A History of American Occultism. Wiccan Ceremonies.* Cern-something."

Athena had come up alongside him. She read, "*Cernunnos Unchained.*"

"Yeah, that," said Max. "What's a Cernunno?"

"Cernunnos. A pagan god from early Celt mythology," said Athena. When Max looked at her in surprise, she said, "My middle name *is* Moonbeam, after all."

"These dudes were definitely into some wild stuff," said Max.

A kind of calm had settled over the kids, safe in the confines of Langdon House – no matter how creepy it was. Archie found himself standing next to Chris in front of the fireplace mantel, as they both studied the dust-rimmed photographs that were displayed there.

"Look," said Chris, pointing to one. "Granny Langdon."

Archie felt moved to speak to his friend, in this first calm of their afternoon's adventure. "Dude, I was so – we were so worried about you," he said.

Chris nodded. "It's OK. At first I was kinda, like, why did you guys leave me. But I was glad you weren't there. Two nights, trying to sleep on pine needles – I wouldn't wish that on anyone."

"What happened up there?" asked Athena; she'd come up alongside them.

"It was awful," said Chris. He sat down on the arm of the leather chair and stared into the empty fireplace. "Scaredest I've been in my life. You guys took off and everything was OK, but then the chopping – it started up again that night. I laid low, hoped it would go away. But it didn't – it kept going the next day too. So that night I went out to finally see what was going on, see if I couldn't catch this dude chopping wood in the middle of the night. And I saw it."

"What?" asked Megan when her brother paused.

"They were – chopping into people."

"We saw that too," said Athena. "But they weren't hurt. It was like, they were made out of wood."

Chris nodded. "I caught 'em, right in the middle of it. And they saw my flashlight. So they started chasing me – it was Brody and another guy I didn't know. I lost 'em in the woods, but I was too scared to go anywhere, so I just hunkered down in, like, the ditch near this tree and waited out the night. Figured I'd leave first thing in the morning. Thing was, the chopping just kept going. It was like they were picking up steam. I snuck back to the camp and started packing, but the chopping – it never stopped. I couldn't deal. I had to get out of there. So I start just booking it for the road when I see those three guys, the ones in the suits."

"The three men," said Oliver.

"Them," said Chris. "And they're wheeling this cart. And..." Here, he stammered. His sister had walked to his side; she put her hand on his shoulder. "And it's filled with bodies. Like, piled on each other. They didn't see me – not yet, anyway. So I followed 'em, and they brought the cart to that building and started loading the bodies into it."

"They must've brought them from town," said Archie.

"Swapped," said Oliver. He glanced at each of the kids in the room, his eyes wide. "Can't you guys see? They get 'em from town, bring 'em up there, and then replace them with those – those wooden ones."

"Dude," put in Max suddenly, "that's why there were all those wooden body parts at Randy's – at the video store."

"What?" asked Archie.

"That's how we knew where you were – Randy had, like, chopped up all these mannequins, it looked like – and they were all over the floor of the store. That's when he was all, 'Go warn Archie.'"

"Wait a second," said Megan. "If they're doing this – swapping people. How come they haven't gone for us?"

"I think they're not swapping children," said Archie. "That's the thing. In that warehouse. It was all grown-ups. I didn't see a single kid."

Athena's face flushed. "Becky," she said. "What about Becky? Oh God." She put her hands to her cheeks.

"We'll find her," said Archie. "When this is all over, we'll find her."

"But why no kids?" asked Megan.

"They don't think we're a threat," said Chris.

"Well, they got another think coming," said Max.

But Archie's attention had suddenly been diverted. While he listened to the conversation in the room, his eyes had strayed to a cracked mug that sat on the side table near the chair. There was a brackish liquid in the cup; he'd assumed it was rainwater and dirt – another testament to the abandonment of the old house. But now he noticed something: there was a string hanging off the side of the cup. A little tag was attached to the end of the string. He realized then: the liquid in the cup was not dirty water – it was tea. Instinctively, he reached out his hand and touched the ceramic surface of the cup.

It was warm.

"Uh, guys," he said.

That's when a new voice appeared in the room, coming from a darkened hall just off the study. It was a low, gravelly voice – a voice that sounded as if it had long since become accustomed to silence and was being heard for the first time in a very, very long while. "Oh dear," it said. "It looks as if I have company."

Everyone in the room collectively held their breath as the man emerged from the shadow of the doorway. Archie stood up from the chair. There was a noise behind him as Max, stepping backwards into a pile of books, dropped clumsily to the floor. He scrambled to his feet and inched towards the kitchen along with Chris and Megan. Oliver and Athena stood to one side of the room, huddled close together.

"S-sorry," said Archie. "W-we didn't mean to…"

"Didn't mean to what?" asked the man. "Didn't mean to trespass on private property?" His voice was cold and weary; there was the slightest tinge of an accent to his voice. It sounded like someone speaking in a very old movie. As he moved into the room, his features were revealed: he was an older man with pale skin and grey hair combed close to his scalp. He was wearing a cardigan over a button-up shirt.

"We didn't know where else to go," said Chris.

The man acted as if he hadn't heard him. "You're some of those town children, aren't you? Coming up here, throwing rocks at the windows. Climbing the fence and sneaking in – on a dare, or something. Is that it?" The man's voice was losing its gruffness as he began to speak louder.

"N-no," said Oliver. "That's not it at all…"

"All these years," continued the man angrily. "All these years. My family's home. Desecrated by transients and school-children." He took a deep breath and said, "I am going to politely ask you to leave, after which I will be alerting the authorities."

"Please," said Archie. "Please don't."

"We were chased here," said Athena, quickly stepping forward. "We had to escape. This was the only place we could hide."

The man paused. "Chased?" asked the man, his eyebrows rising. "By whom?"

"By—" began Oliver enthusiastically, before Archie stepped in to stop him.

"It's complicated," Archie said.

297

The man looked at Archie. "Try me," he said.

"By swaplings," said Oliver, momentarily glaring at Archie. "People who have been changed."

"Pardon?" asked the man.

"Our parents, the police – all the grown-ups. All changed," said Archie.

"Changed..." said the man, musing over the word.

"We honestly had nowhere to go," said Athena. "Our parents – my parents, my friends' parents. They've all been changed, replaced with these ... these things. They've got 'em all stacked up, asleep or something, in a warehouse in the woods. They chased us down from the woods. We didn't know where else to go."

"The hexafoils," put in Archie. "On your gate. They won't go past them."

The man raised his eyebrow at Archie. "What did you just say?"

"Hexafoils. We know about them. How they protect you." Archie glanced at Oliver; Oliver nodded reassuringly at him.

"Fascinating," said the man. He seemed won over by them somehow – or at least less alarmed by their presence in the house.

"They're out there, sir," said Chris. "Outside. And down at the beach. All these things, these swaplings – that's what we call them. And there's, like, three men..."

"Three old men," said Oliver.

"Well, they weren't so old a couple days ago," put in

Archie. They were all talking at once, frantically trying to convince the man of their story.

Chris continued, "Yeah, but they're three old men. They look like they're from another time. They're all wearing these identical—"

"Brown suits?" interrupted the man, his face flattening.

Chris nodded; Athena and Archie exchanged a surprised glance.

The man said, "With whiskers – but three ways. Bearded, big sideburns, and moustache. Is that correct?"

Again, Chris nodded. The room watched the man in silent expectation. Max had edged towards Megan by the bookcase.

The man's look drifted to some distant point as he lifted his finger to his lips in thought. "So," he said after a time. "It is happening."

No one spoke. The man walked to the chair in front of the fireplace, where Archie had been sitting only moments before, and lowered himself onto the threadbare cushion. He reached over absently and picked up the cup of tea; he sipped at it and set it back down on the side table. He remained there, staring into the empty fire grate, not saying a word.

Finally, Max stepped forward and said, "Excuse me? Do you know what's going on?"

The man shook his head and frowned. "I didn't believe it. How could I have believed it? Oh, Grandmother. Oh, Grandfather. If only you had lived to see this day, not me. And I – I alone."

"Sir?" prompted Chris.

The word seemed to jolt him from his reverie as he turned and looked at the kids before saying, "My name is Charles. Charles Langdon."

This elicited gasps from everyone collected in the room; it was a name as familiar to them as their own. It was the name of Seaham's founder; each name, the first and surname, was found on every map of their town, on its two largest thoroughfares.

"Yes, the same. Named after my famous grandfather. He and his brother, my great uncle Edward – together they built this" – here, he gestured to his surroundings in a kind of deflated way – "this edifice. This … tomb. Out of the ashes of Seaham. Out of the devastation. The despair." His eyes then fell on Oliver as he said, "But you, boy, you. You. I can see now. Why you're here."

Everyone looked at Oliver; Oliver's face shaded pink.

"Yes, I can see how this has all led us here," said Charles Langdon. "I've been looking. These three days, searching for the way. But, alas, I am forever frustrated."

"Do you live here?" asked Athena.

"Oh no," said Charles, "I've lived between New York and Paris for years. Haven't set foot on this property – the west coast of America, really – since I was a boy. I have fond memories of the place, I will admit. Playing in the yard out there. Running down to the beach. Watching the waves crash against the rocks. We were a larger family then. Cousins, uncles, aunts. The lot. Everyone gathered. Everyone with their purpose. Except for us little ones, I suppose. We wouldn't have been told then. No, we would not have. And here I am, the last. Yes. I suppose it has fallen on me." Here, he abruptly stood up and walked to the bookshelf. His tone changed suddenly; he was now the deferential host. "Apologies for the state of the place. No one's been in here for — well, I don't know how long. Thankfully, it's been left mostly intact. All these books — my grandfather's books. All here in one state or another. I've searched them, these last few days. Searched them for information, for signs — but I've come up empty."

"Mr Langdon," said Athena, stepping towards the man. "What do those men — those three men out there — what do they want?"

Langdon paused with his hand on the bookcase, and then said, "I suppose they want what they wanted before. They want … well, I suppose they want what we all want, in one way or another. Happiness? Do we all want that?" He pulled a book off the shelf and began flipping through the pages. "But I suppose happiness for one is different for another. Isn't that the truth?"

Archie glanced over at Max in time to see him and Megan exchange a look; the man was sounding less and less sane as he spoke.

The man closed the book he was holding and slotted it onto a nearby shelf. "No — their happiness is very different from ours. It is something altogether much … much darker." He glanced at his listeners, as if suddenly realizing how opaque his language had been. "Where to begin?" he said softly. "There are forces at play here that are beyond our understanding. Cosmic forces. Primordial forces. The sort of thing that humankind, when it was just in gestation, was already meddling in."

"What are you talking about?" asked Megan icily.

"Evil," said the man finally. "Pure evil. That's how it was told to me. It is a force that influences us all – some of us struggle against it, some of us embrace it. But it is always there. It is like a mist, a constant mist. One that surrounds us and yet is, ultimately, intangible. But sometimes – certain events, certain actions – something is enough to concentrate that force and make it almost corporeal. And I suppose that's what they found, those years ago."

"The pioneers," said Oliver. "The first people in Seaham. They found it. We saw the pictures."

"Not pioneers, per se," said Charles Langdon. "They were a generation removed. But the sins of their kind were not easily forgotten. It has a powerful draw, this thing. It draws one – it calls out to one. It has immense powers, transformative powers. The kind that ambitious men seek. But ultimately, it is a corruptive power. What's more, it is a power that creates an echo. An echo that is heard … elsewhere. Certain elements beyond our plane of reckoning have sought out these discoveries. As they have from the beginning of time. They are shape-shifters – they are tricksters. All cultures have names for them, for they have appeared, at one time or another, in all eras, in all guises. They seek to collect these things, these leftover bits of evil, to pull them together. To what end? I do not know."

"The three men," said Archie. "That's them, huh?"

"What?" asked Max in disbelief. "You mean this has happened before?"

"Indeed," said Langdon, frowning. "They have returned. It is my grandfather's greatest folly – the belief that by burying it, he would have nullified its powers. Made it inaccessible. And, I suppose, for a time he did."

"But the cave," said Athena. "The cave at the cliff. That's what they dug up. It wasn't hidden very well if it just took somebody building a hotel on the ocean."

The man looked at her quietly before saying, "This house, this property, has long been in the control of a family trust. Sadly, I have had no control over that trust for a long time; I was pushed out by the many cousins – the many cousins and their many lawyers. They said I was strange, that I was mad. That I had the old Langdon madness. The one that drove Edward and Charles to their folly. I have long opposed the selling of the property, no matter its state, no matter its value. But I had no say. My opposition held, for a time, but now I am superseded. The trust has sold the house and the ground beneath it. I knew then that these creatures, these entities, would be coming for it. As soon as the dirt was unsettled, they would be called."

"What happens if they find it?" asked Athena.

Langdon looked at her sharply. "Very bad things. Very bad, indeed."

"Is it like a weapon or something?" pressed Athena.

"No," said the man, "not as such. You see, these elements

that are searching for it — these ... three men, as they've managed to mould themselves — they serve a higher purpose. A master, as it were. And if they were to retrieve this lost bit of evil and return it to its whole, to add to its whole, well, as you can imagine, the repercussions are very dire. It's the sort of thing that makes plague, famine, war, genocide. The sins of imperialism, of manifest destiny. Always these kernels are the driving force. The things that tear at the very fabric of our common purpose, as living things. Oh no, they cannot be allowed to find it."

"What are we supposed to do, then?" asked Chris.

"We need to stop them," said Langdon. "We need to stop them at all costs. And then we must do what my grandfather could not do — did not have the strength to do. We must destroy it."

It is the kind of storm that is not unusual in early June; it is the first thunderstorm of the summer. The clouds have been absent from the sky for the last few weeks – a taste of the dry, hot summer to come. And yet: there on the horizon, gathering since the sun rose, is a meridian of cloud. As it makes landfall, it reveals its shape: a dense, dark cloud like black smoke. Bright cracks of white in the seams, only highlighting the darkness of the cloud itself. Somewhere, a telltale crash of thunder. Lugg looks skyward, from out of the pit, at the darkening sky.

"It means to rain, Brothers," he says.

The two others do not mind him. They are busy watching the workers remove rock from the hole. The hole is growing.

Lugg says, "I've not felt it rain. Since we've been here, it's not rained on us."

Still, the two men are silent. They do not answer.

Lugg removes his notebook from his jacket; he drops it to the rocky floor. He is surprised by this. He looks at his hands. His hands are old hands. They are wrinkled; liver spots freckle his skin. The hair on his wrists and arms, he can see, is white. He bends down and picks up his notebook; he feels his muscles complain. The notebook back in his hands, he thumbs it open to a page; he brings out his stub of a pencil and jots down words on the page. He looks at Toff and Wart.

"Brothers," he says, "we are old."

Wart turns on him angrily. "All the more reason for haste, Brother," he says.

"I wonder," says Lugg, "if before we retrieve the thing, we might first see the storm."

"The storm?" asks Wart.

"Brothers," says Toff, "now is not time for argument. Our time is short. Our task is before us."

"But for the sake of thoroughness, in the interest of our project, would it not be wise to make note of the storm?" Here, Lugg gives a little wave with his notebook.

Wart strikes out with his hand; he knocks the notebook to the ground. Lugg frowns at it.

"That is not our project," says Wart. "Our project is to retrieve the item. *That* is our project."

Toff and Wart return their attention to the widening hole, for now it is large enough to walk through. Air continues to flow from the opening, suggesting a large cavity within. Soon, Toff and Wart pass through the hole and into the cavern. Lugg bends down and, with some difficulty, retrieves his notebook from the rocky floor. He returns it to his inner jacket pocket. He looks up at the grey sky, what little he can see from his vantage, before following his brothers into the darkness.

"That's nuts," said Max. "There's no way we're going out there."

"He's right," said Megan. "Even if we got past the fence, the whole beach is swarming with swaplings. It was like everyone was suddenly volunteering to work, doing whatever they're doing on the beach."

"Oh," said Charles Langdon. "I'm not proposing we go to the cliff, to this hole they've made."

"Then how do we get to this … thing?" asked Archie.

"If only I had more time," said Langdon, his voice again taking on the tone of someone who was not aware there were others in his vicinity. "If only they'd left more instruction. But no, so great was their desire to keep this thing hidden, they could leave no trail, no trail whatsoever. All I received was conjecture, riddles, veiled meanings. It is always the way with this family – I suppose their brief interaction with this *thing* did seed a kind of madness in our lineage." He laughed a little then, but quickly stifled it, as if suddenly aware of the present company. He cleared his throat and, addressing the kids, said, "This is why I came. And I've been here, these last three days, searching."

"For what?" ventured Archie.

"The way, my boy, the way," said the man. "There was a way, an access that was built. They never meant to seal it off completely. They should have; we know that now. But then, they thought they'd succeeded – that no one would dare disturb it. It would slumber, deep in the ground. And the three had been pushed into the ocean – long gone. But I suppose someone thought there was no harm in keeping a channel open. Just in case."

"I saw it," said Oliver quietly. "In my visions. I've seen it."

The man watched Oliver thoughtfully, a careworn look on his face. "Yes," he said. "Tell me."

"A calling – to somewhere," said Oliver. "For me, it was an animal. A zebra. It leads me, in the dreams. But I don't know where."

"Yes," said the man. "Yes. You must remember." He walked to Oliver and took his hands in his own, cupping them tightly.

"I… I can't," murmured Oliver. "They're so vague."

"That is their power, their secret," said Langdon. "But you must listen. You are a channel, my boy."

"What are you guys talking about?" asked Chris.

"Yeah," said Max. "Mind clueing us in here?"

The man looked at the kids blankly. "There is no time," he said. "We must find the way." He returned his stare to Oliver. "You must help me find the way."

Somewhere, distantly, beyond the plywood-covered windows of Langdon House, out over the ocean, a peal of thunder rolled across the water towards land.

Charles Langdon spoke as he led the children through the house; Archie tried to focus his attention on the man's words, but he was constantly being distracted by the clutter of the house, by the obstacle course of rubbish that they were forced to navigate as they made their way through the warren of rooms. He led them down a hallway off the study, through a bedroom, into a kind of circular sunroom, its windows either broken or boarded up, and down a set of stairs. All the while, he spoke.

"I thought it was myth – all the stories. The stories my grandfather told me. The stories my father and mother told me. When no one was around. When all the cousins and second cousins and aunts and uncles were off, beachcombing or hiking in the forests, they would take me aside. They would tell me – me, Charles Langdon II – that it was my responsibility. My duty as a Langdon. To be a protector. 'Protect what?' I asked. I was so innocent, you see. As you are. I was a few years younger than you are now, I suppose, when first they broke this news to me. Watch your head."

For now they were entering a basement. There was no light here, but Archie could feel the cold stone of the house's foundation at his fingertips as he made his way down the stairs. The air was close and damp here, despite it being summer. The stone walls seemed to retain the moisture. A large iron pipe ran across the ceiling just above the stairway, and they all ducked to make their way under it.

"But then it was silence. My grandfather died. My mother and father separated; she was living in New York, he in London. The house, here in Seaham, became a distant memory. A cousin, I believe, became its caretaker. But they were not a good caretaker. They did not know the story.

The responsibility. What some might call a curse." Here he stopped, bringing the entire procession to a halt on the stairs. "And now the cousins are gone. The nieces, nephews, all scattered to the wind. And here I am, the last Langdon, the only one left to bear that curse."

Archie looked behind him; Athena and Oliver were both there. Athena gave him a worried look, a look that mirrored Archie's own feelings – they were following a madman into the basement of a house that was thought to be abandoned. But then he saw Oliver; Oliver's face wore an expression that reminded Archie of a child coming down the stairs on Christmas morning. A look of powerful wonder.

"What's up?" Archie whispered to his friend.

"I've been here," said Oliver. "I know this place."

"How?" asked Athena.

"I've dreamed it," said Oliver.

Now Charles Langdon had reached the floor of the dark basement. The only light in the room was what little came from the top of the stairs. Charles fumbled with something for a moment; a match head flared in the dark. He had a kerosene lamp in his hand, and he held the match to the wick. As the light grew from the lamp, the basement came into focus. It was an expansive room, surrounded by stone walls. The floor was made of hard-packed dirt, and its surface was heaped with all kinds of rubbish: old, collapsing cardboard boxes; soggy piles of newspapers. There, hanging inexplicably from a rafter, was a tower of empty bleach bottles, all strung together.

"Pardon the mess," said Langdon.

"I'm going to wait upstairs," said Megan, beginning to turn around.

"No, we have to stick together," said Chris.

Megan shared a look with her brother, rolled her eyes, and continued down into the basement. "This is *so* way creepy," she said.

"What's this guy talking about?" hissed Max to Archie. He'd taken him aside on the other side of the flight of stairs.

"I don't know," Archie replied. "Weird stuff."

"Let's keep an eye on him," said Max. "Who knows what this guy's into. Could be some child murderer or something."

But now it was Oliver who was leading the party. He looked anguished, like someone trying to remember a word or a name that was just on the tip of his tongue. He murmured sounds, unintelligible sounds, as he began wandering the dirt floor of the basement. He fluttered his fingers; he massaged his temples. He walked haphazardly across the junk-strewn ground. Langdon shadowed him, holding the lantern high, watching the boy closely as he made his way through the basement.

"What's going on?" asked Athena.

Langdon shushed her. "Don't interfere!" he hissed. "Let the boy find the way."

Athena shot the man a glare. She walked up alongside Oliver and said, "Ollie, talk to me. What's up? Are you OK?"

"I saw it," said Oliver, his speech momentarily lapsing into understandable words. "It led me here. The zebra. Bricks. Bricks."

"Bricks?" asked Athena. "What are you talking about?"

"You mean these bricks?" The voice came from Max; he was standing by a pile of bricks in the corner of the room. They were heaped against the wall as if they'd collapsed there – though there was no source of such a demolition.

Oliver's eyes shone. "Yes," he said. "Those are the bricks. From my dream."

Charles Langdon's face brightened in the glow of the kerosene lamp. He quickly set down the light on an old, crooked chair and began throwing the bricks aside. One nearly landed on Archie's foot.

"Hey!" he shouted. "Watch it!"

"Of course!" Charles Langdon was saying. "So simple. Hidden in the corner. A pile of bricks. Here I was, searching for secret doors and battened hatchways. Oof!" This last word he uttered after having tossed another brick from the pile. He stood up uneasily and began massaging his back.

"Here, let's help," said Chris, and he began removing bricks from the pile. Soon, they had relocated the pile to another part of the cellar floor. Once it was cleared, Langdon picked up the lantern and shone it towards the now-empty corner.

"I…" ventured Max, not wanting to dispel the man's enthusiasm. "I don't see anything."

"But it must be here," said Charles. "The boy!" He looked at Oliver pleadingly. "This is what you saw?"

"It's all muddled," said Oliver. He walked towards the corner and began feeling at the dirty rock face of the house's foundation. Archie felt his stomach drop. He was afraid; he was confused. There seemed to suddenly be so much riding on their actions at that moment.

Just then, Oliver said, "This stone – it's loose." He had his fingers jammed into the grey mortar between the stones. With seeming ease, he managed to pull the stone loose, creating a dark hole in the wall of the foundation.

Langdon ran to his side. "What is it?"

"It's an opening," said Oliver, peering inside. "Let me have the lantern."

Langdon handed Oliver the light; Oliver held it up to the hole he'd made. "Yes," he said. "There's some kind of passage here."

Langdon began to laugh. "It's true!" he said. "It's all true. The way, the way! Quickly, children! We must go!"

With that, the man began hastily removing the stones surrounding the hole. The kids stepped in to help, all six of them in a line, passing rocks hand over hand. Before long, they had created an opening the size of a small door. They all stopped in their labours to marvel at it. It was remarkable, the darkness that seemed to pour forth, like they'd uncovered the entrance to a mausoleum that had long been sealed shut.

It may have been that at one point in the not too distant past, the headlands stretched far out into the ocean. But the earth undergoes rapid changes, and the coastline was eroded, bit by bit, until all it took was the delving claw of a large diesel-powered machine to uncover a rift into the labyrinth inside the cliffside. These two forces – nature and man – work in tandem to undo the projects of the most well-intended individuals. Lugg notes this as he watches his brothers make their way through the tunnels. He thinks briefly that he will write it down in his notebook, to carry with him as a further understanding of this strange and beautiful place. He remembers so little of it, that other life, when they had come before. Again, seeking the thing. He was struck then by the beauty of the place, but had no time to record his findings.

This time, he came prepared. He brought his notepad.

Indeed, he noticed as soon as they arrived that the area looked very different. There were more structures. There were more people. The streets were no longer made of dirt and gravel, but a kind of hard, black substance that he later learned was called asphalt. He made a note of it. The conveyance of people had changed too – while before they had been carried by animals, in a kind of symbiotic relationship, they were now carried about by machines. Constructions, with intricate mechanical parts. This eliminated the need for the animal. He had not seen one of these conveyance animals since he returned, and he marvelled at the humans' ingenuity. Truly, they were a remarkable people.

But now he is called by his brother from the darkness. "Quickly, Brother," says Toff. "Why do you delay?"

"I am thoughtful," says Lugg.

Toff glances over his shoulder, as if to see that Wart is beyond earshot. "Now is not the time to be thoughtful, Brother," he says quietly. "You have angered Wart enough."

"Yes," says Lugg. "Yes, Brother."

The tunnels are dark, but they can see. Darkness does not affect them. They are part of the darkness.

Lugg can see Wart ahead, can see his body moving. The tunnels are cramped and cold; it is dry, the dryness of a tomb. As he walks, Lugg can feel his body weakening. He can feel pain in his joints. He can feel the tiredness in his eyes. He calls out, "Brother!"

"Yes?" says Wart testily.

"Do you feel it?" he asks.

"Yes," says Wart.

"I can feel it. The changing," says Lugg. "The aging."

"We are close, Brother," says Toff.

"Yes, we are close," says Wart.

Wart stops abruptly; he puts up his hand. Toff and Lugg stop behind him. "Listen," says Wart, his voice an angry hiss.

Lugg listens. He can hear voices. Children's voices.

"How is it possible?" asks Toff, his eyes wide. He is old, like Wart, like Lugg. They are now impossibly old. They are ancient.

"They have found another way," says Wart.

"There is another way?" asks Toff. "All this time? Another way?"

"There can be no more delay, Brother," says Wart. "You must stop them. You too, Brother." He looks at Lugg.

"What are we to do with them?" asks Toff.

"You are to kill them," says Wart.

"With what should I kill them, Brother?" asks Toff.

Wart removes a knife from his interior pocket. It is the sort that has a long steel blade that folds out from a wooden handle. He hands the knife to Toff and says, "With this, if you must."

Lugg frowns. Toff says, "And what about you, Brother?"

"I will reach the item," says Wart. "You need not worry about me. I will reach it. You must stop them. For if you do not, we will perish."

"Yes, Wart," says Toff. He looks at Lugg.

"Yes, Wart," says Lugg.

"Go," says Wart.

And so the brothers part ways, Wart moving towards the call of the thing, the great and terrible thing, so near to their grasp, so near, while Lugg and Toff shamble towards the sounds of the children, their voices growing ever closer.

Langdon leaned forward into the opening in the wall and held the lantern out at arm's length; a circle of light illuminated a tunnel that led into blackness. The tunnel's walls were lined with the same grey rock that made up the foundation of the house; it was clear that whoever had built the house had made the tunnel a part of their labours.

"I'm here, Grandfather," Archie heard Langdon say quietly before he walked through the opening and into the tunnel.

Oliver followed close behind, his face set in a kind of mesmerized stare that Archie only ever associated with one of his strange episodes. As they were entering the opening, Archie put his hand on Oliver's shoulder.

"Hey," he said. "You gonna be OK in there?"

Oliver glanced at his friend and said, "I'm fine."

"I just don't want you to ... you know..."

Oliver smiled. "Don't worry, Arch. It's weird but..."

"But?"

"But it's like I've waited for this for a long time." A determined look clouded his face. "I know this is what I'm meant to do."

Archie watched him as he crossed through the hole in the wall, into the tunnel. Taking a quick glance behind him at the wild detritus of the Langdon house basement, Archie followed.

They had to walk single file, so narrow was the passageway. Archie took up the rear; he could see Langdon's lamp as a distant glow at the head of the line, casting weird shadows against the stone wall. Before long, the line came to an abrupt halt. Archie craned his neck over Oliver's shoulder to see what the hold-up was. He could see Langdon at the front of the line, holding the lantern high.

"It's a ladder," the man called.

The pit was lined with stone and descended beyond the throw of the lantern's light. An iron ladder had been bolted to the wall of the hole. They were in a small, cramped chamber, but the lip around the hole allowed them all to spread out and surround it. Langdon looked at Oliver; Oliver shivered and nodded.

"We go down," said Langdon.

Chris volunteered to take the lantern; Athena went first,

followed by the old man. Chris took up the middle, bearing the lantern in one hand as he gingerly descended, one rung at a time, with his free hand. Oliver followed him, then Megan. That left Max and Archie standing at the edge of the pit, staring down into the darkness.

"Age before beauty," said Archie.

"Funny, bug," said Max, smirking. He put his foot on the top rung of the ladder.

"Hey, Max?"

"What's up?"

"I'm glad you're here." The words came out of Archie's mouth in a tumble, as if he had no control over them.

In normal times, such an earnest statement would've inspired eye rolling from his brother. But these were not normal times. Max nodded and said, "Me too, dude." He then disappeared down the hole.

The climb down the ladder felt interminable; Archie had never climbed down a ladder so tall. After several minutes had passed, Archie was relieved to hear Athena's voice echo from down the shaft.

"I've hit the ground, guys!" she shouted.

The last few rungs seemed to stretch on for an eternity, but Archie finally arrived on the hard earthen ground. Here, the stone masonry stopped and the surrounding chamber seemed to be blasted out of the rock itself. It occurred to Archie that they were far enough underground that they'd long left the soil of the surface behind.

"This way," said Oliver. A tunnel led off the bottom of

the shaft, and Oliver began to follow it, Athena close at hand with the lantern.

"What is this place?" asked Megan.

"It's like some kind of cave or something," said Max.

"This," replied Langdon, "is the work of my grandfather and his family. Years they put into this. Digging and blasting. I thought it was all myth, all family legend – but no! They left a channel open, just in case … just in case."

"Just in case of what?" asked Archie, feeling a bit annoyed by the man's confusing speech.

Langdon said, "Just in case they should want to find it again, I suppose. It was unwise. Very unwise. It was their madness that drove them to it. Man's hubris – man's temptation – can never be buried completely. And so we must do what they could not do."

"Which is?" asked Chris.

"To destroy it, once and for all," said Langdon.

"And how do we do that?" asked Archie.

Langdon smiled. "Leave that to me," he said. "It is my duty. You must only stop these three entities from reaching it. That is yours."

Archie saw little alcoves and side tunnels branching off here and there from this main channel; he only glanced at them fleetingly, following the glow of the lantern at the head of the line. Following Oliver.

But then: Langdon cried out. Archie looked ahead of him in time to see a dark figure leap from an unseen path in the tunnel. Something bright flashed in the lantern light; Archie heard a sickening splash against the rock. Athena screamed. The lantern fell to the ground but did not extinguish. It lay sideways, casting a garish light on the scene.

Langdon was dead. He lay on the ground in an ever-spreading pool of blood. His throat was torn open, and blood gushed from the wound in short spurts. His eyes looked heavenward, towards the roof of the tunnel. An old man with a pearl-white moustache and a brown suit stood over the dead man; he was holding Athena in his arms. A bloodied knife, held in his hand, was poised at her throat.

"Don't you *move*," said the man.

A second man, the white-bearded one, emerged from the shadows. They both were far older than they had been only hours before; they looked as if they were on the verge of turning to dust. Archie didn't have time to consider this strange phenomenon, as Athena, his friend, was struggling in the arms of the man with the knife.

"Please," said Chris, "we're just kids."

"Leave her alone!" shouted Megan.

"You won't get it," said the man. "You'll not live to get it." And Archie saw he was speaking in earnest. He could see it in his eyes. In the dead of his cold, old eyes. He meant to kill Athena. Archie began to shout "*No!*" when suddenly, to the man's left, the man with the white beard lifted something and brought it down hard against the man's head. The knife clattered noisily to the ground. The man's arms released Athena, and she leaped away from her captor, bowling into Oliver and Chris.

They stood for a moment in shocked silence.

The bearded man stood over his fellow and looked at him emotionlessly.

"Brother," said the man on the ground. There was blood seeping from a large wound in the side of his head.

Archie saw he'd been felled by a rock; it still remained in the bearded man's hand.

"Brother, why?"

But the man was silenced as his killer knelt at his side and brought the rock down repeatedly into his skull. Archie looked away; he heard Max scream something guttural. And then they were all running, running past the horrific scene, down the tunnel, following Oliver farther underground.

Toff is decaying; he is disappearing before Lugg's eyes. There, on the floor of the tunnel. The other man, the meatbag, lies next to him, having had his life drained from him in little liquid spurts. Toff does not depart this way. His skin shrivels inside his suit, this uniform, this eternal uniform, and his hands creep back into the sleeves like a turtle head retreating into its shell.

Which reminds Lugg: turtles. He found one, there up in the forest. A small one, sitting beside a pond. He stared at it for many minutes, noting its painted shell, its mottled head. Now Lugg pulls his notepad from the interior pocket of his jacket and riffles the pages until he finds the entry he made on this strange animal, this *turtle*. He rereads his words, recalling the thing. His eyes fall on his writing, just below the entry on the turtle. It is a poem, by a human poet. William Blake. He is moved, then, to read it aloud. He reads it over the body of Toff as the man deteriorates into brittle, black ash.

"'Cruelty has a Human heart / And Jealousy a Human Face,'" he reads, "'Terror, the Human Form Divine, and Secrecy, the Human Dress.'"

He is crying; he wipes a tear from his cheek. He can feel the papery thinness of his skin. He, too, is decaying. He reads on.

"'The Human Dress is forged Iron / The Human Form, a fiery Forge / The Human face, a Furnace seal'd / The Human Heart, its hungry Gorge.'"

He closes his notepad softly. He returns it to his pocket. Toff is gone now; Lugg is alone. He stands with some difficulty. He must brace himself against the wall of the tunnel. His lungs are racked by every breath. He walks the length of the tunnel, back to the chamber where first they entered. The rain is falling hard now, down into the shaft and over the metal scaffolding that laces up the side of the shaft. He feels the cold rain on his face, in the tussock of his beard. There are swaplings here, but they are silent and still. They are marionettes without their operators. Their work is through.

He climbs the ladder of the scaffolding and walks back out onto the beach, where the waves are churning and the rain is lashing down. The machines are motionless, unmanned. The mannequin townspeople dot the beach, frozen in time. He walks through them, touching them as he goes. They fall to the ground, one by one. Before long, he is at the place where the ocean meets the land, where the surf laps at the beach. The rain is impenetrable now, and his brown suit is soaked through to his skin. He walks farther out into the water; the cold is bracing, it is sudden.

Then a wave crashes against his body and he is floundering, deep in the ocean, his waterlogged suit acting as a kind of anchor, dragging him farther down below the surface.

He is aged. He is weak. He did not realize the constraints this human body would exert on him, not when he assumed the form. It is curious, this dying. It is something he's often heard about – often read about – but it was still unfamiliar. The familiarity comes on him now, bracingly.

He opens his mouth; water floods in. He closes his eyes. And drowns.

In the first moment of chaos, when the bearded man knocked down his comrade, Oliver had grabbed the lantern and started running down the tunnel. Archie was reeling. He'd witnessed two grisly killings; he could hear his friends' frightened breathing as they leaped over the bodies on the floor and chased the glowing orb of the lantern. Archie's heart rate was galloping; his eyes felt like they were about to pop from their sockets. He kept his eyes intent on Oliver's lantern, tamping down the terror erupting in his gut.

"We have to get help!" Athena shouted.

"Who's gonna help us?" said Max.

"What happened back there?" screamed Megan.

"Just keep running," said Chris. "Follow Oliver."

They were all in a frenzied state; their words came tripping out like the speech of someone in the grips of a hallucinatory fever.

"This way!" Oliver shouted from the front of the line.

They followed a tortuous route; the tunnel wove like a snake, like it had been dug by drunk men. Little alcoves broke off from the tunnel here and there; they once followed such a turn and found themselves at a dead end. Oliver was frantic.

"We have to get to it first," he said. His eyes were wide. If this was one of his episodes, it was unlike any Archie had seen before.

"Keep going. Keep going," Archie said, as much to mollify his friend as to give any sort of guidance to the group. Each time he looked at the others, he saw more terror and confusion in their eyes.

The tunnel seemed to branch at one place, and Oliver stopped, pointing ahead into the dark. "Do you see it?" he asked.

"What?" asked Athena. "I don't see anything."

He looked at Athena, wonder in his eyes. "Right there. The zebra. He's there. He wants us to follow him."

"We don't see anything," said Max.

"Just listen to him," said Chris.

Emboldened, Oliver dived down one of the channels; the kids followed. He held the lantern high, searching. "This way," he said. He began moving faster. Archie found himself trailing the line of kids. The tunnel took a sharp turn, and the light from Oliver's lamp was gone. When Archie turned the corner, there was only blackness. He felt someone come up behind him.

"Arch? Is that you?" It was Chris.

"Where'd they go?" asked Archie. They listened; they could hear the din of their friends' voices somewhere in the tunnels, but it was as if they were ghostly murmurs, blown on the wind.

"I don't know," said Chris. "They were just there."

"This way," said Archie. And the two of them wandered headlong into the darkness.

"What are we doing?" asked Chris. Archie could hear the fear in his voice, in the way it choked his words as he spoke. "That dude is dead. You heard him: he said he would destroy it. How are we supposed to destroy it? We don't know how!"

"I don't know," said Archie. "But we need to get there before they do. That's what Langdon said."

They walked for some time, groping along the cold stone walls as they went. Finally, Chris shouted, "Look!"

Archie looked up and saw light. He assumed it was Oliver's lantern at first, but as they drew closer, the light became blinding.

Archie and Chris froze. The light was strange; it was not electric, nor was it from any kind of flame or fire. It looked to be daylight. Chris began walking slowly towards the whiteness. Archie's eyes smarted at the sudden change; he held one hand on the tunnel wall, bracing himself, as he followed his friend towards the light.

And just like that, the two of them walked out into bright day.

They were standing on a riverbank. The water, dark green river water, burbled over rocks; cottonwoods swayed in a warm breeze, glinting in the light from a sun hanging high in a blue sky. The surface below their feet was no longer packed dirt and rock, but green brush and grass. Archie stole a look behind him; he saw a gently sloping, forested hill. The tunnel was gone.

"What happened?" asked Chris. "Where are we?"

"I have no idea," said Archie, though an odd feeling of recognition was swelling inside him. And then it hit him: he knew this spot. He knew where they were. And, if he was correct, they were hundreds of miles from Seaham and the headlands.

They were standing on the bank of the McKenzie River – Archie knew it from memory. They had gone on a joint camping trip here once, when they were eight or nine. Archie had been invited by Chris's family; they'd spent two days wandering the riverbed, swimming in the cold water and scouring the surrounding hills and culverts for adventure. This was the precise location of one of Archie's fondest childhood memories.

"I know this place," murmured Archie.

"You do?"

He turned to his friend and said, "You don't recognize it? It's the McKenzie—"

"Dude," began Chris, interrupting, "we're, like, miles from—"

"Listen to me," said Archie. "*We* know this place. Remember? The two of us, camping with your dad. We were here. Right here."

A look of realization wiped out Chris's dubious expression. He began to scan their surroundings; his mouth gaped. "You're right," he said finally. "But that's impossible."

"I don't think this is real," said Archie, a new fear creeping into his chest. "This is some kind of hallucination."

Chris was now smiling. "Of course," he said, not hearing

his friend. "We came here. Like, every day. You and me. We camped up there. Up on that little hill. And we'd come down here. I remember that." He'd begun to walk towards the rise of the hill, just upstream from where they were standing. Archie, despite his misgivings, followed. The sun beating on his neck felt very real; the sounds of the trees and bushes, the supple whisper of the river — it was all undeniable.

But then Archie realized they were not alone. He froze and grabbed Chris by the arm. He pointed to a nearby stand of trees on the bank of the river. Sitting against a tree trunk was a very old man in a brown suit.

He was holding a small notepad in his hands. He was leafing through the pages.

Chris and Archie approached the man warily, but it soon became clear that the man was no threat to them. He was the very image of a man on his deathbed, breathing his last. He was improbably old: his suit dwarfed his meagre frame, his face deeply drawn and mottled with liver marks. His eyes were sunk deep in his skull, and his hair, what little remained, was wispy and white. He pawed at the pages of the notebook in his hand with pale, skeletal fingers. When the boys came close, he looked up at them wearily, and then looked back down at his book.

"'I had a dream,'" said the man, reading, "'which was not all a dream.'" He was suddenly racked with a coughing fit, and his reading paused. Once he'd recovered himself, he continued: "'The bright sun was extinguish'd, and the stars did wander darkling in the eternal space. Rayless, and pathless, and the icy earth swung blind and blackening in the moonless air.'"

He stopped and puzzled at the notepad before flipping to the next page. Finding nothing, he flipped back and stared at the words on the page. "So many words," he said. "Byron, poet. English. You know him?"

Archie and Chris shook their heads.

"It figures," said the man. His voice was weak and quiet. "Beautiful words. Wasted on humans. All this. Wasted." He now seemed to be referring to the surrounding countryside: the babbling river, the soughing trees. Archie reflexively looked around him. He looked back at the man.

"Who are you?" he asked.

"No time," said the man. "Look at me. I'm dying. Grown old. And to think we had it. We had it this close. After all this time, it was ours. But no: We were too delayed. Your mortal skin betrayed us. And now I will die, stuck in this … in this … body."

"You – your friends – you're all evil," said Chris angrily. "You took our parents. You took our town. You – you killed that man, Langdon."

"So messy," the man continued, oblivious to Chris's words. "All of this. Never figured for that. How messy it all is. That's all you do, humans, make a mess of things. No wonder they put it here, to hide it. Of all places. You could never control it. It'd only be more of your mess. What a waste."

He coughed again; he adjusted himself against the tree trunk and sighed. "Well, it's all yours now. Go on, take it. You beat us all to it, didn't you? Go on."

"What are you talking about?" asked Chris.

"Go on, it's there," said the man. He was closing his eyes. "Congratulations. Well done. To the victors, the spoils."

The man, with the last of his strength, was nodding his chin in the direction of the riverbank. Archie looked towards the river; something caught his eye.

It was as much a fragment of his memory that drew his attention to the stones as anything else; at that moment, there was nothing there of note. But in his mind, in his memory, he saw two boys. He saw himself and Chris, standing by the river. Children. Best friends. Peeling the rocks from their resting places and studying the dark undersides. The feeling of recognition was overwhelming; he was transported to that moment and his heart was flooded with joy and longing. His breath escaped him momentarily, and he felt a smile spread across his face. He looked at Chris; his friend was looking at the spot too. Chris had clearly felt a similar recognition – he, too, was looking at the spot with a wide-eyed awe, his teeth bared in a wide smile.

Chris looked at Archie and said, "Arch – look." He began to walk towards the spot; Archie stayed frozen in his place.

The man by the tree was no longer of interest to the boys; in fact, the man had quietly died and his body had sunk in on its own skeleton, like a piece of fruit rotting in time-lapse. The bones then turned brittle and crumbled to a fine black dust. Soon, nothing was left but the old brown suit. But that terrible image was no competition for the draw of the riverbank. The river murmured and the grass on the bank rustled; a bird wheeled above their heads. Chris continued walking towards the bank.

"Archie," Chris said, looking over his shoulder, "come on." He was smiling; his voice sounded giddy.

A noise sounded on the far bank. It called Archie's attention away from his friend. It was a bestial moan, a kind of guttural, dying yawn.

But Chris was at the bankside now; he was crouched down by the smooth, ovoid river stones, studying them, assaying them, deciding which would hide the most treasures. He looked back at Archie again and said impatiently, "Come on! Let's see what we can find. Like old times, Arch. Like old times."

The noise sounded again, the moan. Its intensity had grown; it now sounded like a howl.

"Arch, what are you waiting for?" called Chris.

Archie looked across the river, squinting against the bright sun. He saw a figure on the far bank. It was an animal, crawling across the weedy vegetation that lay along the bank. A trail of bright red followed the animal. Then Archie saw: the animal was a half-dead zebra, its viscera exposed to the air, all raw and pink and bloody. It paused there on the riverbank and swung its heavy head to face Archie.

"What?" murmured Archie. "Who – what are you?"

As if in response to Archie's question, the zebra turned away and began walking into the brush, leaving a trail of blood in the grass behind him. Archie blinked rapidly; he then looked back at Chris. He had suddenly become very afraid. This strange feeling of pleasure, this pang of nostalgia, was gone, replaced by a very acute terror.

"Chris!" shouted Archie. "Get away from it! Don't touch it!"

Chris looked at his friend quizzically. He then looked back down at the rocks. He chose one and flipped it over. He craned his neck forward, peering at what was underneath. His body froze.

The world began to shake.

The ground was trembling beneath Archie's feet. Strangely, the surrounding countryside did not appear to be affected by the quaking – the tree branches were swayed only by the occasional breeze; the rocks by the river did not clatter. The zebra was disappearing now, having dragged itself into the brush. But its blood-red trail could still be seen.

"We have to go, Chris!" Archie shouted. Chris was unresponsive, staring at whatever he'd found beneath the rock. Archie ran to him and grabbed him by the arm, dragging him away. He pulled him across the river and to the far bank, shouting his name as he went. But Chris was silent, stumbling at his side.

This way, they followed the zebra. They followed the blood.

The animal had disappeared into a wild thicket, overgrown with brambles. Archie now had his arm around Chris's side, feeling the boy grow heavier and heavier. He urged his friend to walk faster, to try to support his own weight, but Chris was unresponsive. There was no time to stop and gauge Chris's health – the zebra had disappeared into the thicket, and the ground was agitating beneath their feet, a persistent tremble.

They entered the thicket, and Archie could feel the blackberry thorns tear at his clothing and bite his skin. The blood was there, though, on the forest floor, and Archie felt a tremendous urge to keep following it. As they drew farther into the heart of the bramble, the light began to diminish. The blackberries blotted out the sun. The blood on the ground had deepened, somehow, and Archie could feel it seeping into the webbing of his tennis shoes. It slopped between his toes, all sticky and wet. As the bramble grew thicker and the light dimmed more and more, the trail of blood became a rill on the ground. The earth's tremble, too, had grown and was now quaking at their every step.

"C'mon!" shouted Archie, feeling his friend's energy sap. "Chris! You have to move!"

But still there came no response. The blood was at his knees now, a lapping cascade of red blood, soaking his trousers. The darkness was pervasive. They were lost.

Suddenly, Archie felt something; it was a hand, grabbing his shoulder.

"Archie Coomes!" shouted a voice. It was Randy Dean. He'd have known that voice anywhere.

Archie could barely respond. His surroundings had suddenly transformed. He was no longer in the darkness of the blackberry thicket but in a stony enclosure. The now waist-deep pool of blood was no longer blood but frigid seawater.

"Do you have him?" Archie heard a voice cry; it was Athena. Relief cascaded through him as his eyes adjusted to the light. Several klieg lamps lit the shaft of a subterranean cave. Randy was lying belly-down on a scaffolding platform directly above him, his hand tightly wound into Archie's T-shirt. Rain was bucketing down from the open sky, far above.

"I got 'im!" shouted Randy in response. Archie had never been so pleased to see the video-store owner in his life. As he squinted up through the slashing rain and blinding light, he thought he saw something strange: was that a sword strapped to Randy's back?

He had no time to contemplate this as Randy dragged both him and Chris to the safety of the scaffold platform. Chris collapsed to the floor of the platform, and Randy, his clothes and hair drenched from the rain, looked at Archie in alarm.

"What's wrong with Chris?" he asked.

"I don't know," said Archie. "He saw it – the thing. The buried thing. I don't know."

"Well, we don't got time," said Randy. "This whole place is about to go down."

Together, they supported the limp body of Chris Pedersen up the maze of scaffolding that ran along the side of the shaft. Water cascaded down the edge of the pit in great heaves; rain pelted their faces. "The tide's coming in," shouted Randy as they climbed the final ladder to the edge of the pit. "It's a big one."

When Archie reached the top, he saw that he was back

on the beach below the headlands. There were his friends, his brother. They wore looks of amazement and disbelief; Max ran to Archie and engulfed him in a sort of hug Archie didn't think he'd ever received from his brother.

"We thought you guys'd had it for sure," Max said. Athena and Oliver were there; they joined in on the hug, wrapping their arms around the bodies of the two brothers.

"You made it, Archie," said Athena. "You guys made it."

"Did you do it?" asked Oliver breathlessly. "Did you destroy it?"

"I don't know," said Archie. Rain poured down his face; his clothes were soaked through from the seawater. "Chris," he said. "Chris found it." They all turned. Megan was bent over her brother; Chris was lying in a fetal position in the wet sand. She was calling his name. He was not responding.

Randy was staring out at the ocean; the ground, Archie noticed, continued to rumble. Archie followed Randy's look and saw the wild sea, bucking white and frothing.

"King tide," said Randy loudly. "We gotta get out of here."

Max and Randy helped carry Chris as they all ran for the gravel road sloping up from the beach. The chain-link fence had been battered into a mangled heap by the force of the waves; the massive construction machines that had so recently been tearing away at the cliffside were empty and derelict now, obstacles to the rush and pull of the pursuing ocean. As he ran, Archie noticed wooden limbs, tree branches, strewn everywhere across the wet sand – and yet there were no such trees to shed those branches here on the beach. He scarcely had time to consider this, as a monstrous wave could be seen gaining strength out in the ocean, and the ground was trembling beneath his feet.

They had just reached the safety of the road and begun climbing when the king tide descended on the beach and the cliff face. The water exploded against the rock and they saw the headlands shatter.

It was as Peter Coomes had said: the cliff was like Swiss cheese, full of crevices and holes. It was an unsound environment for construction. No one in their right mind would've built on that as a foundation. That was how it was explained later, when all that was left of the headlands was a ragged rubble of rock and mud and trees. It was an environmental hazard, a cataclysmic erosion event waiting to happen. All it took was an unseasonably strong king tide to rip the whole cliff face apart. The collapse triggered an aftershock that went far inland, setting off a landslide in the forested hills bordering the coast. Highway 101 was blocked completely by the destruction, creating a snarl of traffic that plagued the Oregon coast for weeks.

Thankfully, the disaster was presumed to have claimed only one life, that of Charles Langdon II, one of the last surviving members of the storied family. Nothing of the house remained, aside from the old stone pillars that marked the boundary of the property. As for the house, it disappeared into the sinkhole that was created when the headlands collapsed. Mr Langdon's body was never recovered.

The environmental loss was tremendous – the headlands, once a prized and scenic landmark of the Oregon coast, was nothing more than a mass of piled rock and mud.

The scale of the destruction was so great that it tended to overshadow the fact that a kind of strange contagion had laid claim to the towns' inhabitants. Many of Seaham's adult residents, at the very moment of the headlands' collapse, awoke to find themselves lying on pallets in an old timber warehouse some miles east of town. It was as if, they said, they'd woken from a very long and dreamless sleep. They were horrified to find two of their number had apparently been stabbed during their slumber.

No one was ever discovered to have been the killer. The murders, to this day, remain shrouded in mystery. Some will recall that a cable news show, *Mysteries Abound*, did a program on the Seaham Sleepers (as the event came to be known) in the mid-nineties. It was the third-most-watched episode the show had produced, behind their specials on Amelia Earhart and the Zodiac killings, respectively. A tourism boom followed the airing of the show, one that was not necessarily greeted with enthusiasm by most Seahamites. Many residents were keen to put the whole event behind them. Others tried to milk the sensation, selling commemorative coffee mugs and key chains and the like, but it only lasted a few seasons.

The hotel project was abandoned. The same developers opted to move their plan south, to Newport, where it sits today. It is called the Sea Haven and boasts some of the finest views to be found the length and breadth of the wild Oregon coast.

AFTER

The beige stucco walls of Harrisburg High came into view, and Archie felt a jolt run through his body. It wasn't just a single feeling, it was one that seemed to embody several emotions at once: anticipation, fear and excitement. It had been building all summer long, and here he was. His first day of high school.

"You'll be fine, bug," said Max from the driver's seat. He was piloting his Honda station wagon through the car park. He'd only had the car for a few weeks now. It had belonged to Liz's sister, Marion; they'd bought it on the cheap after the Omni had been relegated to the junkyard. Olivia and Annabelle sat side by side in the back seat; Annabelle wore a pair of yellow headphones and was cradling a Walkman in her lap. "I remember my first day," continued Max. "Mom drove me. At least you don't have to deal with that."

As if on cue, the car ahead of them slowed to a stop. A boy climbed from the passenger seat and made his way towards the metal doors of the school, only to be halted when the driver of the car, his mother, called out through the open window,

"Stop — stop, honey. C'mon, let me just snap your picture."

The boy was surrounded by other kids, all making their way into the building, and he had to stop amid the throng to face his mother's car while the traffic backed up behind her.

"*Mom*," the boy complained, "you're, like, holding up the whole line."

The car didn't budge; the boy gave a half-hearted smile. Archie could see, through the car's windscreen, the driver ready a camera. Someone behind them honked.

"*Mom!*" the boy repeated.

The picture was taken, the camera stowed, and the car moved on. The boy, abashed, put his head down and walked into the high school.

"I rest my case," said Max.

They found a parking spot and Archie climbed from the car, throwing his backpack over one shoulder. Olivia and Annabelle gave a cursory nod to their brothers before disappearing amid the crowd of students making their way towards the doors.

"Don't want to be seen with us?" asked Max, smirking after the sisters. He mimed smelling his armpit. "What, do I stink?"

Archie laughed; they walked side by side through the car park.

"Hey, there's your boy," said Max.

Archie looked up; Oliver was standing in front of the doors to the freshman halls. He had his backpack clutched to his chest like it was a life buoy and he'd just been jettisoned from the deck of a ship. Seeing him that way made Archie's own feeling of nervousness evaporate. He suddenly felt protective, in charge.

"You better help him out," said Max. He then turned and made his way to the other side of the building, where the juniors entered. A few of his friends were waiting there, waving him on. He jogged to catch up with them. He shouted over his shoulder as he ran, "See you at the car, three fifteen. Don't be late, bug."

"Hey, Arch," said Oliver as Archie mounted the steps towards him.

"Hey, Ollie," said Archie. "How are you doing?"

"I'm OK. I'm fine. Y'know, I might be a bit nervous."

"You don't say."

"Didn't sleep much. I heard they, like, lock freshmen in their lockers on the first day of class."

Archie rolled his eyes. "Whatever. Just keep your head down; don't make a fuss. You'll be fine."

"Yeah?"

"Yeah. Stick with me." He patted Oliver on the back, ushering him through the doors. "Oh, but first – maybe put your backpack on the normal way."

"Yeah, OK."

The freshman halls were alight with activity, a buzz of kids with their backpacks, navigating these new corridors, these new metal lockers. Some of the kids Archie recognized from Seaham Elementary; most were strangers. Harrisburg High pulled from many of the smaller towns that dotted the coast, as well as the sizable population of Harrisburg itself. Some of the kids seemed to look at Archie and Oliver queerly as they walked past; he was suddenly aware that the strange events that had taken hold of Seaham earlier in the summer had become the talk of the coast. He tried to ignore the fleeting looks, the furtive whispers behind their backs. He glanced at Oliver; thankfully, his friend seemed entirely oblivious to the attention. One of the benefits, Archie supposed, of living life like you were floating, submerged in the waters of your own imagination. He hadn't had one of his episodes since the events of June; there was no more talk of visions and zebras. Whether or not that was coincidence and he was just enjoying a prolonged respite from this phenomenon – it was too early to say.

"Oh, Archie, by the way," said Oliver, once they'd arrived at their lockers. They'd arranged to have them next to one another at the orientation night the week before. "I got this new game. Mom got it for me. Kind of a back-to-school present. It's cool – it's about being stuck in the desert."

"Oh yeah?" said Archie, feigning interest as he placed his textbooks on the top shelf of his locker. Oliver had spent the summer glued to the screen of his family's IBM home computer, playing these so-called text adventures: video games that were just a bunch of writing on the screen with the occasional pixelated picture if you were lucky. Oliver always commandeered the keyboard, leaving Athena and Archie to watch over his shoulder as he played the game. It was not Archie's idea of a good time.

"Anyway," continued Oliver. "I'm kinda stuck on this

one bit. Maybe you and Ath want to come over after school and see if you can figure it out?"

"Yeah, sure," Archie said. "Sounds fun. Though I might be a little late."

"Oh, right," said Oliver.

The bell rang again; they closed their lockers and fell in with the lingering crowd of kids, all making their way towards their classrooms.

Archie didn't run into Athena till after lunch, during his sixth period. They were in the same Algebra class.

"Hey, what's up?" asked Athena, a textbook flattened to her chest. "You have fun in Bend?"

"Yeah, it was OK," said Archie. The Coomeses had spent three weeks in a rental cabin in eastern Oregon during the last part of summer break. It was a far cry from Los Angeles, but it was what they could afford. "I don't know. Guess my mind was kind of elsewhere."

Athena nodded, looking down at her shoes. There was a distance between them that he didn't remember from earlier in the summer. "Hey – Oliver's got a new game, I guess," said Archie. "I was going to head over after school, check it out. He said to invite you, too, if you wanted."

"Oh, I can't," said Athena. "I've got soccer tryouts. Probably gonna take forever."

"Soccer," said Archie.

Athena nodded; she held the book tighter to her chest. The bell rang. "I gotta go," she said. "But I'll see you tomorrow."

"Yep," said Archie. "Tomorrow."

Athena turned to walk away, but then stopped by a row of lockers. She looked back at him and said, "You should really go see him."

Her tone of voice shook him; he felt accused. "I am," he said. "I'm going today."

Athena gave him a nod. "Good," she said. And then she turned to leave.

He watched her disappear around the corner of the hallway; he then remembered his seventh-period government class was all the way on the other side of the building. He dashed away, nearly upsetting an AV cart that had been left in the middle of the hall. He arrived at his class breathless, receiving a dismayed look from the teacher and several bemused giggles from his classmates as he found his seat.

"Now that we're all here," the teacher said archly, "we can continue."

As the class wore on, Archie stole glances at the clock on the wall. Whatever lingering thoughts he had about his interaction with Athena, all the unsaid things that seemed to hide between the words the two friends exchanged, these thoughts had evaporated and were now replaced by a strange dread that seemed to be growing in him with every advancing tick of the clock's hands. He suppressed the feeling. It worked, mostly, until the moment that the bell rang and the dread suddenly bloomed, as if making up for lost time.

He stacked his textbooks in the top cubby of his locker; he tossed his algebra book in his backpack for the homework he'd been assigned that night. He closed the door and locked it. He found himself slowing his walk as he drew closer to the school's exit. It was an unconscious change – when he realized he was deliberately putting off what lay before him, he felt embarrassed, unsettled.

Max was standing at the car in the car park, waiting for him. "You're late," he said.

"I know," said Archie. "Sorry."

"S'all right," said Max, climbing into the driver's seat and starting up the car. "You got a lot to think about."

"Yep," said Archie. He'd sidled into the passenger seat, stowing his backpack at his feet.

"You ready?" asked Max. A note of concern was in his voice.

"Uh-huh," said Archie.

They drove out of the car park, out into the streets of Harrisburg. They fell in with the traffic heading north on Highway 101. Before long, they'd returned to Seaham – tidy, quiet Seaham. The air was warm and the sun sat, unclouded, off to the west, over the ocean. A man was washing his car in the driveway of his home; he stopped briefly to give Archie and his brother a nod as they passed. Archie saw kids in the yard of a house, chasing each other with Nerf guns; he saw their parents sitting on a front stoop, watering plants and watching the battle play out before them with a disinterested eye. He saw a mail truck make its way slowly down Fulham Street, ping-ponging between mailboxes, its red hazard lights flashing.

It all seemed so normal. Three months had passed since the destruction of the headlands; three months since everyone had returned, newly awakened, from the warehouse to a changed Seaham. And now, for the most part, it seemed like nothing had happened. No mistake about it: Archie welcomed this return, this resumption of his boring teenage life. It was an outcome he couldn't have imagined back when everything had seemed so dire. And yet, it was a marvel that everything could come back to normal so quickly. It was almost too clean, too tidy. There were aspects of the adventure that still nagged at him, late at night, nights when he had trouble sleeping. There was no real way of knowing that they had satisfied Langdon's project. They had stopped these other entities from getting to it, sure, but what then? Archie found it easier to simply ignore his suspicions, to enjoy this revival of the old Seaham. Sometimes, he figured, things do work out for the best. Sometimes they do resolve like a movie, no matter how unbelievable that might be. Besides, it's not as if there weren't still repercussions felt from the event. Not everyone got off scot-free.

The Pedersens' house came into view, its gabled roof shadowed by the towering fir trees in their backyard. Max pulled the car in behind Ted Pedersen's Toyota truck; he turned off the ignition.

"Mind if I come in too?" asked Max. "Just want to say hi to Megan."

"Sure," said Archie.

Megan opened the door at Archie's knock. She smiled

weakly. Even beneath the lacquer of makeup she wore, Archie could see her hollowed-out eyes, her sunken cheeks. She looked so much older than the last time he'd seen her. "Oh," she said. "Hey."

"Hi, Megan," said Archie. "I'm here to see…"

"Yeah, yeah," said Megan, standing aside and waving him in. She stayed on the porch, talking quietly with Max as Archie walked into the house.

"Is that Archie?" called a voice from the living room.

"Hi, Laura," said Archie. Chris's mother was sitting in a faded armchair in the living room, watching television.

Archie walked into the room and stood behind the couch, watching the images on the TV. A game show was on. It was weird to see a TV on during the day at Chris's house. He'd always known the Pedersens as a family that frowned on daytime television watching.

"When'd you get back?" asked Laura, her eyes not leaving the TV.

"Sunday," answered Archie. "Saturday, actually. I mean, we stopped in Corvallis to see my aunt and stayed the night. So we got back here on Sunday." He hoped Laura couldn't hear how nervous he was.

"Uh-huh," said Laura.

Archie could hear Chris's dad's voice coming from the next room. It sounded like he was talking on the phone.

"How's the weather out there?" Laura asked.

"Huh? Oh – pretty nice. Sunny."

Ted's voice suddenly boomed through the door: "Listen,

347

the *last* lady I talked to put me on hold for *ten minutes*. Don't put me on hold before… Oh, for God's sake."

Laura looked away from the television screen – first at the door to the other room, then at Archie. "Don't go down before Ted says hello. I know he'd want to see you."

Archie wasn't in a hurry to go downstairs; he accepted Laura's invitation and sat down on the couch opposite the woman. They both watched the TV in silence while Ted, in the other room, continued to berate whoever he was speaking to on the phone.

"Listen," he said loudly, "I've been through this. We met our deductible, what, two months ago? Those were for my son – yes, my son. I was told— Listen to me— I was told by *someone* at your company that these therapies were *in network*. They were covered. You tell me. That's what they said."

Archie shifted uncomfortably on the couch. Laura, seemingly unperturbed by the tone of her husband's voice in the next room, said, "They always get this one wrong."

"What's that?" asked Archie.

Laura gestured to the TV. "This question. The final one. They never get it."

Archie looked at the screen; a man and a woman were standing next to the host of the show, smiling nervously while the host read them a question from a blue card in his hand. Through the door, Archie heard the phone slam down on its receiver; Ted came walking in.

"Oh," he said, seeing Archie. His face was red. His

forehead wore a sheen of sweat. "Hi there, Archie. Didn't hear you come in."

"No problem. I just stopped by to see Chris."

"Oh yeah," said Ted. "Oh, I'm sure he'll be happy to see you. Isn't that right, Laura? He'll be thrilled to see you."

Laura didn't say anything; she was watching the television.

"First day of school, huh?" asked Ted. His voice was strained. "High schooler now, huh?"

"Yep," said Archie.

Ted gave a little laugh. "Good for you. Good for you. I suppose, well. I suppose … we had to give up our spot at that school in Columbus. Principal at Harrisburg High said he'd have a spot when he was ready. You heard, I'm sure. Looks like we'll be here in Seaham after all."

"I heard," said Archie. "Mom told me." He looked over at Laura; the woman's face was vacant, staring at the TV screen.

"Figured we had enough on our plate," said Ted. "Other jobs out there, huh, honey?"

Laura was silent.

"Huh, honey? Ah, well," continued Ted. "Maybe sometime down the line, sometime. I would've missed this place, that's for sure."

"Well, don't let us keep you," said Laura. "You should go on down."

"Yeah?" asked Archie.

"Yeah," said Ted. "You go on down. He's going to be thrilled to see you."

Archie pushed himself up from the couch and walked away from the living room; the sound of applause dwindled as he moved farther from the television. He found himself at the top of the stairs to the basement; he looked back at the living room. Chris's parents were staring at the TV. An advert had come on.

The air became steadily cooler as he descended the wooden stairs into the basement. He listened for a sound; all was silence, except for the diminishing noise from the television. The air smelled damp.

A single lamp in the corner lit the half-finished basement. An old couch and an easy chair were the only other furnishings in what had always been a favourite hang-out space for Chris and Archie – it was like an annex to Chris's room, their own den. Now, it felt abandoned. The door to Chris's room was slightly ajar. Archie could see daylight coming through. He walked to the door and pushed it open.

"Chris?" he called out.

Chris's room was unchanged from the last time Archie had seen it. The same posters were on the wall. His desk was still stacked with workbooks and papers from the end of the last school year. The room's sole window was set high into the concrete wall; its drapes were pulled aside, and a shaft of daylight fell across Chris's bed. A patchwork quilt followed the contours of Chris's body. He was lying on his side, his face to the wall, away from the door.

"Chris?" Archie repeated.

Again, he received no response. Archie looked around at the room, at the posters on the wall – a European sports car idling on some mansion's driveway, a football player Archie didn't recognize smiling, kneeling; an action movie poster from Movie Mayhem's promo leftovers – they had hung on Chris's wall for over a year. Archie wondered if he would've changed them out by now, if things had turned out different. The room felt like a tribute, like a memorial to a disappeared boy. He looked down at the figure of his friend. He frowned.

Archie sat down on the edge of the bed. He could see the back of Chris's head, his brown-blond hair. It was getting longer. It looked matted and unwashed. The rest of Chris's body was shrouded in the blanket; Archie could see the slow rise and fall of the boy's breath through the quilt.

"First day of school," said Archie. He waited a moment for a response, as if by habit, then continued, "My locker's right next to Oliver's. Guy won't let me out of his sight. It's OK, though. I don't mind. Weird being a freshman."

Stillness from Chris; the back of his head, the movement of the blanket with the boy's breath.

Archie said, "Athena's going out for soccer. I kinda wonder how much I'll see her this year. It's a big commitment, I guess. That's what she says. She says hello, by the way." This wasn't true, but Archie was having an awkward time finding things to say. "They both say hello. Ollie and Athena. Going to see Ollie later. He's got some new game he wants to show me – or show him playing it." He let out a soft, forced laugh.

He scanned the room again before saying, "Maybe when

you're, y'know, back — we can get you the locker next to us. At school. Now that you're not moving. So, that's one thing. One, y'know, good thing."

He stopped, here, feeling tears rise. He began again. "I'm sorry I didn't do more. To help you. To stop you. I think, maybe, sometimes, I could've done more. I could've grabbed you, pulled you away from it. But, see: I felt it, too, you know? It had a power. I wanted to see. It called to me, too, that *thing*. I tried to stop you, I swear to God, I tried. But it was too late." Tears were flowing now, freely flowing down his face. "I just want you back, man. I want my friend back."

He wiped away the tears with the back of his arm. He looked at Chris, at the still figure in the bed. The boy gave no indication that Archie's words were being heard. Archie watched him breathe silently for a few moments, the blanket rising and falling almost imperceptibly with the movement. He then patted the mattress with his hand. "Well," he said, "I gotta go. I'll see you around."

Archie stood up from the bed and, without giving a backwards glance, left the room.

In the half-light, Chris lies on his side, his head burrowed deep into his pillow, his body enshrouded by his blanket. The door closes behind him softly, and he is alone in the room. He faces the empty wall beside the bed. His eyes are open, unblinking.

He lies in the half-light, but he needs no light.

For in his eyes are universes.